Praise for *Entropy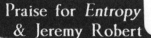
& Jeremy Robert Johnson*

"I sat down, properly, with a cup of tea, read the first paragraph
of the first story, and a disembodied voice shouted, 'You will not
close the cover until you read every word.' The voice, as voices go,
was a prophet. *Entropy in Bloom* crackles with weirdness, style, wit, a
befittingly oddball sense of humanity, and a misshapen dark heart.
I loved every damn story."
—Paul Tremblay, author of *A Head Full of Ghosts*
and *Disappearance at Devil's Rock*

"Jeremy Robert Johnson's stories are, simply put, unlike any others
you've ever read. It's as if an alien life form picked up a pen and
wrote its thoughts in a language comprehensible to humans—reading Johnson, you feel you are in the grip of an immensely powerful,
possibly malevolent, but fiercely intelligent mind. Beware! (But
enjoy—and trust me, you will.)"
—Nick Cutter, author of *Little Heaven* and *The Troop*

"I've seen the future and it's bizarre, it's beautifully berserk, it's
Jeremy Robert Johnson."
—Stephen Graham Jones, author of *Mongrels*

"A dazzling writer. Seriously amazing short stories. While I read
them, they made time stand still."
—*New York Times* bestselling author Chuck Palahniuk

"One of the most exciting voices in contemporary fiction. Jeremy
Robert Johnson's work has always tested the limits of both genre
and literary fiction."
—*Bookslut*

"Jeremy Robert Johnson is dancing to a way different drummer. He loves language, he loves the edge, and he loves us people. This is entertainment . . . and literature."
—Jack Ketchum, author of *The Girl Next Door* and *Off Season*

"I'm a longtime fan of Johnson. A master of derangement, he's been bringing it for years."
—Laird Barron, author of *The Beautiful Thing that Awaits Us All*

"The people populating these stories are real and vital and you WILL care, deeply, about what becomes of them . . . and in JRJ's harsh universe, baaaaad things happen. Often. Prepare thyself."
—Craig Davidson, author of *Rust and Bone* and *The Fighter*

"What makes JRJ's work stand out from his contemporaries' is the strange sense of empathy—in that regard he is not unlike David Foster Wallace's wicked and perhaps deranged younger brother. Sometimes the horror is so understated that it's deadly. JRJ has the ability to balance sheer humanity with sheer grotesquerie."
—*21C Magazine*

"The guy's a genius. Reminds me of William Gibson—the dark interest in altered states of consciousness, the unrelentingly furious forward movement, and the same kind of unlimited imagination."
—Ben Loory, author of *Stories for Nighttime and Some for the Day*

"Jeremy Robert Johnson performs stand-up comedy for the gods. And their laughter is a marvelous, terrible thing. He's the kind of post-Lovecraftian genius berserker who makes the Great Old Ones new again. As with Clive Barker, there is no glorious mutational eruption that Johnson can't nail directly through your gawping mind's eye."
—John Skipp, *New York Times* bestselling author of *Spore* (with Cody Goodfellow) and *The Bridge* (with Craig Spector)

"In its most twisted moments, Johnson's writing is too gleeful to pigeon-hole as strictly horror, and when he steps outside the gross-out game he transcends most other straight literary writers."
—*Verbicide*

"Johnson weaves vivid and fascinatingly grotesque tales."
—*Bookgasm*

"I don't know if Mr. Johnson sold his soul to the devil to give him this gift for nightmare imagery, but by god, this guy can write. Johnson excels at pathology and perversity. A confirmed weirdo and authentic writer of uncommon emotional depth who deserves to be watched."
—*Cemetery Dance*

"Johnson is probably a few books away from doing for horror what Jonathan Lethem did for science fiction. Plain and simple? Forget horror; this is good fiction."
—*Girl on Demand*

"Johnson can write horror, science fiction, crime, and Bizarro. Sometimes he does all of the above within the same story. He's at once brutal and elegant, innovative and an immediate classic, ridiculously talented and an obvious perfectionist."
—*Horror Talk*

"*Entropy in Bloom* is an instant classic, a carefully curated manifesto whose main goal is to tell the world one of the brightest stars in indie lit is now too brilliant to remain hidden. . . . This collection should turn him into the writer everyone is talking about. These fifteen stories and one novella show a powerful imagination, a great talent for storytelling, writing chops that allow him to tackle any genre, and a flowing, dynamic voice that, if Johnson were a singer, would extend to an impressive eight octaves."
—*Electric Literature*

"Exciting, unpredictable, and feels slightly dangerous . . . free of the boundaries of conventional literature in ways you can't quite imagine. *Entropy in Bloom* is emotionally challenging, unpredictable and thoroughly original. I cannot say it enough: I had a great time with this book."
—*Dead End Follies*

"[Makes] readers and fellow authors scratch their heads while wondering 'How the hell did he pull that off?' Crime, horror, bizarro, and everything in between; Johnson can do it and blow your mind in the process."
—*LitReactor*

Entropy in Bloom

Also by Jeremy Robert Johnson

Collections
Angel Dust Apocalypse
We Live Inside You

Novels
Siren Promised (with Alan M. Clark)
Extinction Journals
Skullcrack City

Entropy in Bloom

stories by
Jeremy Robert Johnson

Night Shade Books
New York

Night Shade books may be purchased in bulk at special discounts for sales promotion, corporate gifts, fund-raising, or educational purposes. Special editions can also be created to specifications. For details, contact the Special Sales Department, Night Shade Books, 307 West 36th Street, 11th Floor, New York, NY 10018 or info@skyhorsepublishing.com.

Night Shade Books® is a registered trademark of Skyhorse Publishing, Inc.®, a Delaware corporation.

Visit our website at www.nightshadebooks.com.

10 9 8 7 6 5 4 3 2

Library of Congress Cataloging-in-Publication Data

Names: Johnson, Jeremy Robert, 1977- author.
Title: Entropy in Bloom : stories / Jeremy Robert Johnson.
Description: New York : Night Shade Books, [2017]
Identifiers: LCCN 2016038959 | ISBN 9781597808958 (hardcover : acid-free paper)
Subjects: | BISAC: FICTION / Horror. | FICTION / Short Stories (single author). | FICTION / Fantasy / Short Stories. | FICTION / Occult & Supernatural. | GSAFD: Horror fiction. | Occult fiction. | Fantasy fiction.
Classification: LCC PS3610.O35643 A6 2017 | DDC 813/.6--dc23
LC record available at https://lccn.loc.gov/2016038959

Hardcover ISBN: 978-1-59780-895-8
Trade Paperback ISBN: 978-1-59780-925-2

Cover illustration by Martin Wittfooth
Cover design by Rain Saukas

Printed in the United States of America

For Caleb

Table of Contents

An Introduction by Brian Evenson — *xiii*

The League of Zeroes — 1
Persistence Hunting — 10
The Oarsman — 29
The Gravity of Benham Falls — 36
Dissociative Skills — 48
Snowfall — 56
When Susurrus Stirs — 61
Luminary — 70
Trigger Variation — 78
Cathedral Mother — 97
Swimming in the House of the Sea — 115
Saturn's Game — 129
The Sharp-Dressed Man at the End of the Line — 141
A Flood of Harriers — 149
States of Glass — 165
The Sleep of Judges — 183

Author's Notes — *255*
Acknowledgments — *261*
Publication Credits — *263*
About the Author — *264*

An Introduction

by Brian Evenson

I think it was Stephen Graham Jones who first mentioned Jeremy Robert Johnson to me, seven or eight years ago now. Shortly after, I saw a copy of *Extinction Journals* in a bookstore and picked it up and read the first line—"The cockroaches took several hours to eat the President."—and thought, "What the . . . ?!?" A few paragraphs later, as things really got zany (with, among other things, radiation protective suits made out of Twinkies and sewn-together cockroaches), I decided to buy the book.

In Johnson's world, anything can happen. The most crazed, twisted ideas are given life, pursued to their bitter limit. People have their lips removed in the name of beauty, Tibetan monks sing the human race into death, a boy slits open his own stomach just out of curiosity, a man's body billows out in an explosion of tiny insects. Straight-edge punks might get high on intense violence, even murder, or a treehugger might find more in the crown of a redwood than she bargained for, or a man might discover that a robbery is just the first gambit in a game that will lead to his own destruction, a game whose rules he can't begin to understand. One story even opens, *"You could bite off Todd's nose,"* and it becomes quickly clear that if Jeremy Robert Johnson hasn't actually bitten off someone's (Todd's?) nose, he's spent a fair amount of time thinking about what that actually might be like, and he's kindly willing to share the fruits of that knowledge with you, the reader. Beginning with absurd premises that often swerve into some serious darkness, reading Johnson is a little like believing you're at a GWAR show and in on the joke, and instead suddenly finding yourself a participant in Gorgoroth's Black Mass.

But it's more than that, since Johnson can shift gears and genres between and within stories, keeping you always a little off balance, going from dark to comic, from *Twilight Zone*-style horror to contemporary noir to something almost Lovecraftian and back again. The point is, you never quite know where you're going to go in a Jeremy Robert Johnson story, and even when you get a glimmer of where you're heading, you may still not quite believe it. What makes Johnson so interesting is that once he takes on a premise, no matter how absurd it is to begin with, he treats it seriously. He rushes forward with the concept, often at a dizzying pace, leaving you as a reader wildly trying to find something to hold on to. These stories can be uncomfortable, difficult, unflinching, but they're also always entertaining. Johnson writes with an energy that propels you through some very dark spaces indeed and into something profoundly unsettling but nonetheless human.

One of the great things going on with writers working on the edge of several different genres, with writers simultaneously able to overlay the codes of different ways of reading into their work—providing multiple paths through a book and multiple deliberate dead ends that force you to shift code sets along the way—is that they're both able to offer readers the satisfactions of those genres and to give them something more: the whole is more than the sum of the parts. Johnson's work rewards readers who read widely, who like different genres, and who think about connections across genres. The kinds of readers who are willing to stand on the side of the literary highway and thumb down whatever vehicle comes by, who are willing to take more chances than the average reader.

It'll be a wild ride, but after a little shaking you'll get to your destination, and be able to get out unharmed, mostly, and it'll still be you. Or at least someone who looks and acts like you. Well, someone who will be able to pass for you in most circumstances. Honestly, the real you probably won't even be missed.

The League of Zeroes

It's obvious she's having a hard time sipping her coffee. No matter how delicately she raises her hand or how straight and elegant her posture, she can't help looking awkward when she drinks. Half the damn cup of coffee is trickling its way to the spreading brown stain on the front of her white blouse.

It's her fault, really. She's the one who wanted to have her lips removed.

She'll adapt. We all do.

She'll figure out how to keep her gums moisturized with Vaseline, and she'll carry a small container of it in her purse at all times.

She'll learn to drink with a straw tucked into the side of her cheek. You can still get some good suction like that and the method cuts the mess to nothing.

She'll get her teeth bonded and bleached to emphasize their newfound prominence.

She'll figure out how to make plosive sounds with her tongue against the back of her gums.

She'll be looking good and find it even easier to smile.

I think she's gorgeous, sans shirtfront stain, but I don't think she'd go for a guy like me. I consider crossing the coffee shop and trying a pick-up line, but the three prongs I've had my tongue split into feel swollen and tied up. Still healing, I guess.

Although she might find my iris-free eyes attractive. They're all pupil; very black, mysterious and hard to read. That might work for her.

Deep down I know she'd never go for an amateur freak like me. She's the type of elegant, slightly-modified trophy girlfriend I see hanging around with Body Modification Royalty.

I'll save myself the embarrassment for now. Once I join the League of Zeroes, though, she's mine.

The thought of being a freak show all-star brings my all-black eyes back to my sketchbook. I'm looking at the drawing of my modification design, wondering just how the hell my brain is going to look outside of my body. I hope it's symmetrical. I never had to worry about brain aesthetics until I came up with my plan.

I want to detach my brain from my body. I want to polish it up and put it in a nice display case and carry it around with me, like a sidekick.

My Buddy the Brain.

I jot notes around the sketch.

How do I keep the brain clean and presentable?

What kind of fiber-optics can transmit neuro-signals to my spinal cord?

How do I do this and not die?

Is it worth it?

I look up and across the room at Our Lady of Liplessness. I picture her licking the box I will keep my brain in, asking me what it's like to be in the League of Zeroes.

She'll think I'm special.

It's worth it.

I wonder for a moment longer about asking her for a date, see if she wants to check out the Italian Horror Movie Festival on

Fifteenth. I pass on the idea. Maybe it's just sublimated embarrassment, but she looks a little uptight. She might bite.

I head out of the coffee shop and kick over three blocks in the cold until I reach a telephone booth. I sweep the coin return for change and come back with a finger load of ketchup. At least I hope that it's ketchup. I'm curious, but I skip the smell and taste test and smear the red goop on the glass of the phone booth wall in front of me. I drop in some coins, press seven buttons.

Raymond picks up the phone on the other end and says, "SaladMan here!"

The second I hear his voice I feel like I wasted eighty-five cents.

"Hey, Ray, it's Jamie. Cool it on the SaladMan shit, you don't have to market to me."

"I know, Jamie, I'm just trying to stay on point. I'm picking up a lot of regional buzz and a couple of the BMR's have mentioned me on the website."

Ray, who is my best friend based only on our mutual lack of total resentment, is obsessed with joining the upper echelon of the League of Zeroes. He keeps talking.

"I'm serious, Jamie. I'm like days from becoming Body Modification Royalty. You know Aggie WoodSpine? He's always putting in a good word for me on the circuit, and Marshall Le Crawl has said, and I'm almost quoting like verbatim here, that I have one of the most original modification schemes he's ever seen. That's on the damn website."

"I know, Ray, I'm aware of the accolades. I'm not doubting you. I've got more pressing business, that's all, so if I seem impatient it's only because what you're saying isn't important."

"Thanks, Jamie. What's going on?"

"Meet me at the Italian Horror Movie Festival in twenty minutes, okay. We'll check out some Fulci, watch some eyeballs burst, and then we'll go get coffee and I'll tell you about my new scheme. I think I've come up with something really special."

"Cool. I'll catch you later."

"Oh, hey, Salad . . . hey, Ray."

"Yeah."

"I saw another chick with no lips today. I think that style's about to blow up."

"Yeah. I've seen that around lately. How'd she look?"

"Pretty sharp, man. Pretty sharp."

WE'RE HEADING OUT OF the theater halfway through the movie 'cause we've already seen the best stuff; the scene where that kid gets the drill through his skull, and the one where the demon priest sucks out that girl's organs just by staring at her.

Ray and I are walking in the flickering light of the faded theater marquee and I'm anxious, hoping for something more visceral in my life. No more celluloid thrills and vicarious rendering of the flesh. I'm ready for my next surgery and I can't wait to tell Ray my plans.

I pop in to a Super Saver Mart while Ray waits out front. It costs me thirty bucks for a pack of Marlboro Chronics, a soda, two Charleston Chews, and a dropper of Visine. Half of the money goes to taxes. I have to give the government credit for that one. The same day they legalized weed they went and imposed a sin tax on candy and eye drops. It's almost devious enough to be admirable.

We head over to D. Brewster's Café and find some plush seats far from the speakers where we can have a conversation. I don't order anything because I've already got my soda and chocolate, and Ray picks up an extra large mocha.

Ray is starting to smell. I think some of his vegetables have gone south again, even though Dr. Tikoshi soaked them in preservative this time. The lettuce sewn into his neck looks like it's browning at the edges, and the tip of the carrot emerging unicorn-proud from his forehead has broken off. The sutures around the radish spliced into his right forearm look swollen and irritated.

Right from the beginning I told him SaladMan was a screwed-up scheme. I told him that perishables were always too high mainte-nance. He's right about the attention he's garnering though; even now people are staring at him. Still, on a purely olfactory level spending time with Ray is like hanging out with a big pile of compost.

Despite his odor, he gets big points for ambition. He's got some respectable friends on the circuit and if he can get someone to endorse him as Body Modification Royalty he can do some tour time and then apply for the League of Zeroes.

The League. It's the big money, the endorsements, the adulation, the weekly primetime broadcasts, and the outright worship of the people.

Ray's got his goals set high. If he makes it big he'll be able to buy fresh produce every day, and eventually he'll be able to afford that platinum dressing decanter that he wants to have installed in his ribcage.

I've got him beat though. After my next modification I'll be an indelible image in the public eye. My plan is the fourth ace nobody thought I had.

I lean in through a cloud of thick smoke and whisper my scheme into SaladMan's cauliflowered right ear.

I'M ALONE AND WALKING home with my thin jean jacket wrapped tight around my shoulders.

I hear Ray's voice in the café whispering, "Jamie, that's *impossible*. What makes you think you could live through that kind of modification?"

I brush off his comment, but the concern sounded genuine. I try not to take it to heart. I'm so excited about my imminent fame that mortality has become a second-string worry.

Maybe Ray's just jealous.

I shake Ray's doubts out of my head and remember how great my scheme is. It's worth the gamble. I've never been one to swallow motivational speaker pablum but I've always nodded in agreement at the phrase, "You've got to play big to win big!" So, I'm choosing not to acknowledge the danger. Now entering Ostrich Mode, head firmly inserted in sand.

On my way home I walk past trashcan fires and drug deals and I hear sirens wailing and glass breaking and a bag lady nearby mumbles something about wires embedded in the Earth telling all of us what to do.

A League of Zeroes poster stapled to a telephone pole advertises an upcoming appearance by S. O. Faygus and his amazing translucent throat.

An ad beneath the poster promises a two-for-one deal on mail-order brides.

Another asks me if I *really* trust my gas mask.

It all leaves me with the impression that I'm living in some kind of ravaged nuclear wasteland. The problem with that diagnosis lies in the absence of any level of apocalypse. No one dropped any bombs; no great fire scorched the Earth.

We just ended up like this. We followed a natural progression from past to present. We're not Post-Apocalyptic, we're Post-Yesterday.

One look around, though, and I realize that we must have had some brutal kind of Yesterday.

Ray's voice is still in my head, echoing doubt, stirring up stomach acid.

"Jamie, that's impossible!"

It can't be.

This plan is all I have. It's my only chance of getting off these streets.

It's the only way I'll ever be special.

DR. TIKOSHI WOULDN'T TAKE me as a patient.

Dr. Komatsu had me ejected from his building.

I had to go to my old standby, Dr. Shinori. He's the only one who likes to experiment. He's the only one willing to push boundaries. He's the only one who would take a credit card.

I'm moments from anesthesia and Dr. Shinori is sharpening his diamond bone saw. He has emphasized several times how difficult this will be. He hasn't said anything, and I wouldn't understand a single word he'd say, but we've been communicating with drawings.

I showed him a picture of my design, the new me, the guaranteed League of Zeroes member.

He sketched for a moment and showed me a picture. On the left there was a big, bright smiley face, and on the right there was a little stick figure drawing of my body resting in a casket.

I hope this means my chances are fifty/fifty.

I suspect this might mean he'd be happy to kill me. He gets my money either way. I signed the Goddamn waiver. I'm taking the dive.

I go over the reasons in my head, even though it's too late to turn back. People would assume I take the risks and bear the public scrutiny because there's money in it. They wouldn't be totally wrong. The freak show industry pulls millions every year, and gets more lucrative as time passes. More fame, more attention. Those things don't hurt. Before I started this, before I split my tongue into three prongs and had my irises removed and my toes extended, I was dirt poor and always felt like I was ugly anyway. Now I'm so ugly that people can't look away, *and* I can pull advertising dollars.

The number one reason I do this? People jump to assumptions and whisper asides to each other about parental neglect or abuse or acid in my baby formula. They're wrong.

I do this because when I was little my mom told me I was going to be someone *special*.

I asked her what special meant. She pointed to the TV screen. I thought "special" was Burt Reynolds, until she spoke up.

"Special means that people pay attention to you. Special means you have something that other people don't. Special is having people love you without even knowing you. I know, and have known since the day you were born, that you are going to be special. That's why I love you so much, Jamie."

So, I waited to become special.

By the time I hit twenty, I was just like everyone else.

I still am.

Which is not to say that I'm Mr. Free Spirit Railing Against Conformity, because everyone else does *that* too. I just know that I'm not special, and I have to force the change.

Mom calls me less and less these days.

The hugs are shorter than they used to be.

So here I am, a product of forcible evolution trying to stay one step ahead of the other mutants, hoping my mommy pays attention.

Dr. Shinori puts the gas mask over my mouth and nose and doesn't ask me to start counting backwards from a hundred. I know the routine. By ninety-five I'm floating in a soft yellow ocean made from rose petals. Somewhere further away I'm shaking as the bone saw hits meat.

THE STAGE LIGHTS ARE especially bright tonight, but I can still make out the audience. The women with no lips always look pleased, grinning wide as the valley.

Ray is in the front row tonight. I flew him out here, even though he's Body Modification Royalty now and could afford it himself. He's not wearing a shirt and the baby tomatoes sewn into his chest spell out SaladMan, which is pretty sound promotion.

As the leader of the League of Zeroes I get to make a closing address to our national audience each Thursday.

My mom is in the crowd, like always, and I'm planning a great address tonight, something about how Love Evolves Us All.

They'll eat it up, but they won't understand the costs that come with being truly *special*. They won't know about the white-fire headaches. They won't know about the pressure that shoots down my spine when I change the oxygenated cerebrospinal fluid. They won't know what it's like when your brain signals get backed up and a dream hits you while your eyes are wide open. I keep these things to myself. I don't even tell my mom. She thinks I'm perfect now.

The audience always likes to hear about how I'm doing, first thing in the show. I tell them my brain is getting a little hot under these stage lights and that gets a good, hearty laugh. I'm laughing with them, but inside I'm genuinely concerned and I shift my hands to the left and try to move the clear, titanium-laced plastic box I keep my brain in toward the shadows. It tugs on the fiber optic lines running into my neck at the top of my spinal cord, but I manage.

I adapt. We all do.

Persistence Hunting

Don't act surprised, or shake your bloody fists at the night sky. You chased this down.

Help is coming—maybe a reality check can keep you seething until it gets here. Better than slipping into shock.

Face it—you're lying there in the evening chill, broken and breathless on the dewy suburban grass because of a basic truth:

You've always been a sucker for love.

And being smart enough to know that isn't the same as being able to do a goddamn thing about it.

YOU WERE A MARK from the get-go.

Age seven: All Mary Ashford had to do was smile. You kicked over your licorice. She skipped away, shared it with that red-headed oaf Mikey Vinson.

Rube.

Age fourteen: Sarah Miller asked you to the last dance of the year.

Why wouldn't you help her with her algebra homework? An easy down-payment on a guaranteed post-dance make-out session.

You even gave Sarah your final exam answers.

She passed algebra.

She passed on attending the dance.

Stomach flu—very sad. She cried on the phone.

Two weeks later she went to the final dance at the school across town. With Mikey Fucking Vinson. The rumor mill had them crossing fourth base. In a *hot tub*.

You cursed Mikey Vinson, prayed to God for wolves to snuff the bastard, to disembowel him in a hot tub, a steaming red bowl of Vinson soup.

Revenge fantasies waned. You knew the truth. This was on you. You cried yourself to sleep, thinking Sarah Miller would be the last girl you'd ever truly fall for.

Chump.

Age fifteen: Love got blown off the radar.

Was it world-weary resolve? No, you were a mess of hormones and zero savvy charging headlong into the bayonets of the beauties walking your school halls.

Love caught the boot because your parents burned to death on their eighteenth anniversary. Bad electrical blanket wiring and spilled champagne caused a flash-fire.

As with every anniversary weekend since you were born, you were staying at Uncle Joshua's house—a bungalow off Powell on 58th—in Southeast Portland. The crucial difference that weekend was that at the end of it you had no home to return to.

Uncle Joshua took you in. You didn't speak for three months. You dreamed—your parents screaming with smoke-filled lungs.

Your Uncle did his best. Let you know you were loved. Gave you great pulp novels about druggy detectives and man-eating slugs. Taught you how to swear properly. Let you stay up till any hour, so long as you promised to run with him every morning at seven sharp.

"The morning run blows the morning prayer out of the water," he told you. "Gets you thinking. Breathing deep. It clears out the worry, the garbage, everything."

You ran the city with him—sidewalks, tracks, trails. Portland seemed huge and electric in a way your hometown Salem never did.

He showed you how to run through "the wall"—the utter vacuum of energy that forced you to walk. Soon the wall was pushed further and further out.

You ran to exhaustion—morning jogs with your Uncle and epic evening jaunts that allowed you to collapse far from the reality of your loneliness, from dreams of burning hands reaching for your face.

FIVE YEARS AFTER THE fire, love finally tracked you down.

You were twenty-one. Still a virgin. You'd chased nobility, never exploiting your semi-orphan status for a cheap lay. Besides, that would have meant talking to someone, knowing someone.

You were confident chasing the cat was for suckers anyway. You'd transcended that status because you had a *new* kick, something you'd guessed was better than pussy:

THEFT.

It wasn't for the cash—your parents' trust kept you sound.

You stole because you'd recognized a loophole.

Portland was a runner's city. During daylight it was impossible to hit the waterfront without seeing a jogger, but the nights had their own crews. Doctors or bartenders forced into the late shift. Other running zealots like you.

And Portland's runner omni-presence rendered you a non-threat to the cops. Another fitness freak in fancy gear. You rocked sheer shirts, a Garmin GPS watch, a CamelBak water backpack, a flashy yellow vest, and shorts designed to hug your junk.

You liked to wave at the cops, give them a nod that said, "Here we are, upstanding citizens keeping things safe and healthy."

Sometimes they waved back. Some of those times you ran right by them with a thousand dollars worth of pinched jewelry in your CamelBak.

They never turned around. What self-respecting thief would run by a cop car while rocking reflective gear meant to call attention?

You were just another night runner fading in the rearview.

In fairness to them, you started minor, like some jockey-boxing meth-head.

Your LifeHammer tool was designed for drivers trapped in a submerged vehicle. One side had a hammer specially designed to crack tempered auto glass.

Ostensibly designed for exits, it worked great for entrances.

You trolled the NW hills near the Leif Erikson trail, pulling smash-and-grabs on Suburbans, Jaguars, a smattering of Portland's ubiquitous Subarus and Priuses. You copped cell phones, cameras, MP3 players. You copped hard-ons from the gigs, tracked record runs off the buzz.

You kept the swag in a box in your closet, obsessed over it, deciphering what you could about the people you'd jacked. You fell asleep to stolen playlists. You studied the smiles of strangers in digital photos.

You soon realized that any tweaker could crack car windows.

The buzz dwindled.

You escalated—houses were the logical progression.

Your first pick was a sharp art-deco joint. You'd done your sidewalk surveying—they had a habit of leaving the sliding glass door on the side of their house open.

You almost bailed. Nerves. Visions of the owners polishing rifles inside.

You decided to hit their car instead—a desperation move.

You got lucky, opened the glove compartment, found a receipt. Franzetti Jewelers—$6,000. Dated that day. Scrambled the car, found zilch.

Was it in the home? A necklace, a ring—they'd fit into your backpack so easily. Something like that was much more intimate than an iPod—it represented history between two people.

The gravity of it pulled you to the side entrance of the house.

You knocked on the door frame. "Hello?"

If anyone answered, you'd feign injury: You'd crunched your ankle coming down from Forest Park. Needed a cab, a hospital.

After your third "Hello" echoed dead, you crossed the threshold.

It took five exhilarating minutes to find the jewelry box. Bedroom dresser, third drawer, under a pile of gold-toe socks. A serious square-cut rock mounted on a platinum setting. An engagement in the cards?

You thought about leaving the stone. But then you remembered Mary Ashford and Sarah Miller, decided to save the guy from becoming another sucker.

You hit the streets, the ring secure in your CamelBak.

Back home, the jewelry went into the swag box. You couldn't sleep, reviewing your plunder, tiny pieces of other lives.

B & E's became *everything*.

One a week at first. Monday through Thursday was casual jog recon. Weekends were break-ins.

Jewels reigned supreme. They spent time close to other people, had sentimental value.

You'd take cash when discovered, but never credit cards.

Once a week quickly became "whenever the coast looked clear." Your record was three break-ins in one night.

You wore thin white runner's gloves, hoping they'd prevent prints.

You carried steak-flavored dog treats but never had the guts to break into a house after you'd heard a dog bark. You petted cats when they'd allow it.

If a whole pack of cigarettes was left out you'd take one smoke, save it for the morning, puff on it at sunrise.

Sometimes you went to hip hop shows before your evening run. It was easy to stay chill, enjoy a show solo, hood up, feeling like an anonymous gangster amidst all the fronting. They could talk up the criminal life; you *lived* it.

You tried to maintain the morning runs with Uncle Joshua. He noticed your owl eyes and lagging pace.

He expressed concern.

You dropped the routine. The nights were just too long.

It was in this state—harried, junkie-hungry for break-ins—that you let love back into your life.

SLOW IT DOWN. PAY attention. This is where everything fell apart.

You were coming home via Burnside that night, maneuvering around the bum-clusters near the bridge. An alky with a piece of corn in his beard gave you a wave.

You were astronaut high from a twenty minute break-in session. The entire house had smelled like summer lilac. You'd wondered if the owners paid to have that piped in at all hours.

That sweet smell is what you were thinking about at the moment the little black car took a no-look right turn at 10th and Burnside past Union Jack's. You saw a bright flash out of your peripheral, heard a thump that you ID'd as your body hitting the hood of the ride. Then you were rolling on pavement.

Brake lights made the scene run red. You caught the model of the car . . . couldn't focus on the license plate.

Last-call closeout-boozers were a night run liability. You'd accepted that, but you couldn't accept the fact that you might have been slaughtered by a fucking Jetta with a butterfly sticker on the bumper.

Gorgeous legs in camouflage stockings emerged from the driver's side. The girl stood, giraffe-tall. Five inch heels. Soon she was crouched by your side. You couldn't focus on her face aside from wide hazel eyes, tiny flecks of gold floating in the green.

You sap—you might have been in love before you even lost consciousness.

SHE DANCED UNDER THE name Avarice. When she told a guy he could call her Ava it guaranteed extra tips. When boys pointed out the fitting nature of her name she called them clever. That pulled more tips, too.

She was insanely irresponsible, taking you to her apartment instead of a hospital, but her license was already suspended for another offense. Ava had bugged at the idea of real jail time and was strong enough to get you into her back seat, then her first floor apartment. She watched you sleep on her couch. You kept breathing. She gave you an ice compress for your head. You asked for Advil; she came back with two Valium and a Xanax, delivered by slender hands, chipped black polish on the fingernails.

She asked why you were out running so late. You told her you worked a day job and preferred to run when it was cooler out. She asked what you did. You said roofing. Seemed tough.

She asked you running questions, caught your excitement about the topic, used it. You could see her game—ingratiate until she knew charges would be dropped—but you didn't want to stop playing. You liked the way she was tending to you. It stirred something you hadn't felt in years.

Plus, she was easy on the eyes. Heart-shaped pale face framed with short black hair. Decent lips made more charming by a crooked smile. Legs that seemed to be two thirds of her frame. She wore grey shorts with pink trim piping, a thin green cotton T-shirt that showed off the curves on each side of her small breasts.

You knew most men didn't get to see her like this—casual, relaxed and gracious. She knew you knew and rode the vibe. She showed you her tattoos—two thin stripes, one running up the back of each leg, meant to mimic the back seam of a pair of pin-up stockings. As she got closer you saw that each seam was actually composed of delicate cursive words.

She bent forward, touched her toes so you could see the entirety of each line.

The right leg said: . . . I asked him with my eyes to ask again yes and then he asked me would I yes to say yes my mountain flower and first I put my arms around him

The left leg continued: yes and drew him down to me so he could feel my breasts all perfume yes and his heart was going like mad and yes I said yes I will Yes.

"It's from Ulysses," she said.

She admitted that every time she read that last chapter she felt like "rubbing one out." She made a circling motion in the sky with her index finger and closed her eyes. Then she smiled, full blaze.

You were ready to die for this girl, and she hadn't even kissed you.

YOUR CONCUSSION WAS MINOR. More disconcerting was the new gimpy sensation in your right leg. When you tried to run the iliotibial band next to your knee registered tight, hot pain.

You had to drop running for a week. Better to let it rest than blow it out.

Ava was an Olympic-level tease. When she dropped you off at your Uncle's house she leaned in close, said she wanted to look at your pupils. Be sure you didn't have any brain damage. She locked you in at the eyes. Her lips floated a hair's-breadth from yours, the heat from her face mixing nicely with your Valium/brain damage buzz.

She whispered in your ear, "I think you'll be just fine." Then she told you what nights she worked at which clubs.

She didn't seem surprised that you were there every night. You dipped into the box in your closet, swapped jewels for cash at pawn shops, loved spending ill-gotten gains on Ava.

You bought every lap dance you reasonably could. When anyone else got too close to her they looked like Mikey Vinson.

You turned creepazoid one night, crawled her apartment when you knew she was at the beginning of her dance shifts at Sassy's. You were pro at climbing in through windows. Summer heat had everyone's open. Seemed she barely lived there aside from her disheveled futon and the explosion of clothes scattered throughout. You threw two pairs of her underwear in your CamelBak, rushed home for an epic stroke-fest. You tied her lacy yellow G-string around the base of your cock, huffed the blue cotton pair, and pounded yourself into exhaustion. You never ran short on fantasies—your favorites involved her sneaking into houses with you, violating every room.

If it wasn't obsession, it was pretty damn close.

Things seemed fine, spectacular really, until the night she invited you over for coffee at her place. You accepted, secretly ecstatic, but caught the heebie-jeebies when you noticed she wasn't talking to you on the way, kept looking over her shoulder.

At her apartment she brought you into the loop—She liked you, more than she expected. But she already had a man, on the low, and he was insanely jealous, sometimes to the point where he got rough. She didn't know how to leave him. She didn't want to endanger you. The guy never came down to her clubs, but his friends sometimes did. They'd noticed you. How could they not?

You puffed up your chest. "Who is this guy?"

"Have you ever heard of Stump Lo?"

Shit. You had. You un-puffed your chest.

Stump Lo was a Portland rapper who'd been struggling for years to pimp his pseudo-Cali-gangster-style hip-hop to an audience more interested in commercial hits or backpacker rap. He was the dude you sat through while you waited for the good rappers to come on—tolerated but not loved. You could feel his resentment on stage.

Word was he'd shifted to coke sales a year or two back—he wanted the cred and his album sales weren't churning out the royalties—and had worked his way to the upper echelon of Snortland suppliers.

This moment is when you should've jumped ship.

Instead you looked into Ava's eyes and decided to tell her about your hobbies. It was the best sales pitch available, to offer an alternative bad-ass, one who wouldn't trap her in jealousy.

You told her you weren't a roofer, you were a fucking roughneck criminal. At the top of your game you were Portland's best cat burglar.

You also broke your code and exploited your parents' death, saying you'd even had to see their bodies. You told her you hadn't felt fear since that day. If she didn't want to stay with Stump she could roll with you.

You escalated your bravado with each detail. Her eyes sparked.

She wanted to hear more about your break-ins. You told her about all but one of them.

She loved your runner's scheme for evading the law.

She leaned over, put her hand on your face. Said she had an amazing idea.

You were all ears, you sorry Rescue Ronnie Captain Save-a-Ho motherfucker.

YOU SOLD THE REST of your stolen swag, a whole day of pawn shop hustling.

You liquidated your trust, cashed out your swollen checking account.

Ava found a great place in the Caymans online.

You'd miss your Uncle, but had no other ties and figured that Ava's legs around your back could ease any pain.

Ava told you she'd already bought tickets.

She confirmed she'd found a buyer for Friday night—she knew dealers who liked to show off their cash in the clubs. Now it was just a matter of acquiring the blow.

Stump Lo was going to open a show for Keak da Sneak that night. A small opening, maybe a few hours, but after your score all that remained was a shot up I-5 to meet Ava's connection. Then on to PDX and paradise.

You met with Ava after her shift on Wednesday night. You wanted her to have your best diamond ring, from your first break-in. You couldn't bring yourself to hock it. You waited near her car, not wanting to risk any of Stump Lo's friends seeing you inside.

She ate it up. Even got a little teary-eyed. She put her hands on your hips, pressed her cheek against yours and said, quietly, "I think I might be falling in love with you."

She smelled like sweat, cigarettes, too much perfume. You loved it. You wanted to kiss her but she was gesturing you towards her car. You got in, thinking she couldn't contain her need anymore. You'd fuck right there in the lot . . .

Instead she wanted to review details for Friday. She would drop by Stump's place before the show, wishing him luck. She would make sure that his Rottweiler—named Scarface, of course—was kenneled. You'd watch for Stump to leave. Once he did you'd run around back and disconnect the A/C unit running into his office. That's your access point. After that it was simple—grab the coke/get out. Then a quarter mile jog to your meeting point. You'd roll in her car, make your sale, then get into costume for the airport.

She'd been inspired by your adventures in social camouflage, figured it could work to her advantage too. You'd enter PDX as proud parents-to-be. Her prosthetic belly-bump and draping maternity gear would conceal your collected cash nest egg as well as half a brick.

You questioned the wisdom of bringing drugs. Carrying serious cash was already suspect. The coke made the trip trafficking. Why risk it?

"The US dollar is on the decline. Coke is universal tender. We can turn it into money, connections, favors. I've never seen a pregnant chick getting searched at the airport. Have you?"

You hadn't.

"And now, with this rock on my finger, we'll look like we're engaged. It's perfect."

You considered proposing. Make it real, right then. But it might spook her, and you knew better times were coming. Wouldn't it be cooler to propose at sunset, in the sand, with a buzz kicking from some tropical cocktail?

Besides, you hadn't even kissed yet. For all you knew, though you tried to exterminate the thought, she might still be fucking Stump Lo. But if she was it was just to perfect her cover, keeping things smooth until you could begin your life together, right? You squashed the thoughts.

She pinned you down with her eyes.

"Are you ready for Friday night?"

The version of yourself that you were selling could answer only Yes.

GETTING IN WAS SIMPLE. You saw those window-mounted A/C units as "Open House" signs. You'd brought your LifeHammer as back-up, but all you'd needed to access Stump's residence was a small screwdriver and the ability to disconnect a plug.

You were halfway up the stairs to the guest bathroom where the stash was supposed to be hidden, feeling like the air had been replaced with a Dexedrine mist. Your mouth was dry, your face a sheet of sweat.

You noticed a drop of perspiration fall from the tip of your nose to the carpeted stair underfoot, and wondered if it could pop up as evidence.

You were bent over using your runner's glove to swab up the droplet when Scarface caught your left calf in his jaws.

At first you thought it was a severe cramp. Maybe you'd been favoring your left leg to protect your fragile right and the imbalance caught up with you.

Even when you heard the growl and felt teeth sinking in you couldn't quite believe it. After all, you'd received Ava's text: DG KNNLD, STMP LVG 1 HR.

What neither of you'd considered was that Stump might extract Scarface prior to leaving.

Call it an oversight.

An oversight that was quickly turning your left leg into shredded meat.

You collapsed forward on the staircase. Scarface dug in deeper, swung his head.

Agony.

You'd stopped thinking. You tried to kick out at him with your other foot but couldn't land more than a glancing blow. You wished you'd started running in steel-shanked boots instead of sneaks.

You tried to say, "Good doggy let go doggy" but when you opened your mouth to assuage, all that came out was, "AAAAAAA! SHITSHITSHIT! JESUS!" It riled him; he clamped deeper.

You found the beefy treats you always carried in your pocket for just such an occasion. You tried to extend your arms backwards with the snacks so Scarface could catch the scent.

No interest. So you did your best to wing the snacks at him.

A yelp! Sweet mother of mercy—his jaws cut loose for a second. You rotated, braced for further assaults.

Scarface was pawing at the right side of his face, whining. One of the stale old snacks must have clipped him dead in the eye.

For one tiny moment you felt bad for him. Then his head dropped below his shoulders. He was about to pounce again. You kicked out in desperation, eyes closed . . . .

Both of your feet made contact.

Scarface thumped to the bottom of the staircase, laid out.

Shit! You felt terrible—instantly cursed. Steal a man's coke and his girl and he might move on with his life. But kill his dog? He'd probably hunt you to the ends of the Earth.

Without thinking you were limping back down the stairs, towards the dog, to see if you'd actually killed it. Then you heard a low growl.

Scarface popped up in full bristle, teeth bared, bloody.

Your blood. It took a second to recognize that.

You leapt up the stairs, four at a time. You had to lean more weight on your right. The tightness there turned to razor-wire. Then you were in the upper hallway and bounding, trying to remember what she'd said.

Third door on the left. Guest bathroom.

You collapsed into the third room, no longer caring if it was the bathroom, just wanting to kick the door closed. Shut out the beast.

You heard the door click shut and pressed your right foot against the wood, bracing it.

You could tell he was out there, hear him gnawing at the door with the side of his mouth. You reached up, locked the door. Gnashing turned to barking, guttural eruptions.

You worried about the neighbors being alerted but remembered what Ava told you—the whole joint was soundproofed since they used to get complaints about the studio bumping beats at all hours.

You flipped the light switch and caught yourself in the mirror. Bloody. Shaking. In track gear. The image ran ugly.

But at least you'd landed in the bathroom.

You were glad the mirror had to come down—seeing yourself in that moment brought in a rush of feelings and questions that were better not contemplated. You grabbed each side of the frame, lifted up, and pulled it back off its mounting screws.

The hole in the drywall was there, as she'd described. You reached in and found the plastic loop, pulled it off the nail in the stud. The loop was attached to a vinyl cord. Your shoulders strained to reel in the compressed duffel bag at its far end.

Seeing the loot gave you new confidence. You'd found your grail—your princess was waiting for your return. You re-mounted the mirror, used a towel to clean your blood off the floor and then wrapped it around your leg to staunch further bleeding.

Scarface's paws thumped against the door, nails scraping, not calming down. You scanned the bathroom for a weapon and found nothing that would allow you to confront the hound with confidence.

That left one point of exit—a small sliding window above the shower.

You slid the window open, popped the screen. You tied off the duffel bag to your CamelBak and used the vinyl cord to lower them to the ground.

The drop from the second floor was unfriendly no matter how you went about it. You managed to hang and exit feet first. Both legs felt equally savaged so you couldn't pick one to bear the brunt of the fall. Instead you tried to let your legs collapse and shift your weight to the back so you could somersault out of it.

This did not work.

Your left leg hit first. Before you could shift your weight your knee was driven into your jaw. A world-class uppercut delivered by yourself. For a moment everything was fireworks, copper, dust. Then your brain cleared out.

You'd made it.

Your contraband was to your left, Scarface was a distant threat, and you were only a quarter mile from an angel-in-waiting.

WHAT YOU DIDN'T EXPECT was . . . well . . . any of it.

Ava was at the meeting spot, a dusty trailhead near the Wildwood hiking areas. That part matched up with what you'd pictured.

She'd stepped out of the car, closed the door. She'd left the headlights off. You couldn't see her well. You'd taken longer than expected to reach her, moving along with a limping trot. You began to apologize.

"I know I'm running a little behind but you won't believe . . . "

And then she hit you with the Taser.

You were already on the gravel before you recognized the crackling sound, felt the darts piercing your belly.

For a moment you thought that you'd been shot. That Stump Lo had found the pair of you and you were dead for sure.

But it was Ava holding the Taser, and she wasn't letting up on the volts.

Your right leg was folded underneath your body. With the next blast of juice you felt your calf pull too tight. Your fragile iliotibial band finally gave with an audible snap. You would have screamed if your jaw wasn't clenched shut.

Ava let up on the trigger. She said, "Bag!"

You gestured towards your pack and the duffel bag, thrown three feet to your side.

"Ava, what . . . "

She turned the juice back on. Grabbed the duffel, clearly not interested in conversation. She stepped closer.

"I'm going to release the trigger, but if you start to talk I'll Tase you until your hair starts on fire. Got me?"

You made your best effort at a nod.

She crouched closer. "You're not coming with me, but you should still run. You probably didn't even think of this, but Stump's place has a shit-ton of cameras. They make him feel gangster. He's no killer, but the people who supply him will not be pleased."

She'd been rehearsing this, leaving no room for emotion. Maybe she really loved you. Maybe this was some kind of test . . .

She continued. "You've probably killed me. This is what people will think. They will find a letter at Union Jack's, talking about how you'd been planning to rob Stump. You threatened to kill me if I didn't go along with it. You'd even joked about burying me out here in Forest Park and keeping the drugs for yourself. The girls I worked with last night think I'm scared of you. I really sold it. There are plenty of people who've seen you staring at me for hours. It will read as stalker behavior after the letter gets out."

"But, Ava . . . "

ZZZZRNT! You seized up. She was not trigger-shy on the Taser.

"Don't try to find me."

Another long jolt with the Taser. Then she was kneeling by your side, properly pegging you as too jellied for combat. Even in the dark, you could sense she was smiling. She was back at your ear.

"I did love the ring, by the way, but I had to sell it today. Easier to send off the single mother vibe without it."

Then she was over you. Her breath smelled like black licorice. She leaned in to kiss you on the lips.

And you, you sorry sonofabitch, you still wanted it. When her lips met yours you closed your eyes, hoped time would slow.

But it ended, and she was up and the Taser was left in the dirt.

"You're smart enough to know I'm right. Get the fuck out of Portland."

"Ava . . . "

"Good luck."

Her car door slammed. Headlights slapped you blind and she was gone.

YOU HOBBLE-DRAGGED YOURSELF THREE miles before realizing you couldn't go further. Dawn would come and you were far too savaged for your runner's ruse to help you.

You made it to a house which looked unoccupied. You memorized the street address, crawled to the backyard to keep from being spotted street-side.

You drained the water from your CamelBak, still felt Death Valley thirsty.

There *was* one stroke of luck in all of this. Ava left you with your cell phone.

Call it an oversight.

Your first phone call was to Uncle Joshua. He slurred a groggy "Hello?" but was alert after hearing your voice. You gave him the address. Said to come to the backyard of the house. Don't ask why.

He didn't. You'd run with him as best you could this last Thursday, knowing it might be your last time together. He'd started to ask you questions about late nights, your hitchy right leg. You'd cut him off.

"Things are just kind of crazy right now. I met this girl . . . "

Uncle Joshua had laughed and let out a slow, knowing "Oh." You'd worked hard to ignore your leg, picked up the pace. He got the message.

You hoped he'd pick up his pace now. You'd lost a lot of blood. How long did you have before Stump figured out he'd been jacked? How long before Ava's friends would have the cops scanning Forest Park for a body they'd never find?

A light turned on over the patio at the rear of the house. Could be on a timer—you weren't taking any chances. You crawled across the grass, spotting a large and thankfully empty dog house.

You crept in, found it surprisingly plush. Call it delirium, but you swore the west wall had an on-switch for a tiny A/C unit. Even the *dogs* up in the hills were living easy.

You leaned against the rear wall, set your CamelBak on your belly. Unzipped the pack. Pulled out your accidental insurance policy.

You'd broken in to Ava's place on Thursday night, knowing she was working at Devil's Point, to bring her underwear back. Ever since you'd stolen them you'd felt weird about it. They turned you on, but you wanted to move past connecting to people through their things. You had a chance to be with the flesh-and-blood girl. Starting out psychotic felt wrong.

But once you were in her place you couldn't help exploring. You rifled the bag she'd packed, wanting to see what kind of swimsuits she'd be wearing to the beach.

You'd been living with compulsion so long you didn't even question it when you pocketed the thing. She was going to need it with her. This way you'd be certain she wouldn't forget it.

But you could have left it in the bag. It was already packed. She wasn't going to forget it. Maybe, deep down in the recesses of your memory, you were thinking of Mary Ashford and Sarah Miller, and that twinge of pain kept her passport in your pocket.

Your second call was to Information. They automatically connected you through to a Customs agent at PDX.

You noticed silver sparkles in your vision that couldn't mean anything good. Zoning on the passport photo helped you focus.

God, she *was* easy on the eyes. Too bad she was murder on the rest of you.

You told the man on the phone what she looked like, what kind of uniquely contraband baby she was carrying. You told him that the woman's birth name was Jean Christenson, but that she preferred to be called Ava, which was short for Avarice.

He noted that the name seemed appropriate.

"More than you'll ever know, pal." You closed the cell, thinking of her last words to you.

Good luck.

Your chest began to shake.

You were still laughing when your Uncle Joshua arrived and spotted your running shoes sticking out of the tiny house in the stranger's yard.

He crouched down, looked you over.

"Jesus! Are you okay?"

In between gusts of mad laughter you managed to say, "Nope. I'm in a bad place. I'm going to have to run."

"Okay, we'll get to that. First let's get you out of that fucking dog house."

He managed to get you upright, with your arm around his shoulder and as much weight as you could bear on your dog-mauled leg.

Once he started the car he looked over at you, seemingly relieved that you'd stopped laughing. The pain of moving had killed the chuckles.

Your Uncle had a hundred questions on his face. He asked one.

"The girl?"

You nodded in the affirmative then, over and over, guessing he would understand: Yes I was a sucker I thought it was love and yes I'm still remembering her kiss and the worst part is that if you ask me if I am still in love with Ava gorgeous terrible amazing vicious Ava I might say yes despite it all Yes.

You began to shake, nodding, mumbling, "OhGodohGodohGod . . . ."

"Okay, okay. Take it easy. Trust me, you've just hit the wall. You know that's as bad as it gets. I'm with you. You're gonna get fixed up. You've got to tell me enough to keep you safe, but that's it. We'll go where we need to. And soon as you can foot it, soon as you get past this wall, the morning runs are back. And this time there's no dropping it. No goddamn way. Whatever's got itself inside of you, kiddo, we're going to hit the streets and clear it the fuck out."

He twisted his grip on the steering wheel, gunned his car down slender curving roads on the way to the hospital. Dawn was approaching. It was likely to be another beautiful gray-green morning in Portland. Could your Uncle really be willing to leave his home behind just to protect your mangled carcass?

You wondered at your luck, knowing this man.

He approached a red light, started to hesitate, took one look at you, and then pushed right through.

And you, you love-sick bastard, you finally let shock take hold.

The Oarsman

The same space that envelops my craft surrounds Colony 1, its emptiness floating heavy around two corrupted cells.

A forgotten man in a metal membrane, inevitable death as the nucleus.

Far below—a planet heavy with viral load, perhaps too pregnant to prevent collapse.

Monitor light brings it to me LIVE: The monks on the side of the mountain are still singing, still swaying. But their low-throated hum is tapering. New angles are forming under their red robes, sharp jaunts of bone. A few have collapsed forward, toppled out of lotus position, the metal devices strapped around their necks now useless.

They aren't eating. If they're drinking, I've never caught them. The bastards are starving out, but not fast enough for my liking.

And I just can't stop watching them—the greatest mass murderers of all time, singing themselves to a slow death.

KURYLENKO IS FLOATING OUTSIDE of the station. With some despair I noted that his corpse does not spontaneously ignite even when we rotate into the full face of the sun. I pray for a spark.

Shakyamuni. That was the last thing he said, before he shut down.

We were in Sector C, nibbling vacu-packed peas, watching the news, our respective headphones feeding English and Russian language audio.

Everyone was waiting. Me, Kurylenko, the news cameras, the world—we were waiting to watch someone die.

If you would have asked anybody, they would have laid odds on the monks catching bullets. And that's how it would have gone down, if those cameras hadn't been there. Blame China's new media relations policy, promoting cultural events even in disputed territory. *Check out our beautiful history*—monks balancing on thumbs, fireworks shows leaving days of smoky haze—*and don't worry so much about human rights.*

They promised a beautiful display—the Yang-style chanting of a sacred text invoking empathy and oneness, courtesy of the Pan-Chinese Open Hand Festival, live from the base of the snowy mountains. News helicopters hovered close. Military helicopters hovered just behind them.

I suppose that, to most aside from the Chinese, the assumption was that the circle of white stones and the two great metallic cylinders flanking the monks were part of tradition, perhaps glossed up for the global stage. But when the monitors happened across Chinese soldiers their faces held shimmers of stress and confusion. Tight knit brows. Sweaty foreheads. Something looked *wrong*, but it didn't seem there was any viable order to set things right.

Media speculation filled pre-performance air.

"The purpose of the necklaces is unknown, but they appear to be modern technology, perhaps reflecting China's merger of cutting-edge science and ancient culture."

" . . . those columns, though un-decorated, do lend a certain regal air to today's proceedings."

"We've been asked, for the duration of the performance, to stay beyond the ring of decorative stones."

"Our best guess is this is all part of the sound design, a way to ensure these beautiful voices are heard both here at the foot of these majestic mountains, and around the world."

This may have all been B-roll station filler if a BBC sound tech hadn't accidentally stumbled across those stones.

Just before it happened, you could see him on a few of the other stations' cameras, barely maintaining his footing over the crumbling shale of the mountainside, body hanging with sound gear ballast, trying to get as close to the white-rocked periphery as possible.

Then his left foot slipped, throwing him into a clumsy shuffle, trying not to drop the boom mic. Two steps to the side and he was in their circle.

His hand raised in apology—*Sorry, guys*.

That same hand ignited like phosphorous, sending out white light. Arcs of radiance flashed down on the sound tech's body from the two silver columns. The tech's mouth opened in a scream, his last breath consumed in the fire that swallowed him whole.

Then there were close-ups of the monks, still seated and ready to sing, their faces flashing something . . .

Regret?

Did it matter?

Chaos after that. Chinese military tucking ready rifles into their shoulders. News feeds jumping from B-roll to the Global Now. The charcoal husk of a clumsy man sending off smoke from inside the stone circle. Martin Vilkus spotted among the monks, dressed as one of them, the shaggy hair from his FBI photos shaved clean off.

You could have tried to absorb it, to piece together the feed and find a rational response. But Vilkus was barely on the national radar anymore, his history as the Feds' least favorite virologist-turned-terrorist old news. The guy hadn't issued a manifesto in years, and the Boston Subway Massacre, though leaving over seven hundred dead and internally liquefied to the consistency of fast food milkshakes, was long-forgotten in the wake of more popular atrocities.

Even if you knew what was about to happen, from what I've figured, you'd still be dead.

The monks reached up, each one flipping a switch on the tiny box that sat at the hollow of his throat. Blinking LED's registered "On" status.

Kurylenko had sensed it then. He yelled in Russian, the veins popping on his neck, like his urgency might carry the scream through the vacuum of space.

"Fucking shoot them."

His order yielded no response. And why I couldn't stop laughing at him, at his panicked face, I'll never know.

Then the song began. The monks' mouths were open wide, the tone unified and low. It pulled me into a vertiginous state, as if a door had just opened beneath me in the craft and I was flipping back through empty space.

I started to lose my sight, static spreading across my vision. Reaching up through atmospheric quicksand, I tried an old orientation technique. My fingers found purchase on the soft connective tissue and veins under my tongue, and I clasped down as hard as I could.

As it had so many times before, pain brought me into the present. And I was back in the station, and Kurylenko was collapsed on the ground and whispering something. I crouched and leaned in close.

Shakyamuni.

I would have appreciated less obscure last words. He could have told me I was a good friend. He could have told me where he stashed his best pornos.

Nope—fucking "Shakyamuni" was all I got.

Then nothing. His chest shifted slightly, and I could register condensation on a mirror if I held it to his nose. But that breathing and his heartbeat were already slowing and growing fainter.

The look on his face was the worst. His eyes flooded with tears. The corners of his mouth slightly upturned. If I was reading him right, I'd swear he was *smiling*.

I put his body in Bay 2 after his bowels voided. I considered trying some kind of resuscitation, but by then I'd seen enough news feed to know better.

Helicopters, news and otherwise, were earthbound and aflame. The monks' song echoed off the mountain walls and piles of collapsed bodies. Even Martin Vilkus was on the ground, the first red robe to drop. Whatever part he'd had in this, it hadn't guaranteed immunity. At least he looked happy.

A reporter from CNN had fallen right in front of her camera. The channel, for hours, was just her profile, tears running ravines through her beige foundation.

Flipping stations gave me scores of pre-programmed sitcoms and infomercials but I couldn't find any shows that would require a live human being.

No news. No response. Dead air.

There was a certain and lovely sense of permanence to this.

Kurylenko wasn't coming back. I knew that.

Should I have made sure he was actually dead before I tethered his body to the outside of the station? Some would say so.

But rest assured, that son of a bitch was still smiling at nothing when I pushed him into space.

REGULAR TELEVISION BROADCASTS ENDED days ago, but I've still got my Chinese friends pulled up on the monitor. I suppose this is the saving grace of my job.

Ostensibly this is a way station between Earth—now optimistically referred to as Colony 1—and future homes with nicer things like top-soil and potable water. But if much of the ship's funding came from certain parties in the east and the US that traffic in information, well you might have a better understanding of what we really do. Or *did*, I suppose.

So, for most of my day I tune our cameras in on the monks, watching them sway and starve.

Which contestant is next to be voted out here on Tibetan Idol?

The rest of the time I jerk off, half-sleep, and wonder—*Why am I still alive?*

The broadcast tried to claim me, but it couldn't. It barely effects me, watching it now.

What makes me different? I've been trying hard, so hard for years now, to act like everyone else.

When I was a child Dr. Chodron told me about emulation. I saw him for a few weeks, after the incident with Tommy's cat. Question after question, test after test, hushed conversations with my mother. In the end he sat down with me, wringing his hands, and asked me if I could be a good boy.

The right answer seemed to be, "Yes."

Then he told me I would have less trouble with the other boys if I could learn to make faces like theirs.

Somebody tells you about a naked lady and her dog Free-show; you cough up a few laughs and crinkle your eyes.

Somebody tells you their mom died; you put your arms around them and pat them on the back. Keep your lower lip pushed up.

I've only gotten better at it since then.

But I've never felt much of anything behind the face.

Two other doctors have tried to label me since, but I shook the name. Fighting, fucking—everybody needs a little of that to stay alive. Doesn't mean some quack can tag me.

One thing you *can* call me—survivor.

But . . . I'm starting to think I might have to shake that name too.

There are no transport ships coming. My transmissions are reaching exactly no one.

The monk's broadcast couldn't have reached the whole planet, unless it didn't require the television signal as a medium for transmission. Maybe that was just a catalyst. A bonus, zapping Kurylenko up here in the ether, speeding along the process. Maybe those nasty electric columns were sending the song out in worldwide waves.

Whatever those monks did, whatever sonic virus they used to fuck up the human race, it wasn't going to get un-fucked. And, really, I'm okay with that. They sped up the inevitable, and left us all with a song and a smile. It's a downright kind extinction compared to what we've unleashed in the past.

But I'm not okay with the position they've left me in. Shitty, slow death in this metal coffin, watching my murderers slide softly into nirvana.

I've got fourteen hours until the station is directly over their territory.

With the proper use of the ship's boosters, and a sizable chunk of luck, I'm hoping I can ride this thing all the way down. All the way home. And maybe, just for one moment, they'll look up to the sky.

They will see me then, a terrible and fiery God, and I will descend upon them and ram their bad karma right down their fucking low murdering throats.

That is how this song ends.

The Gravity
of Benham Falls

He's taking me to the place where we lost Michael.
      This thought, more than the speed of the car and the sight of barely illuminated trees blurring past, cemented Laura's unease. She hadn't been up this way since the day her little brother disappeared, and never planned on returning. Now this "date" with Tony was dragging her back.

Laura silently cursed herself for not coming up with a better way to make money. Her current plan wasn't getting any smarter, or easier. Could she even call it a plan? How many small town drug dealers could she seduce and steal from, before one of them caught on and decided to hurt her, or worse? Word would travel; she'd be in danger. Tony, the guy driving, seemed like the type that would own a gun.

When the headlights of the car cut through the wispy road fog ahead of them and illuminated the sign reading "Benham Falls-Fourteen Miles" she realized that this was *not* where she wanted to be. Anywhere else would be better. Then she forced herself to remember her dad, lying in bed at home, under thin sheets, lungs barely pulling oxygen while he dozed in and out of a Vicodin stupor.

He probably still wishes he had a cigarette right now. Well, we can't afford any, damn it. I can barely afford the doctor's appointments, so we're just going to have to disappoint the Marlboro man.

The thought of her freshly divorced dad—mom bailed when the diagnosis dropped—and of his mounting bills at St. Peter's Hospital, re-focused her on the task at hand. The guy in the seat next to her had to fall in love, or at least lust. The faster, the better. The last chump, he was stupid with love after just two days. Love earned trust, and trust earned secrets, like where the guy kept his cash, and that Rolex he wore only on special occasions.

A shoebox. These guys, they all want to think they're Scarface, and they all end up keeping rolls of cash in a little cardboard shoebox.

Laura tried not to enjoy her cleverness, but failed. A smile was spreading across her face, helping to ease the piano-wire anxiety that was sinking into her chest.

She shifted in the tan leather bucket seat of the '68 Camaro, giving Tony an eyeful of leg as her short skirt hiked up her left thigh. Tony glanced over quickly, caught the flash of skin, and turned his eyes back to the road. He grinned.

"Almost there, babe."

It was the first thing he'd said since he picked her up earlier that evening. Laura was fine with that. She didn't want words. She might start talking and mention the wrong thing. Draw suspicion. Or she might start talking about the time her family visited this same forest and came back missing one person. She might mention how they never even found Michael's body.

No, she was content to play with the electricity in the air between them. Better to turn this into a fantasy. Reality could be so unpleasant.

Laura pretended to yawn, pushing her chest forward with her arms raised above her head, moving her legs slightly so that her pleated tan skirt hiked up even further.

It was her turn to grin as she saw Tony shifting in his seat. They were both swimming in tension, nerves on full alert as the stereo blasted and the air that rushed in through the windows grew cooler.

The road became thin and curvy as they approached the entrance to the Tolaquin County Forest, but Tony didn't slow the car for a moment. He slammed through the corners. The rear right tire spit out gravel as it caught the soft shoulder. Laura wanted to tell him to cool it on the alpha-male stunt driver shit, but she didn't want to disturb the chemistry of their little game.

This was a game she had to win. Till now, it had been easy. Asking around town, finding out who the local dealer was. Getting his name. Tracking him down.

In another life I'd make a great cop.

Earlier that day she'd met Tony at the Chevron. Marco at the pool hall had said that Tony kept the Chevron job for appearances, and it was an easy place for people to drive through and buy whatever Tony was selling.

Laura saw Tony squeegeeing the window of a mini-van, checked out his broad shoulders, his jet black hair, his olive skin, the way he filled out his oil-smeared jumpsuit, and shouted, "Hey, nice ass!" She loved playing the aggressor.

Tony walked over and scoped her out in return. He let a slow, straight-tooth smile bloom across his face, and said, "Thanks."

Laura licked her lips, slow, and said, "What's your name?"

"Tony."

"Well, hi, Tony. You got a pen?"

He pulled a pen from his shirt pocket and handed it to her. She wrote her name and cell-phone number on a twenty-dollar bill, folded it, and slipped it in one of his front pants pockets.

Two hours later her cell phone rang. "Hey, Laura, you wanna do something special?"

It now appeared to her that by "do something special" he meant "drive out to Benham Falls and get naked." At least that was the subtext to the tension that hung heavy in the speeding car. Laura was just happy her plan was working. Her dad and home were over a hundred miles away. She'd need a place to sleep tonight. Hopefully Tony had a nice, big bed with a down comforter and some thick pillows. Hopefully Tony had a heavy, hidden shoebox, and slept like the dead.

Hopefully we can head back to town soon, and get the hell out of this place.

The Camaro rolled to a stop as they approached the gate between the paved road and the dirt passage that led to Benham Falls. He hopped out, swung the gate open, and slid back into the car.

He turned to Laura. "They don't want people up here in the spring. It's still pretty cold at night, and the area around the waterfall can get icy."

"So?" she said, trying to maintain her attitude even as she cringed at the idea of stepping into the freezing cold in a short skirt and thin, black tank top.

"So," he said, "people have died up here."

She pictured her own little brother, five years old, smiling in front of the waterfall on a sunny afternoon.

Is that my last memory of him? Has to be. This is the last place I ever saw him.

Laura tried to stop remembering, but the echo of her parent's panicked voices screaming her brother's name still entered her mind. Instant gooseflesh, shivers.

"Don't worry, though, I'll make sure we stay warm."

Tony slid a calloused hand over her knee, then drew it toward the inside of her thigh. As his hand shifted a feminine-looking bracelet, with blue and black beads, slid down his forearm to his wrist, jangling on its way down. The beads formed the outline of a horse's head, raised and proud. Laura wondered if it was a trophy from another conquest, or if he just felt comfortable wearing pretty jewelry. Either way, this guy was different enough to be interesting, and the warmth of his fingers made her cheeks rosy. Laura didn't expect these feelings. Romance, so far, hadn't been par for her twisted course.

She smiled at him and said, "Just make sure I'm taken care of." Laura laughed, trying to come off sly, to ignore her urge to hop in the driver's seat once he got out and drive as far from here as fast as she could.

They drove for four more minutes and then he slowed, killing the lights and the engine. Laura could hear the roaring waterfall through the glass windows of the Camaro. She immediately hated the surging volume of it. It was the soundtrack to the worst day of her life. Laura pushed those feelings down. Right now had to be about Tony and nothing else. She had to earn his trust or soon she'd lose another family member.

He could be dead right now. While you're away robbing lowlifes for medical money, he could have wheezed out his final breath. Alone.

Laura ignored the voice. Listening to her conscience was not an option.

She stepped out of the car and slammed the door, instantly feeling the cold bite of the higher altitude and the dampness of the waterfall's backspray. Tony walked over to Laura and grabbed her delicate left hand, enveloping it with his.

"Follow me. I'll show you something."

She followed him through the woods in the dark of the moonlit night, towards the sound of the waterfall. He walked with a sure-footedness and Laura briefly pictured herself as a notch on his bedpost.

"You bring all your girls up here, Tony?"

"No," he said, through laughter, "just the special ones. My family and I used to live in a house bordering the park so I'm pretty familiar with the area. Used to play here as a kid."

Laura was surprised by how much she liked Tony's voice. The first guy she'd stolen from, her old boyfriend Mark, and the second guy she robbed, Adam, they both had something nasty in their voices. A greasy sort of power. Tony sounded different. Still, she was cold. Her feet hurt. She wore platform shoes with crisscrossing straps on top, picturing this as more of a booze/cigarettes/dancing type date. She didn't plan on this nature hike with Ranger Tony. Still, the firmness and warmth of Tony's hand made her feel safer.

Tony guided her past a patch of trees into a clearing. Laura hadn't seen Benham Falls since she was small, and she was still stunned by its sheer grandness. The nearly full moon reflected off the water, giving the whole area a shimmering, light blue glow. The hundred foot wide river was raging over the lip of the waterfall, about three hundred feet above them. The water roiled furiously at the point of impact, sending out a spray that within seconds coated her like cold sweat.

The memories—the sounds of her parents' voices crumbling and growing hoarse as they yelled for Michael, the look of instant despair on the face of the park ranger who couldn't help them—all of it wanted in to her head. Laura knew she had to stay in motion to keep from thinking. Maybe Tony could distract her.

She leaned in, ran her tongue lightly up the salty skin of Tony's neck and then whispered in his ear. "It's beautiful." Somehow it wasn't a lie. The falls couldn't be denied their majesty.

His hands found the curve of her lower back and he kissed her. She could feel the beads of his funny bracelet pressing against her skin, strangely warm even through the fabric of her tank-top. Then they were kissing, intensely for a moment, then slowly pulling away. Laura found herself thrilled at the newness and willingness of Tony's kiss. The kiss was good enough to make her think maybe this night could be okay; that maybe she was meant to come here and create good new memories to erase the old. The start of a new life. Tony pulled away.

"You've gotta see the cavern."

He grabbed her hand and they continued down the trail towards the base of the falls.

"This used to be called Sotsone Falls, after this Indian lady. She was a princess, like an Indian princess, with the Tolaquin tribe, and back when they were relocating her tribe, she came up here and jumped off the falls in protest. Some way to go, huh? Well, supposedly, she's *in* the falls, haunting them, cursing them, whatever. You're supposed to be able to see her face in the falling water during a full moon. Anyway, people kept dying up here, falling and drowning and stuff, so they renamed the place Benham Falls in the thirties. Weird, huh?"

"Yeah." Laura said. "Pretty weird."

Inside she was trembling. She fought to keep it from showing; Tony was just starting to open up to her. She wanted to tell him that changing the name of the falls didn't stop anybody from dying up here.

Then she looked up to the top of the falls and for a second she saw the Indian woman up there, staring back at her, pointing at her with one long finger.

She shook her head and turned away. A trick of the moonlight off the mist.

They reached the bottom of the falls and Tony led her across a series of lichen- and moss-covered rocks that played hell with her slender ankles. Soon they were behind the waterfall, standing close to each other beneath the low ceiling of a cavern carved out by the falls. The smell of minerals was sharp, and the sound of the falls was deafening. The cavern was barely illuminated with the thin, gray light cast by the moon's reflection off the falls. A cold drop of water fell from the black cavern ceiling and splattered on Laura's scalp dead center. She was about to complain about the cold and her shoes and the hike, to say, "Hey, this cavern's just lovely but we should go *now*," when Tony grabbed her and pulled her in for a deep kiss.

Tony's kisses were so sweet, so genuine in their urgency and attraction, that for a moment Laura was capable of forgetting again. He bit her lip playfully; he kissed her ears. He chewed at her neck and kissed the corners of her lips.

She sighed with pleasure; the shaking exhalation turned to thin vapor. She watched her breath float upwards, away from the shimmering light coming through the waterfall.

Tony kissed the hollow at the base of her throat. His lips felt so good on her skin, like a release from the ugly thoughts this place had forced on her, from the sickness that had permeated her new life with her father.

She tilted her head back, exalted, smiling.

That was when she saw the dead boy on the ceiling of the cavern.

Michael.

Her brother had black sockets where his eyes should have been, two holes in a pale, angry face. Thin trickles of blood ran from his open mouth. His little corduroy pants and yellow T-shirt were tattered and soaked dark crimson. He was floating down from the ceiling towards her, his arms and legs spread wide, and she was frozen with fear, oblivious to Tony's urgent kisses.

The little boy floated closer to her and one tiny hand reached out toward her face. She could not move as she felt four cold fingers press against her forehead.

A black veil fell over her eyes and she couldn't tell where she was, or who she was, or where Tony was. All she could do was *see*.

A small boy, at the top of the falls, picking up an old, beaded bracelet. The child, attracted to the bracelet and its horsehead pattern, slid it on to his wrist. Little Tony was a lucky boy that day. All smiles.

She saw that same boy pushing her brother into the river just north of the falls.

NO! Where were my parents? Where was I?

The vision provided no answers. It could only show her what her brother knew from that point on. The intimacy of his pain.

Michael, in his yellow T-shirt and corduroy pants, went over the falls and hit the water so hard his eyes were forced from his head.

Michael had yelled Laura's name on the way down. She'd always been there to help him before. Helped him tie his shoes. Helped him reach the cookie jar. But at that moment, everyone had looked away. That moment was all it took. Nobody could have heard his voice over the sound of the raging falls.

The vision shifted, became blurry and liquid.

Somewhere much farther away she could feel hands around her throat.

After putting on the bracelet, Tony had been a busy boy.

She saw Tony throwing his new puppy dog over the falls. It yelped before the splash.

She saw him return to the falls as a teen. This time he threw a woman over.

Then another woman, and another. First he choked them, then he threw them from the top of the falls.

It was ritual; Sotsone's final protest repeating without end.

The fall and the maelstrom beneath it tore them all to pieces, collapsed their lungs and filled them up until they sank, swirling in the current with all the others. With Michael. She could hear them all howling under the water, torn, and restless.

She could hear Michael whispering to her.

Wake up.

Laura awoke from her vision to see Tony on top of her. While she'd watched the memories of her dead brother, Tony had pushed her body to the stony ground. The veins in his face bulged and he had his right hand clamped tight around her throat. The beads on his bracelet rattled as he choked her. She gasped for air and found none.

LAURA REGAINED CONSCIOUSNESS AS her hand touched the icy waters of the river flowing beside her. Tony's voice barely broke through the sound of her own blood rushing back into her head.

"You know, Laura, you could stand to lose some weight. Do you know how hard it was to carry you up here?"

Whatever it was she'd liked in his voice, it was gone, replaced by the same greasy confidence of the guys she'd hustled in the weeks before. That all seemed so distant and petty next to her need to pull in a full breath though her crushed windpipe. She couldn't help thinking, "This is how dad feels when he breathes."

Dad. No . . . I can't die now.

"I asked you a question."

She moaned, unable to respond with her maimed vocal cords. Tony continued.

"You tasted sweet, when I kissed you. But then you started shaking, and your eyes rolled back in your head. I couldn't keep kissing you like that. The look in your eyes was . . . wrong. I decided to take care of business."

Unable to speak, Laura raised a middle finger.

"I'm not going to pretend I don't enjoy this. I mean, *she* tells me to do it, she has ever since I found this bracelet, but I love it more every time. I kind of regretted pushing in that first kid, but it was just too easy. It's like fate put him there. All alone. And she was whispering to me. *Push him in. Watch him fall. Do it for me.*"

Laura hated Tony, the way he spoke of her brother. She wanted to say, "That wasn't just some kid. That was my brother, Michael." She wanted to kill Tony and knew that if she could find the strength she'd have no problem performing the act. She might even like it.

She tried harder to breathe, to think a clear thought, to find a way out of Tony's sight. He kept talking, enjoying the sound of his own voice. Something buzzed beneath his words. Something old. Something that had savored so much death it couldn't understand anything else.

"I like watching the women fall. That's the best part. Just for a second, right when they go over the edge, they kind of hang there, like *she's* holding them up, and then they drop so fast you wouldn't believe it. Sometimes they look like they're flying. Especially when they don't scream on the way down. I don't think we'll have to worry about that with you, will we?"

His hands dug into her arms, lifting her toward the edge of Benham Falls.

"You know, none of the bodies have ever surfaced. I guess the falls holds them down there. Keeps them hidden for me."

Laura felt his grip tighten as they approached the edge. The cascade here was raging as the river shot out and plummeted to the stormy water below.

Vertigo reeled through her body as the swift winds above the falls whipped around her.

She wanted to cry, to run, to scream at the madness and cruelty that brought her here. She hated her stupid plans, her father's cancer. She wanted to escape, to get back home and save her father the misery of losing another child's life before his own. Laura could not resign herself to this last, cold swan dive.

Then she heard Michael speaking inside of her head.

His voice a soft whisper, felt underneath her skin.

"Let go now."

She trusted the voice. What else was there to trust?

Laura let go. She let her body go limp and felt her ankles roll out from beneath her. She pitched forward, dead weight over the yawning precipice. Tony, who was still holding her arms vice-grip tight, had no chance to escape the fall.

Gravity took them both. They fell faster than the river had in its thousands of years.

On the way down, Laura saw the women.

Their white faces were just beneath the surface of the water. Over a dozen of them, empty white faces with hair and skin floating loose around them. None of them had eyes. All of them had gaping mouths, teeth bared, locked in a scream.

Tony and Laura's bodies rotated in the fall, and Tony struck the water first, with Laura on top of him. His body crunched beneath her, and then they were underwater, with the women. Cold, loose skin pressed against her as the thundering waterfall pushed them all under. Hands, all bone and sinew, tore Tony away from her. Teeth scraped her skin as they chewed away his hands, releasing her.

Her freedom from Tony's hands did not matter. She was trapped in the plunge pool, struggling to reach air and being pulled farther and farther down.

She heard a terrible tearing and popping sound, and the water around her grew warm. Laura could see that the dead, empty-faced women had chewed open Tony's belly and torn his limbs from his body. His gutted torso was still in their frenzy, his mouth wide in shock.

Laura struggled, trying not to inhale, but her lungs demanded it, and she pulled in a deep, liquid breath. Her lungs filled with water as the dead women swarmed.

No . . . I brought him to you . . . I'm not dead yet . . . I have to get home . . . my dad . . . Michael . . . please . . .

She could taste death in the water, and sank deeper until she felt a tiny, cold hand on hers, pulling with all its strength. The women's hands clamped down like talons, but could not hold her. She closed her eyes and felt the water parting before her, then falling away.

Moments later she found herself on the mossy shore near the base of the cascade, vomiting gouts of water and pulling thin breaths into her crushed chest. She was shattered and bone cold. Her skin wore the deep lacerations of the pale women's rage. In spite of all this, she was alive. With each breath, pain sunk its teeth through her splintered ribs and reminded her she was still in danger. The cold of night was sinking in. She imagined that if she died here the women would crawl from the water and drag her back in, back down to where they were hidden.

She stood and wavered, fawn-like, and stumbled towards Tony's car, away from Benham Falls. Halfway back to the car she stooped and picked up a fist-sized stone. "Please let one of the car windows break easily. Let me remember how to hot-wire the ignition without getting shocked." Laura felt like if there was ever a night someone was answering her prayers, this was it.

As she reached the clearing, and Tony's car, Laura heard a noise, thin and high pitched. She was bleeding from her left ear and turned her right towards the sound. The laughter of a small boy, a sweet echo from her childhood, drifted through the trees.

Somehow, Laura found the strength to laugh along.

"Goodnight, Michael."

Moments later she was in Tony's car, listening to the engine rumble, wondering how far away any hospital was, and how much money she could get for a vintage Camaro with a busted window and a scrapped ignition. Most importantly she thought of home, of holding her father.

She wheeled the car around and slammed the gas pedal. The entrance to Benham Falls became dust, then darkness.

Dissociative Skills

Curt Lawson felt like a surgeon right up to the moment he snorted the horse tranquilizer. He sniffed hard and then raised his head to survey the scalpel/gauze/suture kit layout on the ratty orange shag carpet next to him. His vinyl beanbag crinkled beneath him as he sat upright and set down his powder-dusted vanity mirror.

The digital clock across the room confirmed he had three hours before Mom and Dad would be back from their ballroom dancing class.

"Dance away, little parents." Curt spoke the words slowly in his empty, Spartan bedroom and received no response. Curt's face became Arctic-cold numb, and he looked around his room through the new eyes the ketamine had given him.

The previously drab white walls and wooden closet doors now seemed sleek and stylish. His weathered, hand-me-down couch looked like a plush boat. The empty space between Curt's beanbag residence and his thin mattress across the room became desert-wide and arid. The normally shabby shag carpet beneath his bare feet took on a new puppy-dog softness, and he clenched it in his numbing toes.

The brutal rubber band–flavored drip and paint-thinner burn in his sinuses sent his brain back to his powder purchase earlier that day. He'd found his dealer, Dave "The Wave" D'Amato, by the soda machine outside the drama room at Shelton High. Dave had been wearing a plain blue jumpsuit and a tan backpack.

"Parachuting later today?" Curt had asked.

Dave had smiled, a split-second grin that faded away fast enough to let Curt know his medicine man wasn't in a joking mood. "No, I'm afraid of heights, Curt. What do you need?"

"Well, I missed breakfast this morning and I was wondering if you happened to have some Special K."

Dave gave the short smile again, all business.

"Yeah, Curt, I got some K, but it's on some heavy Ketalar pharmy level shit, and it's been cut with some diazepam for your blood pressure."

"My blood pressure, Dave?"

"Yeah, dog, without that diazepam in there the K would make all your veins bulge out and your eyes would feel like they was going to pop. Also, this shit burns black super-quick, so it's got some kind of speed, probably benzedrine, or something, up in it."

"Is that bad?"

"Naw, dog, it's all right 'cause *that* shit'll keep your heart beating even when the ketamine's telling it to stop. So it's actually a bonus. And, of course, there's probably some GKWE in there."

"GKWE?"

"Yup. That's some God Knows What Else. By the time I get my shit it's been through more hands than I even know. And everybody cuts it a little. *Everybody.*"

Dave wasn't a comforting drug dealer, but he was a straight shooter. Curt had never known another 16-year-old as honest. Or as driven. The kid put half his crooked income into a savings account for his eventual med school tuition.

A Portrait of the Anesthesiologist as a Young Man.

Back in the narcotic now Curt laughed to himself, bowed his head back to the beckoning yellow lines, and snorted another rail of K. He inhaled deep and a lungful of stale bedroom air chased the powder up the straw.

Curt leaned back in his beanbag and let the straw drop from his nose onto his chest. The world went slow motion and the air got souped-up, thick with gravity.

"Am I breathing?" Curt wondered.

He tried to hold up a hand in front of his mouth to check for exhalation. His hand had other ideas and remained inert. The ketamine staple gun had him pinned as he lay.

Motion, for the moment, was a non-option.

Curt's first thought was panic heavy. "What if I drop into a K-hole? If I go zombie right away then I can't use the scalpel."

Reason launched a sneak attack. "This is just the first wave of the high. Let it crest and then get to work. In the meantime, *feel this.*"

His reptile brain locked into the chemical vibe, and his cortex began to sizzle with bad electricity. Curt uttered a low "Gwaaaaah" as his eyes rolled back and began to twitch, blurring the rainbow spectrum of light provided by the string of Christmas bulbs circling the ceiling of his room.

His brain did the wrong things he'd hoped it would do.

Sound came into his system at weird angles. The classical music from his cheap plastic boom box became tiny sonic wasps with sharp violin stingers. They buzzed around his head, a soundswarm that penetrated his ears and nose and mouth and injected him with disjointed musical notes until his skin shivered. Horns like repressed peasants moaning slow. Wrong.

The distance between Curt's head and the surrounding walls fluctuated from fingernail-thin to epic-black-space wide.

He could smell the old sweat and dried semen on his bedding across the room. It was a human smell and made him feel small and weak for a moment. "Maybe I shouldn't be doing this. Maybe I should call the hospital or Mom's cell phone or . . . "

The thought was cut off by another wave of anesthetic bliss.

Then the air of his spare, stale room became warm and safe, except for his moments of mental alarm.

Curt found himself thinking, with nagging frequency, "Am I breathing?" The question was easily written off once he noticed the tiny faces that lived in the wood-grain doors of his closet.

The faces laughed, growled, knew Curt and smiled at him, grew bodies, fought, fucked, killed. It was a tip-top hallucination. Curt could barely look away until he realized that he had sat upright and could now move his limbs.

He inhaled deeply as he regained some level of physical control. He was not surprised when he smelled French fries, and realized that he had vomited his dinner onto his shirt.

The shirt was easily discarded. It had to go anyway. Curt needed access to the soft skin of his belly.

Curt reached over to the scalpel laid out by the beanbag and managed to wrap his left hand around it.

"I thought I'd have a little more control than this. I'll have to be extra careful. I can do this. I MUST DO THIS."

His yell echoed against the plaster walls of the room. The faces in the wood-grain recoiled at the sound.

"Sorry, guys. I just, well, I need to do this sort of thing."

He knew the little faces understood.

Every *wrong* thing done was a show of strength. An exercise in control. Proof that life could be contained and managed, down to the tiniest, strangest detail, if only for a moment.

"You know that. Right, little faces?"

A twisted wood-whorl face winked at Curt and confirmed the understanding. The liquid wood grain folks knew the secret score. They knew that with every wrong thing Curt did, he was separating himself from the predictable degradation of his gin-guzzling, Prozac-popping parents, from the random humanity of bad skin and poorly timed bowel movements, from the After School Special cliché of his generation's own pre-packaged rebellion. The things Curt did were special, completely unique in their own way.

"I'm different," Curt told himself.

Past exercises in control had been successful. Curt would think something, and if the next immediate thought was, "Well, I could never do that." then he'd do it, whatever he'd thought, no matter how wrong. That was the litmus and the litany.

Curt knew how long it took to eat a pound of Crisco. He knew the nervous sweat that preceded smashing his own thumb with a hammer. He knew what it was like to go to a party in a wheelchair, wearing a Skynyrd T-shirt, asking girls if they wanted to "rollerfuck his freebird." He knew the discomfort of spending an entire day with a travel toothbrush jammed up his ass. He knew what it was like to kill a fly, eat half of it, and deposit the remaining thorax and twitching wing into his left ear.

Sometimes he felt as if he was training towards a gold medal in the Dumbfuck Olympics. Sometimes he felt wonderful, like his acts, however bizarre, were taking him closer to some kind of greatness. He constantly reassured himself.

"No one else has ever done this. You are the only one strong enough to make it happen." He stood proud and walked head high amongst the living dead, a man in control of his future, tossing fate aside.

Even his pain was unique. He sought it out and cultivated its strangeness. It trumped the boring pains of the everyday world. The bright burn that shot through his system while gouging his tonsils with a chopstick made his boring, human migraines seem lukewarm.

"Preemptive suffering makes me stronger," he'd often thought.

Curt's secret-subversive diet burned holes in his stomach lining. His belly never stopped grumbling. Indigestion was his constant companion. He wanted to re-write that "footsteps on the beach" poem and replace Jesus with indigestion.

So he did. The last line had read, "That was when I gurgled you."

The experiments in control always had their harbingers. The Crisco-eating incident was set in motion by an embarrassing, in-class sneeze that had very publicly layered his hands with mucous. The toothbrush colonoscopy was predated by an uncontrollable erection Curt had failed to hide from his teacher in gym class.

Yesterday, Curt had sat down to breakfast with his parents. His dad's hands had trembled until he popped the top of his breakfast beer. Curt's mother had noted this and laughed, a dry, quiet laugh which reeked of acceptance. Her laugh seemed to Curt like the sound of a zoo animal finding the humor in its cage.

Curt fell asleep crying that night, unable to tear his mind away from his father's softly shaking hands and the sound of his mother's laugh, hating the dime-store pathos of the moment, hating himself for not being able to distance himself from it.

This morning he'd awakened to the thought, "I'll never know what I look like inside."

So Curt followed his own rules, copped the K, and borrowed the scalpel that now sat centimeters from his belly.

Curt delayed his self-surgery for a second, remembering to sterilize the instrument. The butane from his lighter heated the blade and seared carbon black on the silver surface.

He paused for a moment and pinched his face, which he had a hard time locating. Once he got a large chunk of cheek between his forefinger and thumb he squeezed as hard as he could.

He felt nothing. No skin against skin, only a dull pressure.

Perfect. Numb. Time to operate. Time to tour the belly.

His right hand shook but steadied as the scalpel met resistance. The wood faces flinched as the blade separated skin without a sound.

Curt hadn't imagined there would be so much blood. He hadn't planned on the mesentery tissue being so tenacious, even under the honed edge of the scalpel. He'd also thought that the small intestine would be, well, small. The three inches of tubing that he'd managed to pull through the incision were wider than two of his fingers side-by-side.

Curt stared at the bit of his insides that he'd excavated. He listened to the stream of orchestral music coming from his stereo and wondered if Amadeus had ever had the willpower to expose his own insides.

Curt seriously doubted it. He looked at his achievement with love and softly stroked the moist, red bit of intestine that jutted from his bleeding belly. He stared and watched the previously unknowable part of him shimmering in the colored Christmas lights.

"I am in control. I made this happen. I own my life," he thought.

A tiny twinge of pain crept into the invaded area after a few minutes of intense observation.

"The ketamine's starting to wear off," Curt thought.

This thought was preceded in his mind by the sound of the front door opening and then closing.

"Oh, God. Mom and Dad are home."

The knock on the door to his room came too quickly and sounded wrecking-ball heavy. He tried to speak; he wanted to say, "Stay out, I'm naked."

The ketamine might as well have removed his tongue and wired his jaw shut. Total disconnect had set in.

His mother opened the door.

She stared and then shook her head as if to throw the image of her son from the surface of her eyes.

Then she screamed, the high, operatic shriek of a woman confronting something which cannot be real, something *wrong*. Curt could smell the vodka on her breath from across the room.

It was a nice, warm smell, and it stayed printed on his senses all the way to the hospital, a sensory presence hijacking a spot in his mind. It was the scent of her scream. It was proof that he'd done something incredible, something the world and *certainly* his mother had never seen.

Her vodka-soaked shriek was a trophy. It was the first real, intense emotion he'd heard from his medicated mother in a long time. The sound betrayed the smooth, idle complacency of her everyday life.

He wished that he could have spoken to her. He had wanted to say, "Try to accept this. Laugh at *this*, Mom."

Even his father had been shocked sober, and jumped into action. Dad's hands had held steady while trying in vain to push Curt's intestine back into place.

For just a moment, Curt's exercise in control had enveloped his whole family, and brought them together. He'd forced them to abandon their slow, slaughterhouse fattening for a moment and really live, and fight.

Had they slipped into drunken slumber without first checking in on him, Curt imagined he'd still be bleeding, numb, watching himself die in the Technicolor glow of his Christmas lights.

But they'd fought.

His parents had both held him, one at each side, until the ambulance arrived. Their hands clenched together over his belly, staunching the warm flow of his blood.

Though he couldn't move his limbs or say a word during the ambulance ride, Curt began to feel again, and his own screams found their way into the world.

Despite the fire in his belly, beneath his wounded-animal bellowing, he felt proud.

Inside, and out.

Snowfall

Despite Jake's profound deafness, he swore for a moment that he'd heard something. He'd at least felt the sound, a tremble in his small, feather-light bones. This pushing noise that seemed for a moment to sit on his chest and trap breath in his lungs, it brought him from deep sleep to a sort of half-awake that didn't feel real.

He stayed in this space between dream and waking for awhile, barely shaking in his hammock bed which was buoyed by a loose spring at each end. Deaf since age three, Jake had developed a "feel" for sound, and thought it best to ignore the immense noise that had tried to shake him from his warm slumber. The sound was too big, a sound for Mom and Dad to investigate and deal with.

There was a moment following the noise when the temperature in his basement room soared, and Jake shifted from side to side, sweltering in the heat and memories of the fever which had stolen sound from his young body. He stirred and gently cried, the tears rolling almost cool over his burning cheeks.

He woke three hours later, in a pitch black room full of stale air. He was sweating in his pajamas, and his lower back felt clammy, slick.

He tossed aside the down comforter his parents bought him last year for his fifth birthday, eager to feel some cool air on his sticky skin. He swung his legs over the side of the hammock and dismounted with a small hop. His feet slapped the floor of the basement. Cold sank into the pads of his toes and his heels. He wished his whole body could be filled with that cold, and thought for a half-second about taking off his gray pajamas and lying naked on the floor. His stomach, grumbling and contracting tight, suggested another agenda.

Jake rubbed the sleep out of his eyes and flicked it off his fingers. It took him twelve shuffling steps in the dark to find the far left wall where the staircase was. It was his staircase, the entrance to his lair, his room, his favorite place in the whole house. The wooden steps rising up to the kitchen entrance were trampled smooth by his constant trespass. Halfway up the stairs he knew he would find the light switch.

Jake stepped with care up to the middle of the staircase. His small hand reached through the dark and silence of the basement and he found comfort as he touched rigid plastic. He flipped the switch up, expecting to see the soft light of the bare bulb hanging central to the room. Instead he saw continued darkness, pervasive. He flipped the switch up and down, up and down, with the same result. This happened once before, and he had told Dad, and Dad had run down to the basement with a flashlight and put a fresh bulb in the socket while Jake sat upstairs slurping sugary cereal milk from the bottom of his favorite bowl, the one with the red fishes on it.

The thought of cereal reoriented Jake, and he padded up to the top of the stairs. He'd tell Dad about the light bulb later, and Dad would fix it because that's all the light Jake got down there. Jake chose to live in the basement, even though it had no windows. To Jake it felt like a hideout, a secret dungeon, and it saved him from sharing a room with his two older brothers, Doug and Sean.

Jake opened the door and stepped into the kitchen, which was also dark, though not jet black like his room. The kitchen was awash in the soft gray light that slipped in through the cracks of the curtains.

He walked over to the light switch by the stove and flipped it. No result. He stood in the dim gray light, confused. He thought every light bulb in the house must have broken on the same day.

He opened the fridge and a soft wave of cool air embraced him, causing goosebumps. He couldn't believe what he saw inside. The fridge light was out too. It didn't matter; he knew exactly where Mom kept the chocolate milk. He opened the flaps, and even though he knew it was trouble, started drinking right from the carton. He gulped back the thick chocolate milk with his lips pressed tight against the waxed cardboard, to keep from getting a brown moustache. He closed the carton and stuck it back in the fridge.

With the sweet milk resting in his belly he became more curious than hungry, and wondered where his parents were. Either Mom or Dad usually waited around with him until Marcy showed up.

Jake loved Marcy, the lady that took care of him during the summer while his parents and brothers worked. She smelled like cucumbers and brown sugar, and Mom said she was the only nanny in the county who knew sign language. She also knew where Mom hid the Tootsie Rolls, and when Jake figured something out Marcy would give him a handful. Jake only ate a couple of them a day, relishing the thick texture and the way they filled his senses as he chewed. The surplus Tootsie Rolls he saved were stashed in a brown paper bag that he hid at the bottom of his toy chest.

Jake noticed that the house felt smaller in the dark. Mom said that the house was little and cheap since the Army used to keep soldiers in it. She said that when the base moved to the other side of town the old concrete soldier houses got fixed up and sold off. This made Jake feel safe, like he lived in a castle made for warriors. He thought maybe someday he'd be a soldier.

He began to feel strange as he crept through the house, looking for someone, anyone. He wished, as he often did, that he could hear. He would just tune his ears in and follow the sound of his Mom or his Dad to the source, like he used to before he got sick and hot and the world became silent.

Every room in the house was empty, and Jake began to worry, and figured that Marcy must be on her way. Otherwise his parents never would have left him alone.

He walked into the living room and sat down in front of the television. He thought he'd watch some cartoons and before he knew it Marcy would be at the door, smelling like sugar.

The TV wouldn't work either, which was probably for the best. Mom and Dad didn't let him watch any shows for the last couple of weeks. They said there was nothing on but the news anyway, and he got scared when he watched the news.

Anxious, and a little worried, Jake crawled over to the window at the front of the house. He reached up and pressed his hand to the heavy, dark green velvet drapes. He pushed them to the left, looked outside, and understood what was going on.

It was snowing, and in the middle of Summer no less! The electricity must not work when it gets cold in the Summer. Mom and Dad were probably outside, shoveling the driveway or the roof.

Jake placed his right palm, open, against the glass of the window to see how cold it was. The glass was warm, almost hot, and Jake noticed his breath wasn't freezing on it.

The idea of a Summer snowstorm filled Jake with a sense of wonder and excitement. He thought for a second that maybe God was giving him this miracle to apologize for making him deaf, but he felt instantly guilty for thinking so.

Jake stood up and walked to the front door. His hand reached to the doorknob and found it was warm. Overjoyed at the thought of this unexpected Winter he threw the front door open and ran outside.

The snow was virgin, and rested a foot thick across the whole neighborhood. Clouds hung heavy and black across the sky, and Jake saw flashes of lightning trapped within them. He looked for the sun in every direction and saw only clouds, and the peculiar gray light that matched his pajamas. He wasn't cold, and felt the shift of a warm breeze across his skin.

Jake didn't see a single person outside, including his parents, but the miracle of Summertime Winter had filled his mind and he didn't worry. He was amazed by the storm. The gray snowflakes were coming down so thick he couldn't see across the street.

He held out his hands and caught some of the flakes in his palms. They would not melt, and when he blew his hot breath on them they didn't turn to water. Instead they fell to pieces and swirled away.

He trudged out to the center of his front yard and turned around, gazing at his house in the dusky light.

He couldn't believe his eyes. Someone had painted his whole house the darkest black he'd ever seen. On top of that, they'd painted people, beautiful, bright white people, on the front of his house. There were two people running, maybe playing, and standing closer to the door, near the front windows, the silhouettes of his parents stood with arms outstretched to the sky.

Jake was laughing as he looked at the mural, a soft, rasping laugh that felt good in his throat. Wouldn't Marcy be surprised when she saw the painting?

Upon seeing the shapes of his parents, Jake was filled with a sense of their absence and couldn't wait to see them after work. For now, he could play.

He lay down on his back in the warm sheet of snow that blanketed his front yard and began to move his legs and arms slowly, rhythmically, up and down.

As he packed the soft ground beneath him he felt the wind change directions, blowing fast and warm against the left side of his face.

Jake perfected his snow angel and took a moment to appreciate what he had created. He breathed deeply, instilled with a sense of calm as his chest rose.

Jake watched the snow drift down, blinking and laughing as it landed on his eyelashes.

He let the hot wind flow over him. It soon filled the air with color, and Jake inhaled its lullaby deep into his body.

He slept quiet in the arms of his angel, while the misplaced Winter stormed around him.

When Susurrus Stirs

He tells me their life is the best thing going. He says that I need to imagine what it would be like to crawl into the plushest limousine I can imagine, to flop down into a deep, soft leather chair filled with downy feathers from giant geese, to turn the internal weather controls to "Perfect" and have a constantly changing range of scenery and a non-stop supply of food and fluids.

Then he says, imagine that all you have to do is eat and make babies and watch your life roll by in luxuriant comfort. The American dream, but he's a citizen of everywhere—he's just naturally attained what we're all shooting for. And it doesn't matter how big you get, he says, because when you become too large, part of you just breaks off and becomes another you. No dating or mating required. No awkward social moments, never a viscous string of sticky spit running thick from tooth to tongue while you try to talk a woman of vague sexual persuasion into an allowance of simian grinding.

Never a credit card bill in sight.

And his kids, he says proudly, they all turn out just like him. The emergence of a misplaced chromosome is a non-option. Every little him is a perfect chip off the ancient block, and has been for eons.

He doesn't speak to me as an individual; I can feel that in his voice as it creeps through my nervous system and vibrates my tympanic membrane from the inside. The idea of "self" is impossible to him. When he speaks to me as "You" I can tell he's addressing our whole species, every last human representing a potential host.

"You are more fun than the elephants," he says, "They didn't drink enough water and always fed us the same things. You feed us the soft pieces, the animal bits. We spread faster now. We are everywhere. We are growing."

I picture Susurrus as a "him" because I don't get along well with women. Always felt more comfortable around men. Can't truck with the idea of a lady crawling around in my intestines, judging me, saying, "Look at how you've treated yourself here. Too much red meat residue in your upper GI, and your colon could become impacted at a second's notice. How about some bran? Some heavy green tea? Something needs to be done. This place is a mess."

I named Susurrus after the analog "SSSSS" that accompanies his voice as it crawls around in my head. There's always this hissing noise that precedes his speaking and hangs on afterwards, like an itch deep in my ear. Sometimes the echo stays with me for hours. Then I play jazz CDs through my headphones and it sounds like I've got old records running under the needle.

Susurrus wasn't always in my brain, but I've been cultivating him, making him more a part of me. When I meditate I imagine the fibers of my spinal cord stretching out towards him, like feelers. They sway and twitch and burrow into my belly and connect to him, linking us. His hiss slides up through my spine and connects with my slow-chanted mantra, my mumbled OMNAMA's, until it's all white noise and for a moment I'm inside him, inside myself, feeling his contentment as his mouths reach out and slurp away at acidy bits of the day's meal, tiny snippets of sausage and soda-pop sugars and oil-soaked ciabatta breads.

He is always at peace, a consumptive strand of nirvana.

According to the last x-ray my radiologist took, he's over fifty feet long, and still growing. My doctors have extracted pieces of him from my stool, pulsing egg sacs waiting to find water or flesh and keep the cycle of expansion in motion.

They say he's not a tapeworm, not a guinea worm, not anything they're used to seeing. He doesn't seem to affect my physiology in any negative way, although my grocery bill has ratcheted ever upwards. Still the doctors think I should have him removed. I tell them I'm a pacifist and it's not in my nature to harm a creature, especially if it poses no threat. That gets me worried glances, furrowed brows. But they don't protest much.

I think they're waiting for this thing to kill me so they can take me apart and extract his coiled body. Get a new species, name it after themselves, get published in the right journals, pull grant money.

I'm a cash cow infestation case. On a ticking clock, they imagine. Especially since this thing is spreading. One end is snaking towards my genitals, they say, and the other is coiling its way around my spine, on the way to my brain. There are more mouths showing up, not just the ones that reside in my belly.

"How did it get out of my stomach?" I ask them, not mentioning my meditation, the way Susurrus and I have bonded now. The way I've encouraged him to become part of me.

"Well, we're not exactly sure. It appears to exit through the duodenum as it heads toward your spine. There's a sort of cystic calcification at the point of exit, where it pushed through the stomach tissue. That's what keeps you from becoming toxic via your own acids. Again, this is all speculation. If you'd let us perform a more invasive . . ."

"Nope. No can do, Doc. You say this thing's not hurting me. What're the odds that this procedure would kill it?"

They don't know. These guys really don't know anything. Why should I open up my body, *our* bodies, to guesswork with scalpels?

I THINK I KNOW where he came from, this new part of my life.

Five months ago I was jogging, a beautiful run at dusk through the sloping, rolling green park near my house. I was sucking down deep lung-loads of air when I ran through a floating mire of gnats. They stuck to me, twitching in my sweat, their tiny bodies suddenly swept up in the forward surge of my run. A few were sucked right into my chest, surely now melting to atoms against my alveoli.

But one of them . . . one of them stuck to the roof of my mouth. There was an itch, so close in sensation to the hiss of Susurrus, and I felt an immediate need to take a nap.

So I did. I collapsed to the ground, mindless of the lactic acidosis that would haunt my muscles, curled there among the duck shit and crawling ants and crushed grass, and I fell into a slumber.

When I awoke there was a tight bubble of tissue on the roof of my mouth, where the gnat had stuck. It hurt when I prodded it with my tongue, so I avoided it.

Later that night the bubble had become even tighter, this small mound of swollen pink tissue with a whitish tip. I stared at it in the mirror, unable to look away from its grotesque new presence.

I could feel my heartbeat inside the bump. There was no way I could sleep with this thing in my mouth. What if it kept expanding until I couldn't breathe?

I rubbed down my tweezers with benzyl alcohol and proceeded to poke and squeeze the bump until it bled. A thin rivulet of blood trickled down from the fleshy stalactite, and the harder I squeezed the more the blood thickened, grew darker. Soon the blood made way for a dense yellow fluid that carried with it the odor of rotten dairy in high heat. I pushed one pointed end of the tweezers directly into the spreading hole at the side of the bump.

Then it ruptured.

The relief of pressure was immediate. My mirror caught the worst of the spray, instantly shellacked with dead-cell soup in a spray pattern near arterial in its arc.

Then the colors came. A thin drip from the open wound on the roof of my mouth, two drops like oil spilling out, swirling with shades I'd never quite seen before, just outside a spectrum my eyes could comprehend. The drops sat there in the curve of my tongue, merged together like quivering mercury.

I'd never felt so intense a need to swallow something in my entire life.

The sensation of the drops was not fluid. It felt as if they were crawling into me, too impatient for my peristaltic process.

And again, almost immediately, I collapsed into slumber, this time dreaming of a sea of human tissue, all of it shifting and turning and surging, soft and hot and wanting to pull me under.

I hadn't had so explosive a wet dream since I was in junior high.

And when I woke up, curled on the floor of my bathroom with my underwear stuck to me like soaked toilet paper, I was hungry as a newborn.

FOUR MONTH'S TIME PASSED like nothing, our perception expanded to a broader sense. The human clock thinks small—within seventy-five year death limitations.

We laugh at the idea of death. The upside of being We.

And We are larger now. Eighty pounds heavier, abdomen distended, watermelon tight. One poke with a toothpick just below the bellybutton and we'd tear open like crepe paper. Neck swollen with a circular rash pattern that seeps clear fluids now crusting in the bony pockets of our shoulder-blades. White of the eyes yellowing, thickening. Hair falling out in clumps from soft-scalp surface.

Our penis is heavier. Its skin shifts constantly; there are more veins, white beneath the surface. The head has bloomed from mushroom tip to flower; it is open, flayed, in rose-like petals, red, pulsing. We bandage it to keep it from seeping down our leg.

We have stopped seeing the doctors. They whispered letters last time.

CDC, they said.

Our I-brain told us this means trouble. We cannot accept "trouble" so close to the next cycle. We force-fed the doctors the bits of us they stole from our excretions. So many of us in each segment that even their testing couldn't ruin all the eggs. Our body was shaking then, sweating hands clutching an oily metal tool, eyes crying. It has stopped struggling since. Its feelings are soft echoes now, little more. Things are quiet.

We are hiding. Hiding ends after the next sun-drop.

Our I-brain is remembering passwords, using fat, purpled fingers to stroke language keys.

We are feeling better as we see the screen before us change.

Our tickets have been confirmed. The glowing box has thanked us for our purchase.

"You're welcome," we whisper. The rolling chair squeaks under our ever-shifting weight. We stand up with a grunt and feel that the bandages around our meat-sprout are wet again. Cleaning up is no longer important.

We crawl on four bony-stems towards our meditation mat. Light the incense and try to assume the lotus position. Too much of us; our legs can't fold into the space filled by our twitching belly.

We lay back and stare at the ceiling. Our mantra has been replaced by a new noise. We push our tongue to the front of our teeth and start leaking air, a steady SSSSSS until our I-brain goes soft and quiet and we lie there in the dark room, shaking slightly from our constant eating and squirming. Much of the old us is empty now. Our new muscles, thousands of them, ropy and squeezing against each other, roll us onto our right side.

At some point we insert our thumbs into our mouth and suck the meat clean from the bones.

Anything to feed the new cycle.

THE SEAT IN THE theater can barely hold us, but we are here and we are ready. It is after the most recent sun-drop, halfway through the dark period. We are wearing leather gloves (they barely fit except for the thumbs, which drape and look sharp) and a trench coat at the suggestion of the remnants of the I-brain.

We sit at the rear of the room. No one sits near us but most of the rows in front of us are full. A bright light appears at the front of the room, large, shimmering.

Our I-brain tells us this is a midnight movie, a Spanish film, one of the best. Hasn't been shown in a while. We knew it would be packed. We see a couple of people have brought their children. There is a pained feeling from the old thoughts, but it fades.

There are thin clouds of sweet white smoke floating in this room. We breathe it in deeply, pulling it with a whistling noise into our one un-collapsed lung.

The show on the screen is strange, like the amusing dreams of our I-brain. The humans aren't acting like humans. They are trapped inside a cave lit by a bonfire. They rub each other with burning metal staffs, men and women screaming, skin bubbling and bursting. They paint their eyes with black ashes. They pull a large creature from a cage at the back of the tunnel, many men struggling and falling as they drag the thing in on chains that run through its skin. Some of the fallen men collapse under it as it is dragged forward and it pulls them up into its fluid mass, absorbing them. The space where their bodies merged and melted in begins to ooze a thick white cream. Women ladle this cream from its skin, drinking it and dancing, circles around the fire, ever faster. The women fall to the ground and their chests open up, ribs turned to spongy soft nothing, hearts missing. Slugs ooze out between spread-wide breasts and crawl towards the creature, still just a shape, still cloaked in dark. The men sit before the fire and sweat black oil. Light glows at the top of their foreheads. The slugs turn their stalks to the lights on the men's heads and shift away from the massive beast quivering in the dark. Then the slugs are on the men, long shining trails on shivering skin.

We are touching ourselves while these images glow before us. We have unbuckled and lowered our pants. The leather on our gloved hands is soaking through with seepage. We do not push aside our jacket, but know that the pulsing rose between our legs is emitting a light-red glow. A hissing noise slips from its center.

We are as quiet as we can be. As expected, the audience uproar in the room buries our birthing sounds. The people in this room are laughing, breathing, smoking, fascinated and excited by a world that is not theirs.

We can taste them on our tongues. Two of our heads have emerged, broken through the belly skin, hissing in the flavor of the room.

We slide down to the swollen meat-sprout at our groin and wrap our long bodies around it. Our fanged mouths find each other and lock up, teeth biting into each other's lower jaws. We are a sheath now, squeezing tight, sliding up and down, pulsing, with the blooming rose at our top, its folds filling with an oil-slick rainbow of wet color.

There is now a desert on the screen. The cave full of revelers has collapsed. A lone man in a cowboy hat has emerged. He walks on crutches made of elephant ivory. He leaves no print in the sand.

We are ready for the next cycle. Hissing at a higher pitch. Our human head lolls back, its now soft skull squelching against the rear wall of the theater, bits of gray garbage draining out.

Our mouths unlatch from each other and we stop stroking between our legs. We bite into the rose-bloom and taste our old warm blood and the oils of our gestation and we pull back and then split the meat-sprout from tip to shaft.

What is left of our I-brain thinks it has gone to a place called Heaven. It feels so good. So alive.

It thinks a word. *Enlightenment.*

Our abdomen muscles contract and push down and a thick, bloody sausage-shaped sac pushes out of the hole we've torn in our crotch, the old flaps of our meat-sprout shaking and slipping against its emergence.

It is rare and lucky to reach this point in the cycle. We are blessed.

We quickly grasp the tube with our man-hands and bring it to our mouth, licking it clean, the taste stirring an old sense memory of the day we swallowed a bug in the park.

One of our new extensions crawls up through our man-throat and slides over the slick, swollen man-tongue. We bite into the sac, spreading it open.

We smile.

Their wings are already drying.

The film on the screen is so strange that when the man in the desert is suddenly eclipsed by the shadow of thousands of tiny flying gnats, the audience gasps in awe, breathing in deep, smiling with surprise, stunned by spectacle.

We ride in on the waves of their exhalation and find soft purchase.

And the people sleep, and dream, and awake to a subtle hissing sound. It is familiar to them. They hear it in their blood.

We are the waves of an ancient ocean crashing to shore, washing everything clean.

Luminary

My brother burned to death in the summer of 1967. The doctors never found any evidence of the fire on his flesh, any scar on his skin.

I know the truth. I watched him burn.

My brother's name was Martin Tally.

Marty was a young man prone to daydreaming, and had a distant quality that strangers mistook for carelessness. Those who spent any significant time with him could identify his drifting eyes and long moments of silence for what they really were—an intense thoughtfulness, the focused kind of calm needed to contain boundless energy. His deep brown eyes, often hidden below a furrowed brow, seemed permanently etched with question marks. At moments of understanding his eyes shone with blazing exclamation points.

His eyes were full of light the day he tried to explain the human body to me. He rattled off Latin words and the names of bones and tissues and organs until he was almost breathless, concluding with, "You and me, Petey, we're the most magnificent machines ever built." Then he laughed, this deep laugh, and he seemed to marvel that the sound was coming from his own body.

His eyes were on fire when he took me up to the roof of our one-story house to watch the stars fall. He ushered me up our rickety wooden ladder and climbed behind me, carrying three blankets, two cans of soda, and a pack of saltines. We sipped on our sodas and crunched our crackers until we were covered with crumbs and giddy from the sugar and we watched the night sky produce star after star. He had heard about an expected meteor shower, and laughed as he saw the first stone streak fire in a straight line towards the Earth. We watched for two hours as flaming rocks painted the sky with thin brushstrokes, our silence punctuated by the occasional sound of his laughter.

Toward the end of the meteor shower I turned onto my side and watched him observing the sky, his eyes shining. As if he could sense my eyes on him he said, "Pete, I know Mom didn't raise us churchy, but I want you to always remember what you saw tonight, okay, bud? 'Cause that, that up there, what we just saw, is proof of God."

My brother's eyes were ablaze the time I got caught skipping school with Percy Brewston and Mark Bowling, and tried to shift the blame to my friends. I said, "Well, it was Mark's idea and I just thought . . . "

Marty didn't give me time to finish the sentence. "If it was Mark's idea then you didn't think anything, you followed. At least Mark had an idea, and he acted on it. You had no idea what you were doing. You acted without the conviction of your own decision, and now you have to suffer the consequences. Lemmings follow, Pete, and men think."

At the time I didn't even know what lemmings were, but from the sharp glint in his eyes I knew that it was far better to be a man.

I learned most of the lessons I still consider valuable from Marty, who, although only seven years older than me, was the closest thing I had to a father.

The real deal, the biological Pops, was a door-to-door salesman who Mom said became a door-to-door husband, performing the service for women in need. After spending days looping through microfiche at the library, I discovered that Pops' final sale was closed at a house in Cronston, Ohio where he was caught rendering his husbandry service with the wife of an infuriated carpenter. It turned out that the carpenter had enough energy for a little overtime, and a hammer to the face ended my father's illustrious career.

I didn't need my dad. Mom kept me warm and kept food in my belly. My sister Vanessa made me laugh. Marty taught me about science, and math, and writing, and during the summer of 1967 he taught me about miracles.

Marty was seventeen years old, I was ten, and Vanessa was five. We were all old enough to know something was seriously wrong with our cat, Teddy. Teddy had taken to pissing freely anywhere he felt like losing some fluids. He also maintained a Rip Van Winkle-esque sleep schedule, surprising for a cat that used to spend all hours chasing invisible antagonists and terrorizing birds in the acreage near our house.

One afternoon I found Teddy resting on his side in the front yard. He was mewling just loud enough for me to hear through the screen door. His furry chest was matted and was barely rising with his breath. His head was resting in a small, dark pink pool of his own vomit.

I didn't expect Mom home from her job at the cannery for another three hours, and I couldn't leave Teddy lying there in that condition, so I went and knocked on Marty's door.

I *never* knocked on Marty's door, especially after school. Marty tended to cloister himself away for long periods of time, focused on his books and his beloved chemistry set, and he didn't take well to interruptions. The last time I had interrupted him it had taken me two minutes to un-lodge the resultant wedgie. Still, Teddy appeared to be knocking on death's door with both paws.

Marty appeared at the door. "Aw, for Christ's sake, Petey, don't bother me. Go play with Vanessa or something. I have reading to do!"

I peeked past him and scoped out his alway-tidy room, the small bed, the neatly kept wooden desk and desk lamp, the toddler-size stack of text books by his bed stand.

Tears welled to the surface. I sobbed, "Marty, you gotta see Teddy!"

Moments later we were in the front yard, crouched over the gaunt and barely breathing cat.

The question marks had entered Marty's eyes, and I watched him watch Teddy, breathing calm as he softly stroked the cat's head. He turned to me and said, "Bring me a blanket from your room, one you don't mind not getting back."

I ran to my room and grabbed an old ratty yellow blanket that made my skin itch upon contact. I ran back and presented it to Marty, who was whispering something to the cat that sounded like, "It could work, Teddy. It could really work."

Marty used the blanket to clean the vomit away from Teddy and then pressed the fabric across his palms and scooped his hands softly under the cat's neck and hindquarters. He wrapped the rest of the blanket around the body of the cat, who had stopped his sad mewling.

Marty carried the cat to his room and shut the door. I heard the lock tumble. I panicked and ran to Marty's door and was about to yell, "What the hell are you doing to our cat?"when his voice came calmly from the other side. He said, "Pete, listen very closely. I am going to fix Teddy, but it's going to take me a few days, and I'll need your help. We can't tell Mom about this because she'll want to take Teddy to the vet, and they will want to kill him. They don't know what I know, or at least what I think I know, and I think I might be Teddy's only chance to live. Petey, will you swear, on Teddy, and God, and everything, that you won't tell Mom?"

"Yes, I swear."

For the next few days I played coy, suggesting to Mom that Teddy might have run away. She seemed less concerned than I expected. I guessed that three kids and a full-time job was enough responsibility without having to worry about the disappearance of our incontinent cat.

Each night I asked Marty what was happening and each night he offered no answers, instead insisting that Vanessa and I follow him out into the rolling fields near our house.

Each night, for six nights in a row, the three of us walked into the field during the soft light of dusk and caught fireflies. Marty supplied us with bug catching nets and jars with metal lids that had holes punched in the top. We swung our nets through the air and captured the little flickers of light that buzzed around us. We coerced the glowing luminescent beetles into our jars, where they grew frantic and flickered even faster.

While we were in the field Marty taught us about our tiny prey. We learned that the males flashed every five seconds, the females every two. Vanessa laughed and devoted herself to catching only the fastest flickering of the bugs. We learned the fireflies came from the family Lampyridae, which I remember only because it has the word "lamp" in it. Marty said the beetles made light out of two chemicals, luciferin and luciferase, both named after Lucifer, the angel of fallen light.

Each night Marty took the bug-filled jars from us and locked himself away in his room, occasionally appearing in the kitchen to grab a bag of cat food or some ice. Every once in awhile I would see a light green glow coming from beneath Marty's locked door.

Things disappeared from around the house.

The fourth day after Teddy collapsed I noticed the absence of several items, most notably a card table, a small wooden chair, my mother's razor from the bathroom, and my father's old insulin injection kit from the medicine cabinet. It made no sense at the time, and I began to doubt Marty.

THE SEVENTH NIGHT AFTER Teddy fell ill, my sister disappeared.

My mom had set out dinner, meat loaf with onions and mashed potatoes, and she called for us. Marty and I arrived at the table, but

Vanessa was nowhere to be found. We walked the perimeter of our small residence. Marty noticed that the fireflies were out early that night. The exclamation points sparkled in his eyes. He ran to our tool shed, with me trailing behind.

Marty threw open the doors of the shed and gasped. Only two insect nets were on the rack.

"Oh, shit, Petey, she went firefly hunting without us."

We ran back to the house and grabbed Mom, explaining to her about our nightly trips to the field to gather the glowing insects. She asked "Why?"and Marty offered no answer. He was too intent on getting to the field and finding Vanessa.

We trudged through the field as the sky grew ever blacker. I felt my heart drop into my toes and my stomach rise to my throat when I heard Vanessa's voice, screaming somewhere far away. We followed the sound, the three of us now running, and I skinned my knees when I tripped on a downward slope in the field.

I looked behind me and saw the third insect net lying on the ground. Where the hell was Vanessa and why would she drop her net? My body was instantly soaked in sweat and my mouth dry as a tomb. I felt sick to my stomach but held the gorge back as Marty and my mom rushed towards the sound of my sister's faint screams.

We found Vanessa on the far southeast end of the field, in the area just before a jutting line of trees at the edge of the thick and boggy marsh. She was trapped under a collapsed deadfall of old, heavy whisper oaks. We could see her little arm sticking out, torn with scratches. What I could see of her body was either incredibly pale or bleeding. Worse than that, she had stopped screaming as we reached her. There was no comfort in that quiet.

As my mom reached forward to grasp Vanessa's hand she pushed aside a thick branch and the deadfall shifted. Trees crackled and smashed through each other, pinning Vanessa deeper and pulling a desperate scream from my mother's throat.

In the growing darkness I saw the metal in Marty's eyes, the calm and the wisdom beyond his years. He said, "It's going to be okay. No one move. Any motion and those trees could collapse further. I am going back to the house, and when I return things are going to be okay."

My mom and I stood silent. I felt a sudden calm as I watched Marty run up the field, his legs graceful beneath him.

The blanket of darkness dropped over the sky.

I agonized over each second that passed without Marty's return. Each moment slammed into me, heavy and punctuated like the heartbeat of a giant.

I saw Marty first, out of my peripheral vision, and then my Mom saw him. "Look," she said. Light filled our senses. Marty ran toward us at incredible speed, streaking sharp green light behind him. As he got closer to us, about halfway across the field, I could tell it was no illusion. He was glowing, bioluminescent. Tiny fireflies rose from the floor of the field and circled him, like planets orbiting the sun.

Marty's veins were on fire, glowing bright green. Every artery, every twist and turn of his body through which blood flowed was emanating a blinding light, and his eyes were saturated with it. The whole field within thirty feet of my brother glowed like daylight. The left side of his chest was shimmering, too bright to look into where his heart was circulating the liquid fire of his blood, so filled with light that his chest had become translucent.

We watched him then, stunned.

We watched as he lifted the mass of shattered trees that hung over my sister.

We watched as he reached one glowing arm into the deadfall and gingerly eased my sister's broken body out and placed her at my mother's feet.

We watched as the deadfall finally crashed in on itself, splintering, sending shards of old wood flying around us.

We watched as my brother, his flesh on fire, pulled one of my father's old insulin syringes from his pants pocket and slid it into his femoral artery, drawing blood. The blood shone so bright in the glass syringe that I couldn't look at it directly. He carefully placed the needle in Vanessa's left arm, at the bend, and depressed the plunger.

Her breathing became steady, her color returned, and a faint glow came from her veins.

Marty spoke to us. He said, in a voice amplified with a strange, buzzing undercurrent, *"Vanessa's going to be all right. I must rest here for a moment, but you need to get Vanessa to a doctor right away. I think she's bleeding on the inside. I love you so much, and I know you love me the same, so you have to trust me, and go now."*

My mom and I rushed Vanessa back to the house. I ran inside and grabbed a thick blanket off the back of the couch, which we used to keep Vanessa warm on the way to the hospital.

Mom and I remained silent the whole time Vanessa was with the doctors, both of us floating in a strange sort of daze, knowing we'd just witnessed something incredible, maybe impossible.

Later, when Vanessa had stabilized and we returned from the hospital, I ran around the house looking for Marty, searching for that bright glow. I found him in his bedroom, lying under his covers.

His chest did not rise or fall. His light, which hours before had burnt itself into my retinas, was now extinguished.

As I walked over to Marty and crouched down by his body I felt the first of a torrent of tears stream down my face, and hardly noticed the soft glow that had entered the room. It was Teddy, padding softly towards me and purring, his eyes glowing green.

I held onto Marty's body and cried until my Mom pulled me away and we called an ambulance. The medical technicians arrived and placed him on a stretcher to take him away. To them Marty looked like a boy, barely a man.

I knew what he really was. I held on to my mother as they carried away our fallen angel of light.

Trigger Variation

Does *he know about the Mercabol? Damn it. Did I hide the gear last night?*
Jackson pretended to stretch his neck as he scoped out his Spartan charm-free rental unit.

Thin mattress/weight bench/jugs of protein powder and amino fuel in the closest corner. Jump rope on the floor. Boom box with a stack of CDs placed neatly to one side, sitting next to a digital alarm clock.

No needles. No tiny glass bottles. Thank God.

But what if the shit's still out in the bathroom? Keep him busy right here. Keep talking.

Kane had just arrived, an hour earlier than expected, and was pacing Jackson's apartment, clenching and un-clenching his considerable fists.

Okay, what was I talking about?

Jackson started up again.

"I mean, didn't you ever think, for just a second, that maybe this lifestyle . . . "

"Maybe this lifestyle *what*, man?"

Jackson paused.

Okay, wrong tack. Focus, man. Don't act so shaken up.

He let his arms drop to his sides and hissed out a deep shaking breath. Felt the blood flow to his hands, veins bulging.

I'm heavy. Getting heavier. Finally. I don't think they know . . .

Jackson eyeballed Kane. Big, hair-trigger Kane. His superior by about 60 pounds and a few months of training. Thick, razor-shaved symmetrical skull and over-prominent brow. Gorilla physique. A guy prone to misunderstanding nuance. A guy deeply loyal to the EndLiners ideals. A guy who might just put a fist through Jackson's throat that very second for questioning said ideals.

Jackson cancelled his query/feigned mental drift.

Kane was watching him—studying him with his head turned slightly to one side, waiting for a response.

"Shit. I don't know. Having a fuzzy-brained moment. I haven't slept much the last few days."

Jackson noticed the oily rings around Kane's eyes and figured he was equally exhausted. They'd been training so hard . . .

"Yeah, man, I know what you're talking about. My brain's a little jacked at the moment, too. Last night I was curling and while I had the bar all the way up I started staring at the weight on the right side and seeing all the patterns in the gray metal, and then I looked up at myself in the mirror and I didn't know who I was for a second and I wanted to jump across the room and just fucking mash the dude."

"What?" Jackson asked the question with excitement in his voice, glad that Kane was going to let Jackson's earlier thought drop. Better for both of them.

Kane continued. "Seriously. I was so pumped that the sight of what I thought was another human being made me want to go kick some ass. It was like this force was behind me, pushing me towards him . . ."

"Towards *you?*"

"Well, yeah. And that's why nothing came of it. Because if I would have swung on the dude all I would have got for it was a broken mirror and a fucked-up hand. But I was *close*, man. Some borderline shit . . . "

They both smiled at that. Things had been sketchy for weeks, chaos sliding into their lives a little more as each day rushed by in anticipation of the big night. Jorge had gone to jail for trying to steal a crate of eggs (ostensibly, they all guessed, to be used for protein binging). Nate got pinched for rape, his own girlfriend the accuser, her broken right wrist making it an easy case for the cops to close. Kyle was arrested for brawling downtown, and was still wearing his "Your Mom is A Rotten Cunt" T-shirt when he was bailed out. Mitchell broke his ankle trying to clear a fence after getting caught in the middle of prowling an upscale residence (for reasons none of them could readily ascertain). And Frank had . . . well, Frank had crossed a line but *hadn't* been caught.

Their fearless leader, the man behind the EndLiner ideals, had gone out one balmy Thursday to spend the night sniping zoo animals with a rifle.

Frank saw it as further proof of human dominion, of the absolute power accorded our species, but Jackson could tell a lot of the guys were holding back a flinch or two while watching the footage.

Ex-straight edge kids, he guessed. Wanted the extra hardcore aspect they could get as EndLiners but still harbored their old pro-animal affection (or *affectation* as Frank would call it). Jackson got the feeling from Frank that his empathy ran as deep as a creek in Death Valley, and that all EndLiners were expected to exhibit that same coldness. And many of them did run frosty, these ex-edge kids who'd realized how much easier it was to deride and destroy. They discovered how *fun* it could be if you didn't mind abiding by their leader's occasional extremes.

As shaky as Frank's digicam footage was, it had been rough watching him drop the tiger. And the monkeys. A few of those twitched as they bled out. Other monkeys came right to the freshly-plugged bait, tearing out their fur in tufts, screaming at nothing until Frank scoped them down too.

And always, in the background, Frank's laughter. Like a sponge full of joy being squeezed out by his throat, his love for the midnight mercenary mission on full display.

Jackson had been paying close attention to the tape. He'd heard Frank whisper, "We win," after the last monkey dropped. Jackson had rubbed the goosebumps off his skin quick and mustered up the best laugh he could. It sounded as false as it was.

Kane had looked at Jackson then, too. Watched him closely.

He can tell something's off. Does he know about the 'roids? What is he telling Frank? We've been friends for so many years, man. Jesus, I shouldn't even be thinking about Kane like this.

But Jackson had been out on his own midnight missions with Kane and knew the kid that helped him limp home after his first bike wreck wasn't around anymore. Kane had developed a strong taste for the rough stuff, and there'd been a shift. They were EndLiners and now everything—everybody—fell into two categories.

The weak and the strong.

And God fucking help you if were even a momentary member of the first party.

THE PILLOW FIGHTS WERE, of course, Frank's idea. Loosely, anonymously organized, being wholly un-associated with anything EndLiner. General net shenanigans got it done. Emails, IMs with an address and a single message: *Bring a pillow and be ready for battle.* Frank paid a guy to pay a guy to set the ball in motion, and the results were great.

The first fight—at McGrady's public park—pulled a few hundred combatants and ended with a ration of bruises and grass covered thick with expelled feathers.

Arrests: zero.

Jackson had watched the officers from the periphery, studied their faces, guessed at their reactions. Some smirked—writing it off as the further infantilism of a worthless generation. A few cops kept their itching hands hovering over their pepper spray canisters. Some wished they'd brought their own pillows.

The second fight was in the town square and pulled double the numbers. This time the media was invited. Everything stayed anonymous but now people who'd never even heard of the term "web browser" knew about the events.

Those crazy kids, they commented, there's worse things they could be doing.

WHAT JACKSON COULDN'T TELL Kane, or anyone else for that matter, was that he was starting to have doubts about the big night.

There was no name for the event. Frank wasn't big on marketing.

"No catchy slogans or simple images to tag up on a wall," he'd said. "Being an EndLiner means respecting one thing: Human survival. If you need a ten-step plan or a secret handshake or a goddamned secret Mason reach-around, then we don't need you."

Keeping the idea at the forefront—that humans were the one great species on Earth and that they must, at any costs, become ever-stronger—that's what Frank did. He tapped into primal urges and desires. Fighting/fucking/feasting. The things that came with power and strength.

But you had to work for it. You had to get big. Local stores ran short on protein powder/milk/eggs/chicken/steak. The guys involved with Frank stayed loosely connected, per his instructions, but when they did meet in person their conversations invariably drifted to three topics—lifting programs, combat techniques, and music (predominately of hardcore variety).

The straight edge kids ate it up because Frank thought that their power should come without the taint of drugs. His ideology freed them from believing in the nobility of anyone other than themselves; saved them from the inevitable letdowns that the rest of humanity had to offer.

And they liked the fact that he allowed meat and promiscuity back into their lives. Many of them had grown skinny and anemic without their old diet of animal flesh. Surging sex-drives had made the ascetic lifestyle a bitch. Now they were bigger/more dangerous/ sexually aggressive to the point where you could taste the hormones when a group of them entered a room. And they were going to the same punk/metal shows, throwing around considerable added weight, and getting blown in the parking lot while blast beats still rumbled against the roof of the venue.

It was ape heaven.

At least that's how Jackson was starting to see it.

He'd been enchanted at first. Like a lot of the EndLiners he came from a shitty household scenario. It was close to standard issue with their crew. Jackson's particular brand of bullshit was father-oriented.

His Pops was an unshakeable, almost admirably tenacious alky. Even the drunken traffic wreck that broke his dad's right leg and put Jackson's mother in the grave hadn't slowed down his bottle draining mission (his time "in the cups" as he called it; shooting for charming but coming off resigned).

After that particular mom-slaughtering indignity, Jackson had been taken away by the state and started the eighth grade as a technical orphan before his dad figured out who to pay off—with money from mom's life insurance policy—to get his kid back.

Back home. Two years of listening to the fucker sobbing over the sound of empty bottles clinking. And then it was legal emancipation/dropping out/working groceries at the Shop N Save for rent money. Freedom, pretty much, aside from the occasional late night phone call filled with promise and apology.

I'm so sorry, Jackson. I hope you know it. I try so hard but I don't think you'll ever see that. Enough talk though, right? Show and prove time. I've been thinking about joining a gym, and maybe I can even go back to AA if they don't keep pumping God up my ass and . . . I don't know. I'll quit talking, Jacky, and I'll show you something.

Once in awhile the old fucker sold it sincere enough to tease out a sliver of hope.

It was that hope—and how his father used it—that led Jackson to hate the man. When Jackson was teased by those chances to see his father as a *father* and not just the drunk that spawned him—and when those chances were inevitably smashed like empty bourbon bottles—that was the worst of it.

That was what made him want to be *hard*. To be big, and better, and clean, and powerful.

To be an EndLiner.

But as Jackson stared at the injection kit in front of him—a slim needle and a small glass bottle with a label reading Mercabol, underscored by some Asian writing he couldn't translate—his doubts returned.

I'm just as hooked as Pops.

Jackson killed the bad thoughts, recognized they could only take him in one direction. He drew fluid into the syringe, wondering if it was really horse testosterone like the web ad had said, and then pushed the needle into the meat of his left thigh. He grimaced at the intramuscular burn, pulled the needle, and watched one drop of fluid emerge and slide loose down the side of his leg. His thoughts ran so morbid that he felt the expelled drug drip was his only way of crying now, and his face flushed red with embarrassment at the lameness of his own maudlin bullshit.

Can your fucking emo lament. Lift. Don't think. Get bigger.

He pressed Play on his mini-stereo and then hit Shuffle. As Death Shall Fall/Morbid Descent/Strength Over All on rotation. Great, raw shit by men bloodied on their own instruments, singers collapsing lungs to let you know that the world was a brutal place, that will was all you had. The first disc was from Denmark and Jackson didn't know what language it was in, but he could *feel* it regardless. Power had little to do with language.

The Mercabol kicked. Jackson hit the bench and pumped the barbell until he had to roll it off him and onto the floor. His blisters popped and oozed blood. He'd been hoping they'd callous more—he wanted 1800s whaling-ship hands. But the sight of the blood made him feel right.

I'm hard. I'm doing what others cannot. Will not. They're sleeping now, and I'm growing stronger.

Visions hit his brain.

Terror-type: murder/rape/destruction. He pictured his fists calloused over, cement-hard, smashing anything that got in his way.

Visions of fear: Frank finding out about his 'roid habit. Frank
setting the other men upon him for training. Dog meat in the center
pit.

Doubts: Needle worries—did he have guts like this without his
secret injections? EndLiner worries—just what the hell was their big
night really going to be like? Always worries—what made him think
he'd ever be better than his father?

Shake it off. Don't overthink. Keep pushing. Get bigger.

He dropped to the floor for crunches and supermans and then
did push-ups on his fists to keep the filthy carpet fibers out of the
ruptured blister pools in his palms. He popped up and grabbed the
jump rope. He worked the rope triple-fast, setting time goals on the
clock, not relenting until the right minute clicked over.

More push-ups. Deep-lung breath like spoiled meat popping
back off the carpet.

He chugged water. He smeared the blood from his hands across
his face and chest. He flexed just to flex, to feel his new size. He
silent-screamed along to his music, face straining the way he'd seen
in the videos.

He desired—anyone to contradict him right now/anyone to
suck him off right now.

He wondered—how had he ever questioned that this was the
right path?

He flexed again, shaking in the dark, whispering "Fuck you"
because it felt right.

HOME FROM WORK, JACKSON always checked his answering machine
before doing anything else. He was one of the five people left on
Earth that didn't have a cell phone so he spent most of his work shifts
at the Shop N Save wondering who was calling him and what he was
missing. EndLiners moved in small groups for their "training"—to

tint their activities as the sort of random violence people brushed off when they caught it on the nightly news—but Jackson was connected to four of these small groups and didn't ever want to miss out. He'd learned a lot during their short forays—how quickly he could run with a stolen crate of Rapid-Bulk powder in his arms (pretty goddamned fast), how hard it was to break a man's arm (not very), how to make a noisy bar turn quiet (return to the place where you broke the guy's arm, accompanied by five guys who look just like you).

He noticed his finger was shaking as he reached out to press the Play button next to the blinking red light on his answering machine.

Look at that, champ! The shakes, just like Pops . . . way to go! What're you hooked on?

Jackson ignored the nagging thoughts. They crept up now and then, although he'd acknowledged his new reality—he was addicted to the life of an EndLiner. So were his friends. They were getting off on violence, but at least it was violence with a purpose. They were fast-forwarding human evolution, bringing . . .

Jesus P. Christ, man! You believe that? You buying what some crazy monkey-sniping fuck sold you through your MySpace account?

Jackson pressed the button, anxious to hear something other than the voice inside his head.

"Message One," said the digital woman.

"Hello? . . . Anybody there? . . . You there, Jacky? Okay, well, I wish you were home. I've got some great news and . . . well, I'd rather tell you in person . . . Okay, so you're really not there. I'll just tell you. I've met a great lady. Her name is Rhonda and she's been *so* good to me, and helped me see some things straight. The part I need to tell you about is that, um, she found a way to get some financial assistance through the city and she's going to pay for me to go to rehab out at Pinebrook and I've agreed to go and that's pretty much that . . . Shit, bud, I really wish you were home . . . The thing is I've got to go in today, like three hours from now, and then I'm cut off from everybody for the whole first month as part of the deal. I was really hoping you'd come see me at her place. She's at 6705 Kent on the northwest side and I'll be there with my luggage in the next hour and I was hoping . . . Well, I don't know what I was hoping. It would be good to see you, Jacky. It would be really good. I know you don't have any reason—"

A sharp beep cut the message off.

"Message Two," said the digital woman. Jackson expected to hear his father's voice continuing. Instead it was Frank's, slow and determined.

"Bring a pillow and be ready for battle."

That was all Jackson needed to hear.

The big night was going down in about three hours.

Jackson pressed Delete on his answering machine, clearing out the false hope and the call to arms.

He ran to the cache in his bathroom, where two glass containers marked "Mercabol" were waiting.

He placed the gear reverently by his front door. He'd inject at the last minute to make sure he was cresting high tonight.

Then he was back in his bedroom, hunched over his pillow with a pair of scissors in hand.

His music was on blast. Fuck the neighbors.

Jackson smiled, thinking one word.

Tonight.

CAR ENGINES RUMBLED AROUND them, dust floating ethereal before headlights. There were maybe one hundred men, perhaps a few less than that. Jackson estimated their combined weight at about ten tons.

Ten tons of muscles and gritting teeth, and each man holding a pillow.

Each pillow a tiny Trojan horse containing: brass knucks/bil-ly-clubs/wrenches/hammers/fist packs/etc. No guns—Frank had been explicit about that. Any idiot could wield a gun—tonight's message would be delivered by the flesh of these men, with the help of a few handy tools.

It would be a show of human strength. Of what the species could be, of what it had to be if it wanted to stay on top of this rock.

Frank addressed them, his voice clear and booming and without the slightest tremor:

"I'll keep this short. You don't need any propaganda to put a fire into you, because *your* fires are already burning. They always have been. That's why you've heard the call. *That's why you're here tonight.* You see the world for what it is. A giant rock, floating in space, over-run by beasts. And you see the world for *how* it is—teeming with life, which means it's also teeming with death. Destruction. Entropy. *We* haven't been convinced otherwise by our strip malls and safe, tightly packaged industrial lives. Nature is *not* sentimental, nor does she respect intellect. The apex predators of this planet are still here because they understand the way the world works."

Frank's volume increased. The words came faster. Jackson found himself swaying from left to right, stirring up more dust. He noticed Kane was doing the same. Knuckles cracked around him. Heads rolled/neck vertebrae popped from the strain of over-pumped muscles.

"The strongest beasts *crush* the weak. They consume *without sentiment. They conquer!* The laziest of beasts are slaughtered *and those that struggle most survive!* This is the truth of our world and any opposition is founded on whimsy.

"The people of our country have gone soft without true opposition. They compete with each other in bullshit corporate games to earn fancy SUVs, desperate to protect their soft, weak bodies with a steel shell, so *afraid* of the world around them. They tell themselves that they are enlightened, that they've escaped their animal roots and have taken humanity on a higher course. These are easy to believe when your food arrives shrink-wrapped and drinking water comes with the twist of a faucet. *But take those things away and see what happens. See how fast the laws of survival take hold.*

"Each of you has a mission tonight. Some of you already know what that is, and you *will* succeed! The rest of you will follow me as we begin our path to glory.

"Tonight you will show the world what the human race was meant to be.

"Tonight the fire that I see in your eyes will sweep through this city and bring it back to life!"

Jackson watched Frank watching them, staring down each of them and none of them, playing up his messiah moment for all it was worth.

"This is your time to define who you are and what you are! This is your time to take your rightful place in the world! So I ask you . . . "

Frank put his fists up in the air.

"ARE YOU WITH ME?"

The roar that filled the air left no doubt about the response.

With that the tribe of born-again savages began their march into the night.

JACKSON KNEW HE WAS bleeding from a deep gash over his right eyebrow, but the wound seemed to be gumming shut, and he'd washed the blood out of his eye at a public water fountain.

I think I shattered that guy's jaw.

The man was about two blocks east of Jackson now, likely still lying in the pool of blood that had been spreading wide under his splayed face.

He had it coming. Try to cut me with a fucking broken bottle . . . he's lucky I didn't kill him.

"You should have killed that guy, Jackson."

Kane had found him.

"I think he'll die, but you could have made sure."

Kane had dived all the way into the big night. His wife-beater was Pollacked with blood spatter in varying degrees of dryness. Jackson thought he could see a glint of white bone where Kane's knuckles had split open, but it may have just been the weird arc-sodium light from above. The black S (for Strength, he'd said) on Kane's forehead was now smeared with sweat from exertion.

"You take care of that gash?"

Jackson nodded in the affirmative.

"Good. We have to keep moving. Frank said that if we stick to our small groups and stay in motion it'll take them way longer to pin down what's going on."

"I know what he fucking said, Kane."

"I know. Just making sure that bummy bar fucker didn't cut loose your brain with that busted bottle. Being all stoked on steroids doesn't make you Superman."

Shit, he knows.

How does he know? Does he really know? Don't let this escalate.

"Yeah, right, man. I'm all juiced up. Whatever."

"Jackson, I've sparred with you. I've been in the group shower with you at the gym. And I'm not as fucking stupid as you think. Your arms are big like mine, but they feel puffy. You've got a nasty patch of back zits going. You put on 20 pounds in two months."

"Hey, I've been working my ass off, just like . . . "

"Shut the fuck up. You're going to lie to me? To *me?*"

Kane had him pegged. This was a no-graceful-way-out scenario. Best he could do was damage control and be ready if Kane charged.

I'm big now. Maybe I can take him.

"Okay. Yeah, I've been cycling. I wanted to be ready. I was so stressed out about tonight and I needed to be sure I could hold my own. I know it's not *pure* like Frank wants it to be, but . . . "

"Excuses. You know who you sound like right now? Kill it, man."

"Does Frank know?"

"No, but he will if you don't end it right now. Things are only going to get rougher after tonight, and you need to be stronger than that. Not in your body, in your mind."

Jackson guessed he might have felt relief at hearing this, were his system not so awash in the chemical stress-bath this night had become.

"Alright, man. I swear. I fucking swear on everything—no more of that shit."

This is another chance. I'll show Kane I mean it. I'll prove I'm an EndLiner. The next asshole that gets in my way is going to find out what kind of a man I am.

"Okay, then," Kane said, "let's keep moving."

Jackson agreed. Staying in motion kept your blood pumping. It would keep the thoughts about Jackson's lies on low/conflict on high.

The beast who struggles most survives, and all that.

Besides, if we slow down we'll have time to think about what's going on. About the fact that we're running around town assaulting people at random. Because Frank said to.

And because it feels good. No, great. It feels great.

Some part of Jackson's mind felt guilt at this last thought, but he started to walk with Kane and let the feeling fade in the face of motion. The air across his skin felt warm, almost a caress over his throbbing forehead slash. He'd ditched his pillowcase back at the first rumble, as had Kane, and he felt streamlined by their forward inertia. Jackson's weapon of choice, a five-pound barbell he'd planned to hold in his fist, had proven unwieldy. Kane still had a small, steel rod–enforced bat with the word "Grendel" written on the side.

They'd grown up in this town, and now Jackson felt they were wandering its streets like a Death Squad. The idea gave every second a bizarre power.

"Kane, we're changing everything tonight."

"I know, man! It's fucking awesome! I'm so glad we're on this team and didn't get stuck with the grocery store run. Maybe those guys will catch up later tonight."

On the short walk from the clearing to downtown, Jackson and Kane had managed to listen in on a few mission details. Rumors or not, neither had any idea. Supposedly there was a crew headed up to the reservoir. Frank had instructed everyone to stock up bottled water the week prior, so Jackson guessed this detail might be true. Another crew was likely headed to the warehouse-sized grocery store on Berger to inject the butcher shop's meat with some homegrown bacterial culture. A third crew was headed to the *real* pillow fight at the Sternwheeler Mall parking lot that Frank had set up as a decoy. They would watch the cops there and walkie-talkie out to Frank when the lawmen were made aware of the more serious rumbles that were being launched elsewhere.

Jackson pictured the cops there at Sternwheeler, laughing, watching the feathers fly, thinking, "Man, kids these days . . . " while downtown had gone slaughterhouse.

He actually hoped they'd catch on sooner than later. Part of him wanted an excuse for their crew to slip back into the shadows, and part of him just really wanted to beat up a fucking cop.

The faster he walked with Kane, the more the latter felt like the truth. They walked like giants. They were lions/Kodiak bears/sharks that never slept. And this town was theirs until someone else could prove otherwise.

THE BLACK RABBIT WAS a dive bar on the southernmost tip of downtown.

It was here that Frank had begun his series of public executions.

The public, of course, had no idea that this was to be the case. Nor did Jackson until he and Kane approached and saw Frank bring the mallet down.

The man in the brown corduroy jacket let out a scream that squelched on impact. Metal met skull and kept moving, bone went smashed-pumpkin wide and slid curbside on brain. The man's body spasmed until Frank brought the mallet crushing down again, this time at the neck. A woman in a red denim skirt and cowgirl top screamed out, "Harold!" and two EndLiners held her back, one seizing the opportunity to score a fist full of tit.

Frank lifted his head from his work, smiled, and shouted out, "NEXT?" He used one thick leg to roll what used to be Harold to one side, clearing a space on his impromptu killing floor for whoever else was to be randomly doomed.

Two EndLiners Jackson knew by their nicknames, Chud and Scam, walked forward with another man from the belly of The Black Rabbit. Jackson guessed that there was a whole crew in there, that EndLiners had taken the place over. They'd likely have secured whatever firearm the owners had behind the counter.

And Harold, poor brain-panned Harold, must have tried to oppose them.

This new guy, he was *definitely* an obstacle to Frank's game-plan. Hugely obese, three chins deep, barely contained by a too-small Schlitz T-shirt and a faded pair of blue jeans wrapped around surprisingly skinny legs.

"Kneel down," Frank commanded. Jackson edged closer, as if his proximity would reveal to him whether or not this was real.

This can't be happening, right? This is happening. I think it is . . .

The fat man hocked a snot-ball at Frank that hit his left forearm. Frank slopped it off with his right hand and stepped closer to his captive.

"I like that spirit, man. Where the fuck was that when you sold your soul to the Yumm Corporation for ten-cent tacos? It's too late for you."

The man tried to throw his girth around but Chud and Scam weighed as much in pure muscle. The big guy quickly recognized that and slumped.

"That's what I thought," Frank said. Then he brought down the fist-sized steel end of the mallet. It didn't kill the man but was enough to make him lose his legs. Chud and Scam dropped the body and let Frank finish his work.

Jackson's heart beat faster. His breath had doubled and he couldn't tell if he was smiling or grimacing.

Am I enjoying this? Is it just the Mercabol?

Frank took two more decisive swings at the fat man's head, and then—almost as if he hadn't been involved in the murder that was bleeding out below him—he was holding his walkie talkie up to his head and listening intently.

He leaned over to Chud and whispered something. Cops must be on their way.

Frank had said he had a plan for dealing with law enforcement, but not one that allowed for direct combat. At least not yet.

"Okay, folks, only time for one more." Most of the "folks" watching Frank were EndLiners, although a few were bar rats who'd edged towards the front but couldn't muster up the guts to take any action.

Chud and Scam were back quickly.

The man they held was small, and curled in on himself. He wore a blue dress shirt tucked into a pair of khakis. Jackson noticed one side of the collar was buttoned down while the other was loose.

Why would I notice that at a time like this?

The man already looked as if he was resigned to death. He could barely keep his feet under him. Had he been crying?

Again, a woman rushed out after him, but she was quickly restrained by a few of the gathered EndLiners. She had a short, permed haircut and a pair of round wire rim glasses on. And she looked furious.

Her face was bright red. The veins at her neck bulged in a way Jackson found admirable. She screamed, "Don't you hurt him! What the fuck do you think . . . "

Scam backhanded her and she would have dropped to the ground unconscious had Frank's men not been holding her.

The captured man lifted his head. "No, Rhonda!"

Help help me, Rhonda . . .

Jackson almost had time to laugh at his own joke.

Wait, Rhonda?

Jackson looked at the man.

Dad?

The man looked at Jackson.

"Dad? *DAD?*"

Frank was lifting his mallet as if he hadn't noticed the development.

"Frank!"

"What?" His voice rolled out in a low monotone. No inflection. Nothing human about it. And Jackson guessed that gave Frank great pleasure.

"That's my dad."

"So what? We found him here, drunk off his ass. He's just another one of them. The weak. The failed. The wasted. Should he live because you're sweet on him?"

They were all watching him. His brothers-in-arms were around him now, their mania disturbed, eager to continue their takeover, waiting for the next kick, the next snuff. Even Kane was twitching to his left, "Grendel" in hand, his face twisted and unreadable.

Shit. I'm alone here.

Jackson eyed his father, the man who had seen fit to bring him into the world despite the fact that he'd always love his boozy oblivion more. He felt the grunting breath of the animal tribe he was running with, could smell them around him.

There was no opposing them. He could give them a hell of a fight, but turning on them now probably meant death for his dad *and* himself.

Why is the old bastard here anyway? What happened to Pinebrook?

Is this man worth dying for? Dying with?

Who the fuck is he?

Jackson looked his father in the eyes and said a single word. "Rehab?"

The old man shook his head from left to right as his eyes drifted to the ground. His voice came out small from between his hunched shoulders.

"I just wanted you to pick up the phone. I just wanted to talk to you, bud. I'm sorry. I . . . "

Jackson cut the old man short by stepping forward and planting a kiss on his forehead.

Then he stepped back and things felt still. None of them knew how to react. The scenario didn't fit into the new code they'd chosen.

His father was shaking, his face hot-red and streaked in new tears.

Frank raised the mallet again, although Jackson didn't know whether the next blow was intended for him or his father. Jackson sensed Kane at his side, saw his fist tight around "Grendel", ready to swing.

None of these things mattered. Jackson had said his goodbye to this man.

All that was left now was survival.

Jackson threw all his weight, from the legs up, into his right arm. His fist connected with the top of his dad's low-slung head causing Jackson and his father to topple in unison and from that moment there were no more EndLiners and no more lies and Jackson couldn't blame the Mercabol for this because the fury he fell into ran deeper and truer than any chemical reaction. His fists clenched like they had at his mother's funeral where his father had asked for a chair at graveside because he was too drunk to stand any longer and now Jackson clasped his hands together and swung them down on his father's head.

If there was a face that resembled Jackson's under all that blood, it was disappearing.

Jackson's arms grew tired. His rage began to subside. A soft gurgle pushed its way from his father's throat.

He was never me.

Never me.

But maybe he loved me. Maybe . . .

It doesn't matter.

Don't think. Finish it.

Jackson could tell that the men he'd been with were running away because Rhonda was trying to pull him off and saying something about the cops and it became obvious to him that he was the only one who could see he was saving the man they called his father from a slow and terrible death to be suffered at the foot of sadness— this immense sadness that the man had fallen in love with and then cultivated and tended to like a rare and exotic flower.

And so Jackson's fists fell again, sure and steady, the echoes of his final mercy sounding long into the night, saving them both from the burden of being human.

Cathedral Mother

O *ne little piggy dies and the whole crew goes soft.*

Amelia saw things for the way they were. No bullshit. You had to see straight or The Machine would grind you down, leave you blind, fat, and confused. *Stare at the hypnotic box. Have another slice of pizza. There's cheese in the crust now!*

She brushed aside a chest-high sword fern, feeling the cool beads of a just-passed rain soaking into her fingerless climbing gloves. The redwood forest was thicker here, and the gray dusk light barely penetrated the canopy. Amelia tried to force herself calm, taking in a deep breath through her nose, picking up the lemony tang of the forest floor, a hint of salt air from the Pacific, and the rich undercurrent of moist rot that fed the grand trees and untold species. She imagined herself in the time of the Yurok tribes, when man had a fearful respect for this land, before he formed the false God of the dollar and built McMansions of ravenous worship.

She found no calm. All thoughts trailed into spite. All long inhales exited as huffed sighs of disgust.

Goddamn fucking humans. The worst.

WHEN SHE JOINED THE Assemblage she had felt like they understood. They *got it*. They could see The Machine for what it was—a vast system established solely to allow the human virus to replicate and consume at any cost. And The Assemblage had formed to restore balance.

She'd only met one other member of The Assemblage, as a precursor to her redwoods mission. Their group thrived in the anonymity of a subnet supposedly facilitated by a sixteen-year-old kid who'd been vying for membership in a hacker group with a classy name—World Wide Stab. So instead of having a batch of finks and fuck-ups gather in somebody's musty patchouli-patch living room with an inevitable COINTELPRO-variant mole, The Assemblage existed only as a loosely organized forum of people who understood The Machine and challenged each other to disassemble it in as many ways as possible.

Minks were liberated from a farm in northern Oregon, their pricey cages devastated after the exodus. Two Humvee dealerships in Washington got hit, one with well-placed Molotovs, the other with thousands of highly adhesive bumper stickers reading "NAMBLA Member and Proud of It!" Chimps were saved from HIV testing at a biotech development firm outside of San Diego, and subnet photos showed them being returned home to a preserve in Africa (where, Amelia guessed, their lack of survival skills probably got them torched as "bush meat" shortly thereafter). Every Wal-Mart in New Jersey arrived to glue-filled locks on the exact same morning.

Not everything The Assemblage pulled was to Amelia's liking, but overall they seemed to be one of the only groups out there worth a damn.

That was until the Oregon tree spiking incident shook them up.

She'd been shocked too, initially, when she opened the forum thread. The title read, "97% of Oregon Old Growth Gone—Don't Fuck With Our Last 3%." Two quick clicks on the title and she was staring at a grainy, zoomed-in digital photo: a logger's face turned meatloaf, head nearly bisected, left eye loose of its orbit. Text beneath that: No more warning signs for spikes! Let's *really* put Earth first! Feed the worms another tree killer!

The Assemblage, for all its rhetoric and snarky misanthropy, was not prepared for murder. Buddhist members cried bad karma. Pacifists quoted Gandhi. Anarchist kids sweated clean through their black bandanas, wondering if eco-terrorist association charges would make Mom and Dad kill the college funds. Membership dwindled in anticipation of Fed heat.

Amelia, however, was applauding. The Oregon spikers got it right. Now The Machine was short a cog, and she knew any loggers working that territory had a new thought in their heads: *Is this worth dying for?*

She was inspired. She knew that acres of redwoods south of her home in Eureka were about to be offered up as a smorgasbord to a conglomerate of corporate interests, one of the final parting gifts from King George's administration.

She had hiked those territories since her childhood, and even now she trekked there with her son Henry. The trees there were giants, vast even among redwoods, some topping thirty-five stories tall, with trunks over twenty feet around. To her they were great and ancient things, representatives from better times.

To grow for thousands of years only to be destroyed for the "cubic feet" needed to house more goddamned MOB's (Morbidly Obese Breeders, Assemblage code for the common-folk) . . . Amelia couldn't stomach the idea.

She planned. There were only a few months until the virgin forest was to be royally fucked by bulldozers and cat-tracks and chainsaws and cranes.

Despite being consumed with finding a way to stop The Machine from gaining penetration, she tried to stay balanced.

Nights were for plotting—surveying and copping gear and staying tuned to those few voices on The Assemblage that still raged and let her know she wasn't alone.

Days were for Henry—homeschooling and hiking and lessons in doing no harm. Late summer heat let them swim in a pond near their property, sometimes until dusk brought out flurries of gnats and insect-chasing bats. These were the sorts of things she pointed out to Henry, to remind him that he needn't be jealous of the TV shows his friends talked about.

Not that she let Henry see those friends too often. Their life was very contained, and she couldn't risk outside influence turning her son into another one of . . . them.

She never intended to become a Breeder and had a hard time accepting the extra pressure she was creating for the taxed environment. But she reminded herself that she had not had Henry for selfish reasons. She'd been young and confused, and had made the mistake of being seduced by a gangly hippie boy named Grant, who was drifting through town with a few hundred other friends on their way to a Rainbow Family gathering.

She was pulled away from the boredom of her grocery store stock clerk gig in Eureka, and spent over a year wandering the US with the Family, dropping acid and shitting in woodland troughs, shoplifting steaks and air duster (for cooking and huffing, respectively). Free love gave her a nice case of genital warts and a disappearing period.

Grant, lover that he was, offered to sell off his Phish bootlegs to pay for an abortion, but by the time she'd really put the pieces together she was already in the second trimester, and the kicks in her belly had her feeling like this kid was closer to alive than not. She killed the LSD and nitrous habits and smoked a lot of weed and ate buckets of trail mix and waited for the Rainbow Family train to circumnavigate back toward Eureka.

The train didn't quite chug fast enough and she ended up having Henry on the outskirts of a field in eastern Oregon, near the Blue Mountains. A girl named Hester, who claimed to be a midwife, shouted at Amelia to breathe. Then, once she confirmed Amelia was indeed breathing, she shared what she must have thought was comforting wisdom.

"The Armillaria mushroom that grows near here is the biggest living thing on Earth. It's underground. It's like three miles wide."

Then she wandered off into the distance, perhaps to find this giant mushroom, leaving Amelia alone to have the most primal experience of her life.

She felt abandoned for a moment, cursing Grant for his carelessness, herself for being seduced by the irresponsibility dressed as freedom that brought her to this Third-World state. But loneliness was swiftly crushed by a series of contractions and a sense of animal purpose. Then everything was waves of pain, and a sudden release, and the sound of tiny lungs taking first air. Amelia collapsed with her boy, loneliness long forgotten.

She was cradling Henry in her arms when a dirt-bag named Armando wandered by and offered to help. He also, she later realized, wouldn't stop looking at her crotch. Still, he had a Leatherman, and in cutting her umbilical, was the closest thing Henry had to an obstetrician.

With her infant son in her arms she'd found it easy to beg enough change to get a Greyhound Bus ride back to glorious Eureka.

Since then she'd done her best to raise Henry outside of an ever-sickening American culture. If she had to be a Breeder, she'd make damn sure that her contribution to the next generation gave back to the Earth in some way. Since she couldn't trust Henry to the goddamned Rockefeller Worker Training Camp they called Public School she'd had to reconnect with her parents and beg enough of a stipend to support her and the kid.

It meant her parents got to visit Henry on occasion, but she was sure to let him know that these were Bad People. Industrialists. Plastic makers. Part of the Problem. They were piggies.

Still, they kept her and Henry in the food and clothes business, and Amelia took a secret joy in spending their money on the various laptops and servers that maintained her connection to the subnet and The Assemblage.

And lately she'd been spending their cash on climbing gear. It had taken her a precious couple of weeks to come up with her plan, but if she pulled it off she'd be able to protect the forest *and* keep it from being tied to her or her new associate.

She'd drafted "Cristoff" from another subnet board called Green Defense, where he'd developed a reputation for being too extreme. His avatar was a picture of Charles Whitman with the word HERO embossed at the bottom.

They vetted each other via subnet friends. "Cristoff" agreed to drive up from San Francisco so they could get to work. Real names, they agreed, would never be exchanged.

Posing as husband and wife—Mr. and Mrs. Heartwood, har har har—they hooked up with a local arborist named Denny who gave lessons in recreational tree climbing down by the Humboldt Redwoods State Park.

Henry was allowed to spend a week with his friend Toby (whose family she found the least disgusting).

She and Cristoff were quick learners. They picked up "crack-jam-ming" on day one, which allowed them to free climb a redwood's thick, gnarled bark by pinning hands and feet into the crevices. Day two taught them how to use mechanical Jumar ascenders, rope, and a tree-climbing saddle to get much higher. This was called "jugging," a term which Cristoff found amusing.

"I'll tell my buddies I spent all week crack-jamming and jugging with a new lady friend."

Who was this guy? *And* he had friends? That was concerning.

Still, he could climb, and was willing to help her with the delicate work they needed to do up in the unprotected redwoods.

At night she wore a head-lamp in her tent and read up on great trees: Forest canopies held half of the living species in nature. The top of the tree was the crown, which could be its own ecosystem, several feet across, filled with canopy soil up to a meter deep, host-ing hundreds of ferns, barbed salmonberry canes, even fruit-bearing huckleberry bushes. These crowns were miracles of fractal reiter-ation, with some sprouting hundreds of exacting smaller versions of the main tree, all of them reaching for the sun. The redwoods were one of the last homes for legions of unnamed prehistoric lichen and some canopies even inexplicably harbored worms and soil-mites previously thought to be extinct.

She was particularly happy to read that both HIV and Ebola were postulated to have come from human interaction with canopy-dwelling primates and bats. These trees were already fighting back. It gave her mission a sense of camaraderie. She would work with these noble giants as an advance warning system. *Don't fuck with our last 3%.*

Amelia and Cristoff spent the last part of their lessons learning a technique for which they'd paid extra. Skywalking was a way of manipulating multiple ropes and knots in the upper canopy, allowing you to float from branch to branch without applying too much weight. Properly done you could even move from crown to crown.

They *had to* be able to do this, as the crowns they'd be leaving would be far too treacherous to allow return. They were going to create a logger's nightmare up there.

That was the plan—To spend a week camped among the canopies, working to saw dozens of branches just short of the snapping point. The loggers and climbers call these hanging branches "widow-makers" and with good reason. Falling from stories above they could reach terminal velocity and they typically tore loose an armada of forest shrapnel on their way down. One turn-of-the-century account of a widow-maker dispatch simply read, "Wilson was ruined. Pieces were found five feet high in surrounding trees. The rest of him was already buried beneath the branch. Most could not be retrieved for proper interment."

How many loggers would be splattered by her old growth nukes before they asked the crucial question?

Is this worth dying for?

THE WAS THE PLAN, at least until Cristoff decided to get in a fight with gravity.

There are different types of branches on a redwood. The higher branches can be thick as most regular trees and are rooted deeply into the trunk. The lower branches are far narrower. Between handfuls of strawberry granola Denny had told them these lesser branches were called epicormics, or "dog's hair" for slang. They were easily shed and not to be trusted.

Cristoff was getting comfortable in the trees, pleased with his progress. Denny told them not to be surprised if this felt strangely natural, since all other primates were at least partially arboreal.

Cristoff's inner monkey had him gassed up and proud after a few strong ascents. Cristoff's inner monkey started feeling an imaginary kinship with the tree. The kind of false trust that let him think a batch of epicormics would hold as well as a single trunk-rooted branch.

He was sixty feet up, ten feet past the climber's "redline" cutoff for survivable falls. He ignored Denny's request that he rope a higher branch. The last thing he said through the walkie talkie was, "I've got this."

The redwood, clearly disagreeing, decided to shed some weight.

The sounds were as follows: a sharp crack as the branches separated, a shocked yell accompanied by a terrible whooshing sound as gravity got serious, and at last a chimerical whoomp-crunch as Cristoff created the first and only Cristoff Crater at Humboldt Redwoods State Park.

Technically, per Denny's lessons, he was supposed to yell "Headache" if any object was falling, even himself. His neglect would be forgiven the moment Denny and Amelia approached his body.

Cristoff was breathing, but the crimson gurgles at each exhale screamed hemorrhage, and compound fractures at the femur and clavicle had happened so fast that the bone still jutted white and proud with little blood to emphasize how shattered the man was.

Still in shock, Denny informed Cristoff that he shouldn't move.

As far as Amelia could see, this was a non-issue. Whoever this Cristoff was, she had a hard time imagining he'd ever move again.

Denny held out hope, lucking into a cell phone signal and getting Air Life dispatched.

Amelia tried to get Cristoff's eyes to focus on hers, but his were glazed and the left had gone bright red. She could hear a helicopter in the distance.

She prayed for telepathy. She stared at the broken man and thought, "Don't you say a motherfucking word."

With that, she turned and walked to her rental Chrysler. Denny's eyes stayed fixed on the injured man as "Mrs. Heartwood" gunned the car out of the park, leaving an odd impression, some cheap camping gear, and the crushed shell of a man she hoped would die, and fast.

WEAK MEN WERE SHAPING Amelia's world. First Grant left her with an STD and a kid. Then the spiked logger's greed and split skull became the catalyst that weakened the resolve of The Assemblage. Now the man she knew as "Cristoff" turned snitch.

It wasn't intentional, but the bastard (real name: Richard Eggleston) had managed to make it to the hospital, and the opiate mix they pumped into him for pain management left him delirious. His night nurse picked up enough chatter about "tree bombs" to feel comfortable playing Dutiful Citizen and calling the Feds.

The Feds got to his computer gear. The subnet that hosted The Assemblage was fluid enough that they were able to block Fed access and re-route themselves, but speculation about what might have been on Eggleston's hard drive had a variety of already-freaked underground groups on full black helicopter alarm.

Worse still, The Assemblage had gone even more limp-dicked. Even staunch hard-liners she'd once trusted were calling the glimmers of her plan that had gone public "monstrous and irresponsible."

She put her stress in the wrong places, snapping at Henry for minor transgressions like leaving his crayons out. She was forgetting to eat.

Then a new voice joined The Assemblage—Mycoblastus Sanguinarius. *Black bloody heart.* She looked it up and discovered the namesake was a tiny lichen that revealed a single dot of blood-like fluid when ruptured.

He signed his posts as Myco. She assumed the member was a "he" since the writing had a masculine terseness, but there was no way to be sure.

Myco posted an open letter to anyone who might have been involved in the aborted "redwoods plan." He begged them to contact him privately, saying that he might have a way to help them reach their goal without shedding any blood.

He had to be a mole, right?

She ignored Myco and tried to come up with her own new plan. Random spiking? Fire-bombing bulldozers?

The stress amped her self-loathing. *You say you hate humans. Well, what do you think you are, bitch? What do you think Henry is? Chain yourself to a tree and starve out. Pull the media into this. How much explosive could you strap to your body? To Henry?*

These were not safe thoughts. She pushed them away. She tried to stay focused on a real option. The loggers would gain access soon.

She sent a non-committal message to Myco. *What's your plan?*

Two days later Myco sent a response, and it felt legit. He *was* government, and he was upfront about it. He held a position of some influence, and if he had the right information he could get it in front of someone who might have the power to halt the government's release of the property.

The problem was that the property was in a weird transitory status, off limits for government-permitted climbs even for the research sector. He needed someone who knew the area to engage in a "ninja climb" and acquire a number of biological samples. Depending on what was found, the rarity of the species and its "viability for government use," he might be able to prevent the destruction of those groves.

But who was this guy? This was a classic COINTELPRO move. He wrote like a professor, which could place him with DARPA or one of its extensions. Could just be an FBI grunt telling her what she wanted to hear. And would it be any better if the property was retained "for government use?"

Or was this some old hippie college teacher trying to regain his idealism after trading it for a BMW in the 80s? Maybe his son was in the California legislature? Maybe his nephew was the goddamned President?

Who knew? But she trusted this subnet, and if he promised they'd never have to meet then she felt there was enough safety in the agreement. There's no way he'd be able to guess which trees she'd climb. The groves were too dense, the old timber too wide.

He assured her that all he needed were the samples, and she could leave them in a place of her choosing, as long as it was temperate and hidden. Then she just had to forward the location via GPS coordinates.

It would be a shame to waste her climbing lessons. And she'd been dreaming of these trees, somehow still standing proud for another thousand years, after all the little piggies had destroyed each other. In her dreams the skyscrapers fell and the redwoods swayed in the moonlight, returned to their post atop the world.

She responded to Myco—Please check Assemblage regularly. Location of samples to follow.

After sending was confirmed she crawled into bed with Henry and spooned him, despite a few sleepy grumbles. She pulled the blankets tight around the two of them and kissed the back of his head.

I'll protect us, Henry, from these humans.

ALL OF HER GEAR was black, from boots to ropes to pack. Even her Treeboat, which would allow her to sleep in the tree hammock-style if needed, was damn near invisible at night.

Dusk had passed now, and her anger was shifting to nerves as she tried to recall climbing techniques. She moved quietly. The yielding forest floor, rich with decomposed needles and ferns, absorbed much of her noise. Where moonlight broke through the thickening canopy it revealed large clusters of redwood sorrel, the heart-shaped leaves still glowing emerald green in the slight illumination. It was beautiful.

I will save this place.

She picked a full moon night, thinking it would give her better natural light once she cleared the canopy and reached the crown. Until that point she'd have to stay to the shadows.

Myco told her that the older the tree was, the more likely it was to be biologically diverse. She searched for the base of a redwood that looked about three cars across, and briefly shone her headlamp to check the coloration of the bark. The "newer" trees, only a few hundred years old, would have reddish brown bark while the eldest would have shifted to a stony gray.

Her tree finally presented itself, after forty minutes of hiking deeper into the grove. Light had simply ceased to find a home. To her right she saw the outline of the blockage, a tree thick as a blue whale reaching up to heights she couldn't perceive.

She ran her hands across the bark, imagining herself at the foot of some planet-traversing colossus who was standing still to allow her up for a visit.

She used a pair of night vision–equipped Zeiss binoculars to scan the base for a solid climbing branch on which to start. The best option was about one hundred and forty feet up, though several epicormics presented below that. She thought of "Cristoff's" ruptured eye and wrong-angled bone shards and immediately canceled any thought of risking the lower points.

The best solution was to shoot a weighted fishing line over the good branch, then use that line to pull a rope back up and over. It was a patience game, and she set herself to it, unpacking a crossbow with a pre-threaded dull-tipped arrow.

Four tries and she found purchase. After that it seemed easy to rig up the rope and lock in her climbing saddle and Jumar ascenders.

She began her climb beyond the world of the humans, praying that the tree's nightlife would yield something Myco needed. She stopped at each major branch and briefly flipped on her headlamp, extracting a plastic container with a microfiber lid as instructed by her mysterious correspondent. The lids allowed oxygen in, but nothing, even water, would find its way out.

At mid-height she managed to pry loose a tent spider entrenched in a bark pocket. Its eyes gleamed purple in her headlamp.

She scored fragments of lichens, some shaped like leaves of lettuce, others like tiny clothespins, and still others that looked like green beard hairs.

Just before breaking into the crown she spotted an inverted blackened chamber about three feet wide, the damage from some fire that likely burned before the birth of Christ. Tucked just inside the fire cave she found a blind salamander, its damp wet skin speckled with orange dots. She grabbed a chunk of moist canopy soil to include in its container so that it might survive the voyage.

The salamander wiggled in her fingers. She stared at it, wondering how the hell it got up here.

Speaking of which, how did I get up here?

Strung between two branches, hundreds of feet above the Earth, staring at some tree lizard. Way out of cell phone range and one mistake away from instant death. So far from home, from Henry.

Aside from the thought of her son, she was filled with exhilaration rather than fear. This was a world so few had ever seen. And she was going to save it from her terrible species.

Emboldened, she pushed upward to the crown. The moon was there to greet her, blindingly bright and so close she could touch it.

AMELIA WAS CONFUSED DURING her descent. Happy, ecstatic really, but confused. She felt as if her time in the crown was a dream. Beautiful to be sure, but . . . those things couldn't have happened, right?

She'd been gathering more samples—a variety of berries, more lichen than she could count, even a bright white worm she spotted nosing out of the canopy soil. But then she'd . . . what?

Shimmers of light. *She'd found the trunk pool.* Dead center in the crown, the main trunk had collapsed inward and hollowed out, allowing water to collect there.

She'd reached in with a plastic sample container and immediately felt a sting in her exposed fingers. Was it the cold? But seconds later her hand filled with warmth. It spread up her arms and unfurled in her chest. She'd closed the sample container and tucked it into her pack.

Then she remembered feeling an overwhelming sense of joy, and safety. Thoughts of rotten Grant or all the pigs snorting around down on Earth turned to sand and were blown away. A dumb grin slid across her face and the moon blurred through her tears—a white puddle surrounded by oil.

But did she really unhitch her tree saddle and carabiners? Did she really let her body drop into the trunk pool, and float there, picturing herself as a tiny red hummingbird sitting in the palm of a kind and loving God.

It seemed insane. But when she reached up to feel her hair, it was still sopping wet.

"I had a moment of rapture," she thought. And she didn't care if it was real or not.

She descended carefully, methodically, and placed her cargo in a safe place before the sun cracked the horizon.

AFTER CLEANING UP AND communicating her drop spot to Myco, she drove to Toby's parents' house to pick up Henry. She still hadn't slept, but she couldn't wait to see her son. There was something so lovely about him. She smiled at the thought of him and her chest ached in his absence. She sped across Eureka, keeping an eye out for the erratic driving of the tweakers that inhabited early morning commutes like this. Not that she hated the tweakers. Everyone had their problems.

Jesus, what?

Amelia had been clean of the poison of drugs for a long time now, but she could swear she was being washed over by waves of euphoria. She wrote it off as sleep deprivation and adrenaline.

But when she got to Toby's she found that instead of honking and waiting for Henry to come running out, she practically jumped out of her car and ran to the front door.

Shit. I'll have to talk to the parents.

I love the parents.

Oh, God.

Thankfully only Henry emerged from the front door. Amelia saw him recoil as she crouched down to sweep him up. What a boy . . .

"Momma, you smell funny."

"Well, kiddo, you smell, too. You smell *great*. God, I just love you SO MUCH!"

She kissed him full on the lips, a big wet smacker that she was sure would have embarrassed him if Toby were watching. Oh well, she'd slap one on adorable little Toby too.

She set Henry down. He looked up at her, his brow furrowed. "You okay, momma?"

"Yes, honey, I'm better than ever. You want to go get some pancakes?"

With that he nodded "Yes" and took off running for the car. He *never* got pancakes. High fructose corn syrup was a poison, one of the favorites of The Machine.

But it felt so right to make him happy. She wanted to hold him close and kiss him all over his little face.

He was already buckled when she got in the car. He was rubbing his sleeve back and forth on his lips.

"It tingles, momma."

"Bad tingles, like burning?"

"No, like peppermint. It's kind of nice, I guess."

"Are you sure?"

"Yup. It's really nice, actually. Really nice."

SHE AND HENRY WERE barely eating anymore. They felt constantly tired, though they found they were happy just cuddling and drinking water. Lots of water, to the point where Henry would laugh at the sloshing sounds when either of them moved around.

Their temperatures ran hot, but never to the point where she started thinking Emergency Room.

Amelia did worry when the sores appeared on Henry's chest and arms. They reminded her of the splotches on the tweakers that tried to shoplift at the grocery store she'd worked for. Her boss had told her that was caused by battery acid in the meth.

She applied A + D Ointment to Henry's sores and got a cool washcloth for his forehead. That seemed to give him more energy. He asked her to tell the story again, about climbing the great tree and meeting the strange creatures and swimming in the sky pool and saving the woods.

He loved the story. He loved her and told her so, over and over again.

HE WAS DEAD WHEN she woke.

She could tell right away. She was so hot—sweating under the blankets—that his body was like ice against her chest.

And something was very wrong. Because his chest was not expanding, but his belly was. His abdomen was thrumming like it was filled with boiling water. Worse, while her animal instinct got her away from his body, she found herself back in front of the sink, refilling her favorite glass with tap water. Good God she was thirsty.

And happy.

Happy? Fucking Christ—Henry is dead. Something is moving in his belly.

They'd both been crying for days now, but they were tears of overwhelming joy, at their luck that they might be alive and filled with so much love.

Amelia wanted true tears. Part of her brain was screaming, begging to collapse to the floor, to crawl back to Henry and wail.

What was happening?

For days now, their lives were only bed/water/love. They'd heard helicopters roaring overhead last night, and it was a wonderful sound. That man should fly was so amazing.

No. Henry is dead. Nothing is amazing. Figure out what's going on.

Drink some water.

No.

Go to bed.

No.

She hadn't turned on her computer since sending her last email to Myco. *What a beautiful name. What a great man!* Amelia wanted to scrape all this love out of her skull, but it came at her in insistent waves.

Myco had responded: Your woods are saved. Your collection efforts provided us with not just one, but *two* viable interests. Rest assured that this grove will be protected for some time to come, though public access will be greatly reduced. However, the trees will be saved, and I would like to let you know, in the confidence afforded to Assemblage members of course, that one of the lichen you provided us may hold the key to boosting white blood cell counts in patients with severe immune deficiencies. The other sample of interest was a microscopic parasite found in the water sample you provided. We expected protozoa but actually discovered a never-be-fore-seen type of copepod, a tiny shrimp-like creature. We can't tell whether it has been self-sustaining in the tree for thousands of years, or if it was just recently dropped there by a wet-winged osprey, but we do know that it possesses an ovipositor for egg delivery and that the eggs have this miraculous viral coating that likely induces confu-sion in the host. It's similar to how a parasitic wasp breeds, but it is *so streamlined.* You've done our group a great service and we believe that this little management tool may help us to control invasive fish species off Florida and elsewhere. Congratulations!

She deleted the message.

Henry's body was twitching under the blankets.

Drink more water.

Get in bed. Love your son.

Protect him.

She refused the voice. It was a virus. Myco's precious stream-lined management tool had killed her son, and it would kill her too. And for the first time in her life, she could embrace her death.

But not Henry's. Poor Henry.

Before she died she was going to send a message to some of the piggies. Somehow they'd led her to this terrible place. *All these humans . . .*

AMELIA CLEANED HERSELF, IGNORING the shifting in her own belly and the "love" that whipsawed around her brain.

She dried and put on her only perfume and spotted a few sores blooming on her skin. Nothing some foundation couldn't cover up.

She slid on a short skirt and an old black T-shirt. It fit perfectly—the last few days' fast had done right by her looks.

No underwear. None needed.

She would walk to the outskirts of the grove, where she guessed gun-sure soldiers and salivating businessmen were already setting up perimeter in anticipation of harvesting what she'd found.

There was an old redwood stump there which had refused to die. It was fifteen feet across and rimmed on all sides by new redwood trunks growing from its edges. The locals called these "fairy circles" and a few romantic visiting botanists had termed them "cathedrals."

She would claim this cathedral as her own and would invite every last man to join her.

She licked her lips in anticipation. She was already wet. Her upper thighs tingled. Like peppermint. It *was* really nice.

Humanity needed a management tool. And she would give it to them.

With love.

Swimming in the House
of the Sea

The retard is finally asleep, which is great because now I can head down to the hotel swimming pool and relax. I can finish off this gut punch of a day without thinking about the blown engine on my sedan, or the lung-sucking heat tomorrow's sunshine will bring.

It's time to get this nasty, reeking desert sweat off my skin and just float in the clear, chlorinated water. I picture myself, arms and legs extended wide, a big floating X in Hawaiian print shorts. I'll close my eyes and hover there in the safe, sanitized water, floating static and alone while the world rotates around me. I can let the cool water roll into my ears and amplify the sound of my heart.

I grab my plastic key card with its generic sun-and-palm-tree logo and the words "Casa Del Mar Resort Hotel—Bakersfield, CA" across the top. I slip it into my swim shorts pocket and seal the Velcro shut. I don't grab one of our ratty, dishrag-thick room towels; there should be some plushies down by the pool.

I take a quick look at my brother, Dude, who is seventeen and still wearing pajamas with Looney Tunes on them. His too-far-apart eyes are twitching beneath his eyelids, which I read as deep sleep. The sound of his breathing fills up the room, eclipsing even the hum of the air conditioner. His thick snore is the final nail in the coffin of my evening's eligible bachelorhood. Even if I could find a girl to hook up with in this festering armpit of a city, I can't bring her back to the Snore Suite at Casa Del Mar.

I close the hotel door behind me, clipping off the sound of my retarded brother's stertoric breathing. I hate the sound of Dude's breathing, when he's asleep. It's like he has to fight the air to pull it in, all sniffles and snoring and open-mouth rasping. Or, as my dad once said to my mom, before their divorce two years ago, "Maybe Dude can't breathe right because God wants him to stop."

"Stop what?" asked Mom.

"Stop breathing, living, all of it. Maybe God's hoping he'll give up and die."

Dad was a charmer back then, right before the marriage fell from its hippie foundation. Mom decided that Jesus was her new savior, and told Dad that he had to stop making acid in the tub. Dad got turned off by Mom's newfound fire-and-brimstone, her nightly Bible readings, her orthodox self-improvement. He shuttled his drug engineering to placate her and secretly reinvested his energies in the pursuit of free love.

Free love turned out to be an ex-Hell's Angels harem member who claimed to have been in a gang-bang with Sonny Barger and Bob Dylan back in '65. Her name was Jasmine and she still lived in LaLaLand, Dad's preferred real estate.

Jasmine lets my dad drink Jack Daniels from her cooch.

Dads will tell you this kind of shit after a divorce. They think it affirms a newfound buddyhood. The illicit info just bugs me out, but I don't tell him. He seems happy, to a degree. The older I get, the harder it is for me to question the guy's decisions. He's just some older version of me that got caught up in responsibility barbwire.

My mom's Christ fixation popped the wheel on their party bus. Dad scoped out the life ahead of him, realized living with a bum, a mongoloid, and a Bible-thumper wasn't going to cut it, and bailed. His decision to run makes sense to me, but it kills the odds on us ever being buddy-buddy.

I only have to see him once a month anyway, when I pick up Dude in LA and bring him back to my mom's place in Modesto.

I run the errand for Mom, Dude's custody deal stays smooth, and I get free rent at my mom's townhouse in lovely northern Cali.

The free rent soothes the sting of being a twenty-one-year-old college drop-out, and it opens up a lot of bonus cash for things like clothes, weed, and new tattoos. So, to supplement my video store–clerk income, I make this long, hot drive once a month.

It's retard trafficking, and I dig the kickbacks.

Casa Del Mar is a shade short of seedy. The wallpaper varies, floor-to-floor, and there's an odor hovering in the air, with the particles of carpet sanitizer. It's the smell of trapped people, desperation; it's the smell of nervous drug deals, inescapable affairs, lonely masturbation, junk-food binges that spray the air with fructose and crumbs. It's the smell that's coming from me, the stale sweat that a bad auto-breakdown in the middle of the desert has soaked me with.

I can't wait to get clean; there's just one more set of stairs till I hit the lobby floor and the swimming pool. The elevator is, of course, stationary for the time being, although a lovely computer-printed sign did apologize for the inconvenience.

I get to the pool entrance, scan my room card, unlatch the door, and walk onto the tile floor. The pool is standard hotel issue, nothing fancy, and the depth tops out at six feet, which means no diving unless I want to surface sans teeth. There's a hot tub to my right, full of foamy bubbles. Someone must have had laundry detergent on their shorts when they went in.

There's a large, square skylight over the pool, but it's been steamed opaque by the overactive hot tub, and I can't see all the stars. Shit, the star view's got to be one of the only reasons to inhabit a Godless desert like this.

There aren't any plush hotel towels in the area, so I'll have to drip dry on the walk back to my room. Hopefully the hotel catches a little carpet mildew as a trade off for my inconvenience.

The chlorine smell to the air is pervasive, which I find comforting. Caustic chemical odors make me feel safe inside, protected from the bacterial traces of other hotel residents.

I set my key card on the tile in the far left corner of the pool area, looking over my shoulder as I do it, despite the absence of any other pool-goers. Then I jump into the deep end, feet first, and the water splashes up and feels perfect on my skin. Cool, and clean, and mildly astringent. I dip my head under and push off of the wall with my feet, shooting to the other end of the pool with a few strokes of my arms. I open my eyes just before I hit the wall, and the chlorine burns, but the view saves me from smashing headfirst into the circular light mounted at the shallow end of the pool. I close my eyes again, and stand up.

My heart is beating fast as I surface, and I feel the water rolling down my skin, sloughing off the sweat, and engine stink, and frustration of the day. I reach up to push the excess water away from my eyes with the back of my hands. I hear the door to the pool area slide open, then hard, flat shoes on tile. Then, a voice.

"All right, sport, up and out. Pool's closin'."

I open my eyes and see an eighty-year-old man wearing a hotel security outfit, the type of outfit that's vaguely cop-like, but not so derivative the guy could spend his after-work hours impersonating a real officer. For example, there's a white iron-on reading "Casa Del Mar Security—Rollins" where a badge would normally be. Still the guy's got a take-no-shit demeanor to his creaky, old voice, and his shoes are so spit-shined I can see my pale face reflected in the tips. I'm confused by what the geriatric justice dealer is croaking at me so I ask him a question.

"Excuse me, Rollins . . . "

"Mr. Rollins, young man."

"Okay. Yeah, sorry about that. Mr. Rollins, the brochure up in my hotel room said adult swim is until eleven."

I can see the guy looking me up and down, catching the tattoos, the earrings, making quick judgments, deciding to take the zero bull-shit approach.

"Brochure's wrong. Pool's till ten, hot tub's till eleven."

I'm not sure how I can respond to this, but I know that I need to swim more, that one lap hasn't shaken the dirty aura of the day off me. I smile and shoot for polite, even though inside my head every single one of my friends is laughing at how soft I'm playing this situation.

"Okay, Mr. Rollins, I certainly understand hotel guidelines, and intend to respect them, but do you think I can swim for maybe twenty more minutes? I swear I won't drown or make a mess, and I'll be a happy hotel resident. I could be here for days, you know, my transmission blew out today and I'm pretty much stranded until my Mom FedEx's some cash."

Rollins looks like he wants to throw up on me, on my hokey obse-quiousness, on my reliance on my mother. I can see inside his head.

The little puke needs money from his Mommy. When I was his age I'd already fought in the Great War and started a 400-acre dairy.

"Nope, hotel needs you out of the pool at ten. We've got auto-matic chlorine. Stay in past ten and you'll get burnt. Up and out."

So there I am, up and out, dripping but not ready to go back to the room; back to Dude and his loud, sickly breathing. I turn away from Mr. Rollins like a sullen thirteen-year-old, walk past him with my feet slapping wet on the tile like soggy fish, and twist the bub-ble-jet knob by the hot tub. I can hear his ancient voice-box rattling behind me again.

"Hot tub's only till eleven. Then it's up and out."

I don't even respond. I stare down at the mountain of foamy bubbles and wait for the old bastard to hobble on to other duties. It's a relief when I hear the door close again.

The hot tub is a poor substitute for the calm, cleansing waters of the pool. The heated water doesn't smell half as chlorinated and there's a dead wasp floating near the drainage bucket, little legs raised to the sky, frozen in a permanent backstroke.

The water feels too hot; the steam from the surface is on my skin like new sweat. Unclean. Hot and unclean. Too many Goddamn bubbles; I'm waiting for a floating Lawrence Welk to pop up and play me a tune. I consider making a beard out of the bubbles, Abe Lincoln-style, but the urge passes. Mr. Rollins already infantilized me enough. I lean forward with my hands in front of me and watch the bubbles squiggle through the interstices of my fingers. It is mildly soothing, and I start to relax until I hear the pool door opening again.

I'm ready to fight Mr. Rollins tooth-and-nail to stay in this rotten little tub. Maybe if I splash him he'll melt like that witch from Oz.

I crane my neck and notice with a little relief that Mr. Rollins has not returned. My new pool buddies are a couple of guys. The guy on the right is bald, with ruddy red cheeks, white chest hair, and a bit of a paunch above his black swim trunks. The guy on the left is younger, maybe my age, and has a full head of black hair, a slim moustache, a flat, nearly concave chest, and is wearing a pair of long, green surf shorts.

The young one's carrying an inflated beach ball, which seems a little off. Screw it, maybe people are really into beach balls out in Bakersfield. This is definitely the kind of town where you have to make your own fun. Earlier today I was spitting on the hot concrete beside my broken-down ride, timing how long the saliva sizzled before evaporating.

I watch the new guys for a moment, to make sure they don't steal my room card. My paranoia goes into overdrive when I travel. Everyone wants to steal everything I own. I relax and remind myself that all I really have right now is my gimpy brother, some stale bagels, and a business card for the auto shop I left the sedan at earlier today. Not exactly the Ark of the Covenant, but you never know what some people will try to steal.

The two guys step into the pool, and I contemplate telling them about the automated chlorine, but decide not to. It could have been a deviant lie on behalf of Mr. Rollins. Besides, it might be more fun to watch these guys get a chemical burn before Rollins comes back to lay down the law.

I turn back to my tiny bubbles and try to ignore the splashing noises to my right. I massage my right leg, aching from the pedal pushing I'd done until the tranny blew out on the highway. The jets seem to have cooled down the water in the hot tub a few degrees, so I decide to put my face under the water. I want to let the water rush into my ears so that all I can hear is my heart and the movement of the water around me.

The water seems a little grimy, so I just hover there, with my face an inch from the surface of the water, running my hands through my hair. The warmth of the water and the mist from the bursting bubbles is actually pretty soothing, and pushes me towards drowsy. I snap out of that right away, and lean back against the tub wall. The idea of passing out in the tub spooks me to the marrow. What if I didn't wake up? Would the hotel staff find me in the morning, a skinny, tattooed slab of roast beef, pink flesh floating off the bone ready to carve? I picture Mr. Rollins throwing a sprig of parsley on my corpse, then gesturing to the hotel staff. "All right, he's done. Up and out."

My guts are starting to heat up and the tub doesn't feel fun anymore, but if I bail too soon I'll feel like Mr. Rollins has won. Won what?

I start to look for an answer in my head but I'm distracted by the sound of my new pool buddies batting the beach ball back and forth. They're laughing and saying things to each other, but the weird tile acoustics in here muffle everything. They seem happy.

I wonder if Dude would like to play a game like that? Simple fucker, I'm sure he would. I could wake him up, bring him down here and introduce him. The beach ball guys would laugh when I introduced my brother as Dude, myself as Wolf. People always laugh at our names. I don't bother to explain the situation to them, how our parents spent the seventies on some tripped out Kahlil Prophet shit and decided, in all their addled wisdom, to let us name ourselves. If I ever bother to breed, I'm naming the kid before it even pops out the womb. Some nice, Biblical name. I'm sure Mom could help me come up with something.

The paunchy older guy gives the beach ball a good whack and sends it flying above the pool, a high arc of rotating color, blue, to white, to yellow, to white, to red, to white, to green, and it lands outside of the pool, rolling towards me. The heat of the tub and the noise from the Gidget brothers has killed any chance I had at relaxation, and as the ball gets closer to me I swear I'll pop it if I get the chance.

The twentysomething kid with the scrappy little moustache jumps out of the pool and picks up the ball before it has a chance to reach me. He regards me quickly as he grabs the ball, and I give him a hard look, the good old aimless ice grill.

Aggression without reason is a bit of a stress reliever in itself. Let somebody else absorb the shit I've been through today.

The kid nearly runs back to the pool, and jumps in with a splash. I'm sure Mr. Rollins would consider that horseplay. I wish there was a convenience phone right by the hot tub so I could rat these guys out and simmer in peace.

I lower my shoulders beneath the water. I sink my head so that my eye-line is just above the tile border of the hot tub and watch Paunchy and the Moustache Kid play their mutant beach ball game. There are no apparent rules, they're just batting the thing back and forth, but the Moustache Kid asserts he is winning. He screams it up at the skylight. "I'm winning! I'm winning!"

Watching them play makes me think about Dude, about how we used to kick a soccer ball back and forth for hours in the backyard while Mom and Dad sat on the porch and roasted Js and listened to Iron Butterfly. Special times, right? Didn't last though, because I kept growing and Dude didn't, really. By the time I hit high school Dude had left standard issue brother status behind and become My Retarded Brother. Our parent's marriage was beginning to crack around the acid-fried edges, and a lot of the responsibility for Dude got sent my way.

I dodged it, begged out, and abandoned the duty. I figured I'd only be young once, what right did my parents have to saddle me with their mutant chromosomes. I hadn't even really talked to Dude for two years, when Mom offered me the free rent/mongoloid transport trade off.

We still don't talk much, although Dude likes the sound of his own voice, and will go on at length about cartoons, and sailboats, and his beloved Elton John. When he gets agitated on car rides, we listen to Elton John's "Carla Etude" over and over again till he chills out.

I hate Elton John. I hate "Carla Etude." I hate bad transmissions and overpriced mechanics and crying brothers that can't be reasoned with because the Elton John tape is stuck in the deck of my broke-ass sedan. I hate all these movies that make retards look like saints and idiot savants, because I spend a lot of time with Dude, and all he seems like to me is a fucking broke-ass person whose brain won't click over and work. Yeah, I sort of hate Dude.

I hate these guys to my right, playing baby games in the pool I was supposed to be relaxing in.

I keep watching them and now they're wrestling with each other, and I wonder if this place is turning into a Roman bath house. They're smiling, and laughing, and pulling each other's hair. The Moustache Kid leaves long scratch marks on Paunchy's back.

I couldn't see it before, but I do now. I thought they might be businessmen ending a long day of conferences, or some kind of daffy foreign sports enthusiasts.

No, these guys are together.

This beach ball business is foreplay. Some kind of weird, childish foreplay killing my last shot at chilling out.

My dogshit day has fully invested itself in me. I'm seething, angry in my bones.

I have to do something.

I pop out of the hot tub, jump into the pool, and snatch the multi-colored beach ball from the Moustache Kid's hands before he can even comprehend what's going on. Then, as quickly as I got in, I'm out, dripping on the tile with their ball clutched under my left arm. I turn to face the guys.

The Moustache Kid looks five seconds from crying, and it's a weird, questioning look on his face that I can't fathom, so I turn to Paunchy and say, "Pool time's over. Up and out."

I pop their beach ball between my hands, and feel the stale air move across my wet skin. Paunchy is coming towards me, his face and bald scalp bright red.

I hit the light switch and bail out of the pool entrance, leaving the buddies back in blackness. I begin to run, wanting to enjoy this but not quite able to bring any laughter to the surface.

I hear the pool entrance open behind me, then slam shut. I run a little faster as heavy, bounding footsteps rush up behind me.

Before I can react, there are wide, heavy hands upon my shoulders, spinning me around like a little top and grabbing me firm again. Then I'm being slammed into the wall behind me, and I'm face to face with Paunchy, feeling cheap plaster tinkling down on my scalp where my head impacted the wall.

Paunchy's breath is on my face, hot, and he's got me looking right into his wide, brown eyes.

"Why?" he asks.

"Why what?" I play dumb. Paunchy won't stand for it and gives me another good smack into the wall.

"Why? Why do people like you have to ruin everything?"

"Ruin what? Your stupid little game? Your faggy little pool party?" I'm about to piss myself, but Paunchy's reaction is so unexpected that part of me is still tweaking, playing tough. And I don't know where the "faggy" business comes from. The whole straight/gay thing is a non-issue to me. Pick a hole, have at it. I don't care.

Paunchy shakes me again, demanding my attention, his eyes on the verge of tears.

"You think we're gay? What do you know? You don't know anything; people like you just want to take things away, to hurt people like me, like my son. My son is crying now, back in that pool, and I've left him alone."

I'm nervous, beginning to stammer, confused. "Yeah, but the guy should be able to handle himself, he's like twenty . . ."

"You fucking jerk, my son is schizophrenic. He can't handle things like a normal twenty-year old. That's why he's crying right now. Because of you. The kid never has fun, his brain's got him all twisted up, and he's scared all the time, like he's stuck in hell. But he was smiling tonight, he liked the game, he liked the pool, and you took that away. And for what? I mean, can you tell me why?"

I have no answer for the man. Which is bad, because he's balling one of his fists and I'm thinking he might want to beat an answer out of me. Where's Mr. Rollins when I'm about to be maimed?

Paunchy shakes me again, just short of furious.

"Why did you have to mess with us?"

I have no answer for the man.

His son exits the pool and approaches us, stops just short of my right shoulder. His eyes are red and bleary. He speaks. "Hey, Dad?"

Paunchy takes a deep breath, then responds, "Yes, Michael?"

"Dad, there aren't any towels by the pool."

"Well, there should be some back at the room. Do you know where that is?"

"Yeah, Dad."

"Okay, well, head on up and I'll meet you in a sec', okay?"

"Okay." The Moustache Kid walks away and turns to the stairwell. He is shivering, although the hotel is stifling hot.

The kid is shivering because of me, because I popped his ball and left him behind, in the dark. His dad leans in close to my face, our lips almost touching, his eyes deadlocked to mine.

"I'm going to go take care of my son."

I want to say sorry, to say something, but nothing comes across my lips.

Paunchy throws his meaty right fist into my soft belly and I hit the floor. He spits a quick, harsh "Fuck you" before turning to the stairwell.

I manage to retain my lunch and start breathing again. I half walk, half crawl my way up the stairs to my floor.

I reach into my Velcro shorts pocket and come up with nada. My Casa Del Mar room key is still down at the locked pool, but I don't want to risk running across Mr. Rollins, or head to the front desk and ask for a replacement.

I knock on the door for two minutes before Dude wakes and opens it. He's confused, and tired, and wants to know why I'm bleeding.

I tell him I took a bad dive, down at the pool, that the deep end wasn't deep enough. I don't mention the large, angry man who decided to crack some drywall with my skull.

Dude walks me over to our bathroom, the legs of his rayon pajamas whisping against each other. I sit down on the toilet and Dude puts a towel to my head, which has developed a steady, jackhammer throb. Dude presses the towel down too hard, while he's trying to staunch the blood seeping from my split scalp. It hurts, sending quick, white-fire pain down my spine, and I lash out with my left arm, pushing Dude into the bathroom counter.

"Stay away from me, you fucking retard." He's out the door quick, and I flop off the toilet, then reposition myself to vomit.

I take off my clothes and crawl into the shower. I start the water up, sharp and cold, to try and wash away the whole day, the whole evening, everything. I can hear Dude crying in the other room. I'm good at that, I guess. I try, but I can't work up any crocodile tears for myself.

The shower isn't helping. I'm trying to make things right inside my head, trying to replay the pool situation in a way that doesn't make me feel like a total asshole. The cold water isn't helping my noxious headache.

I get out of the shower and dry off. I throw on some flannel pants and wrap the last clean, ratty towel around my head, and hope my scalp wound will clot soon.

I walk out to the air-conditioned hotel room and see that Dude has cried himself to sleep in his twin bed on the left side of the room. I sit on the edge of my bed and look at my brother.

My vision is blurring, and I probably have a concussion, but it feels right to look at him like this, like for once I'm the vigilant and caring older brother. I think for a moment about all the times I've told My Poor Retarded Brother stories, playing the pity card to get into some drunk girl's pants. I think about the times I've seriously considered abandoning Dude at some rest stop along the highway, picturing the guilty relief that would spread across my parents' faces when I tell them Dude had disappeared.

For the first time, the thoughts feel like poison in my bruised belly. I don't know how to shake the feeling. The digital clock on the bed stand reads 3:23. I collapse into my bed.

I can't sleep. Things are too wrong to sleep.

So, at 3:27 I slip out of my bed and into Dude's. I let one of my arms flop onto his thin chest. He wakes for a moment; his thick, unsteady breathing smoothes out. He turns his head towards me, and opens his eyes, surprised that I'm there.

"Wolf?"

"Yeah, Dude, it's me."

"Okay. Are you going to sleep by me?"

"Yeah, Dude."

"Okay. Hey, Wolf?"

"*Yeah*, Dude." The irritation I'm trying to shake comes back into my voice.

"Sorry I hurt your head earlier, Wolf. I didn't mean to."

I'm thinking, "It's okay, I know you didn't mean to, and I'm sorry I hit you, I'm sorry for so many things." I can't get the words out of my mouth. Looking at Dude's wide eyes, hearing the care in his voice, I'm almost paralyzed.

Then my whole body is shaking, and I can tell I'm a moment away from sobbing. I wrap my arms tight around Dude, and shake against my will. I don't cry out loud, because I don't want to upset him anymore. I hold the tears in and feel heat radiating from my face.

He can tell I'm upset and he runs his fingers through my hair for a moment, each finger tracing a soft line across the side of my head. Dude whispers to me.

"I know, Wolf. I know it hurts. But you're going to be okay."

It's like the little fucker wants me to cry. So I do, I break, and I cry for longer than I ever have before, and Dude just keeps running his fingers through my hair until I stop shaking.

When I'm done, all I can think to say is, "Thanks, bro."

Dude repeats it back to me. "Thanks, bro."

Those are the last words we speak before Dude slips back into sleep. I want to pass out, but I consider my probable concussion and fight to stay awake, while my brother fights to breathe.

Should he stop breathing, I'd be there to save him.

This is the oath that I swear into the too-bright sunrise, as the desert heat returns and our room at the Casa del Mar fills with new light.

Saturn's Game

Y*ou could bite off Todd's nose.*

That's the thought at the back of my head.

That's the thought I ignore. I squelch the sinister sentiment and refocus on my friend.

Todd is saying this and that about motors and camshafts and gear shifts and custom something, and the whole time I'm nodding my head like one of those little plastic dogs people think add character to their dashboard.

My eyes focus on the little divot underneath his nose where today's stubble is starting to grow, but I have these slick "Alien Eye" Arnet sunglasses on and it's approaching sunset, so he can't tell I'm not making eye contact.

Shadows are lengthening on the sidewalk in front of the coffee shop. My mind is wandering, making electric connections, chaotic. I'm thinking about the inadequate elastic in my sagging left sock, the razor burn sting by my Adam's apple, the smell of barbecued chicken in the distance, the cool edge that's creeping into the air. I can't wait until Todd goes away, but I'm too polite to say anything.

The bad thought slingshots back into my brain, echo-heavy.

What if I grabbed Todd's head and then bit off his nose?

It's a poison thought, the kind no one is supposed to think, or at least no one is supposed to *acknowledge thinking*. The thought came from a different part of my brain, and it feels like a misfire, a still-born idea.

Still, what if?

Could I do it? Could I bite off someone's nose?

I'm trying to think something new but now I'm preoccupied with the idea of biting off Todd's nose.

I wonder if he's sensed the shift in my mentality, and how much danger he could potentially be in. I know I'm not supposed to think like this anymore, Dr. Marchand was pretty direct about that, but now the thought is looping, building speed, swirling down the brain drain.

It's a sick thought. Squash it. Just my frontal lobe fucking up again. If I do something crazy tonight, then Saturn wins.

He's been winning for twenty years.

Then the setting sun shifts one millimeter down in my field of sight, and one razor-thin ray of light shoots directly into my optic cone and strikes the nerve like a match, and I'm overwhelmed by the smell of motor oil. Something . . . Oh God . . . and I look down and see a tiny green plant poking up through the crack in the sidewalk, and the plant sways a little bit in the breeze, and its motion blurs as it enters my eyes, and an electric jolt shoots up my spine and buries fire in my gut and I have to quench it.

So I grab Todd's head.

I've never bitten off anyone's nose before, but I figure that if I get a strong grip on the hair at each side of his head I could have a fair amount of leverage. From there, with the element of absolute surprise standing in my favor, all I have to do is open wide and clamp down.

My teeth sink through the skin of Todd's face after a split second of resistance and the teeth at the left side of my mouth crunch something. It might be that bony ridge at the top of the nose, or maybe the thin sliver of cartilage running down to its tip. Regardless of anatomy, it really crunches.

Todd is screaming now, his warm breath is in my face, and his hands are at my wrists, trying to loosen my grip. But I'm too focused on the task at hand. I pull back as hard as I can, with my teeth sunk as deep as they can go into Todd's nose, and I tear my mouth downward at the last of it. The motion doesn't quite sever all the tissue so I have to make a couple of hard sawing motions with my incisors, like you do when you're eating sinewy flank steak. Todd's nose makes one last attempt to stay on his face before the wet tearing sound and the coppery taste in my mouth tell me I've succeeded.

Oh shit.

I just bit off Todd's nose.

It's in my mouth, and it is otherworldly warm. I spit it out onto the sidewalk where it lands with a moist plop. It looks fake, like it's made of rubber. It looks smaller than it did on Todd's face.

Todd is collapsed in a fetal ball on the ground. He's moaning, mewling, groaning, screaming, something. I can't quite tell. He doesn't sound good, and a crimson pool spreads around his head.

Oh shit.

I don't think either of us expected this, Todd or I.

The view out of my sunglasses is warped and liquid. A drop of Todd's blood is on the right lens, smearing a trail toward the ground. The sunglasses are tight against my face, too tight, like they want to press into my skull and cleave the top third of my head. It reminds me of the time when I was five and I got my head stuck in a plastic wastebasket. I tear the glasses off my face and throw them to the ground. My view feels instantly improved, my skull is safe.

I look back down at Todd.

One of Todd's Puma sneakers is unlaced, and I can still smell motor oil. My brain is buzzing, dull static numbing my ability to think. I've got to do something.

People will see Todd soon, police will come, medics will come.

I'll be arrested.

I should just stand here.

My voice is falling out of my mouth and I sound all of twelve years old.

"Hey, Todd, oh fuck, Todd, I'm sorry, I'll just, um, wait, just . . ." I say to Todd, but he seems to be in another world, and he's making these horrible moist, gargle noises. I'm confused. Static. Interference. Synapses are not connecting. I'm sniffing the air, feeling like my nostrils are coated with something dirty, black factory air. That thick industrial smell is saturating my head, covering my skin.

"Fucking motor oil! Can you smell it, Todd? The motor oil?"

I look down at Todd, who I think just said something like, "Gwaaaah, uunnaaa reggg, God, uhhh." Todd is definitely not smelling the motor oil.

I can't take the scent anymore. It's making my chest convulse, and I'm taking all these tiny excited breaths, like I'm trying to hyperventilate, only I don't want to, and my heart is beating so fast now that it's probably just vibrating, not even compressing, and I feel like passing out. My limbs are tingling and I'm sweating profusely, drips rolling down my face, and so I just shake my head back and forth, back and forth, fast and hard.

I'm trying to jar my brain into action.

I'm not dealing with this very well.

Todd's trying to stand up. Someone just walked out the front door of Berenger's Pub across the street, and I can feel them looking at Todd and me. I can hear a Foreigner song coming out of the jukebox inside the pub. "Cold Blooded," I think, but I'm not sure. They all kind of sound the same to me. Songs do.

The man who just left the pub is looking at us and he's crossing the street. He looks tubby, with big, meaty ham-hock arms, and if he sees Todd like this he might think the wrong thing. He might think I did this on purpose. He might not know I have problems, and try to beat me up. I don't ever want to get hit again.

Now I am running.

Running to where?

Fuck it; I'm just running, pulse erratic, sweat streaming from every pore. I'm oozing sweat like a soggy sponge squeezed tight, positively soaking now, and my skin smells electric.

I'm still tasting Todd in my mouth. I have to run faster. Can I? My lungs are at capacity and then some. My eyes are burning and I think tears are coming out, but I can't tell. It could just be sweat.

I'm about six blocks away from Todd and his severed sniffer, and I'm trying hard to run but it feels like someone just stuck a prison shank in my chest just below the heart. Damage to the port side, Captain!

I'm heaving myself forward, trying to ignore the pain, laughing at my own little joke in short gasps, slowing down, trying to get some air.

Stop. Stand still. Breathe deep. Where can I go?

There's a defunct Sooper Saver-Mart to my left and a series of industry offices packed with cubicles and small green plants to my right. I can see inside one of the cubicles, past my reflection in the glass. The lady who occupies the box has a tiny porcelain picture frame on her desk. In the frame sits a photo of a house cat that looks like it might have eaten one too many servings of Atta-Kitty. A tiny, hand-written sticker on the picture frame says "MY GERGEN!" The lady has chosen *that* as her one tiny token of self. A picture of an overweight cat called GERGEN is her life preserver; the one thing she has decided will save her from being sucked into the corporate undertow.

Maybe I'm not so bad off.

The Northside Liquor Store is only three blocks away from me. It is still open, and although I already feel sick and queasy I can't help thinking that maybe a huge bottle of rum is just the thing to make a bad, bad day turn better.

Prescription, Doc? 750 ml of self-administered distilled spirits should fix your malady, my good man!

I can already taste it on my tongue as I walk into the air-conditioned booze shop.

DING-DONG!

Oh, Holy Lord Jesus they've got their customer alert bell turned up loud. The store clerk turns to look at me and as he rotates I see a hearing aid manufactured at some point in the late seventies is wedged in his ear. A beige octopus made out of plastic appears to be burrowing into his ear in an attempt to suck out his brains. He seems to pay the grotesque plastic apparatus no mind, which some-how makes it look all the more malevolent, like maybe it already got to him.

Then the old guy with the non-ergonomic and mechanically malicious hearing device says, "Hey buddy, stop starin' and buy something or I'll call the cops and report your ass for loiterin'."

Loiterin'. The worst of my crimes.

I hear him but aside from loitering I can't make much sense of the words. He seems antagonistic. My brain is turning increasingly fudgy and I'm thinking, "Is he going to bite me?"

I turn to my left and the wall trails by me in slow motion. Colors are blurring together like I did the wash wrong again. Things are not up to speed in my brain.

Another psychotic break, Doc?

I grab the first bottle of cheap, rotten rum that I see and boom up to the front counter.

I move forward so fast and so intently that the clerk shrinks back a bit. The strange and worried look spreading across his grill says he can't wait for me to leave. Can he sense I'm not right today?

The total bill comes to $14.56 and I've got a jug of shit rum in my left hand and a pack of Mini-Thins in my left pocket.

Pop pop fizz fizz and I'm washing back cheap, legal speed with liquid fire.

Walking faster now, towards the park two blocks away, hoping to God that the shit I just swallowed will clear my head and help me to deal with this situation. Do I have a way out? Do I have to deal with this? Will they put me back in the fucking hospital? Can't I just see straight and fly right for once?

Too late, kid. Done is done.

Yeah, and I'm pissed, feeling like this was never in my control. Blaming Saturn.

Your excuses won't reattach Todd's nose, will they?

The voice in my head is louder and somehow not my own.

My insides warm up, which is good because the sun is setting and the air will cool. Swigs off the bottle, two three four, in rapid succession, and now the world looks a little friendlier.

Then I hear the squelch and beep of a police car's radio and everything runs ugly. The air is alive with white noise and my eyes have static on their surface. I look back over my left shoulder and see a black and white patrol car rounding the corner of Ward and Meeks. Adrenaline flushes through my system. My eyes burn, instantly dry. My throat fills up with booze and acid and I have to re-swallow, hard, to keep my liquid lunch from relocating.

Options: few to none. A voice at the back of my head says, "Stand very still. He will not see you if you stand very still." Fucking five-year-old logic, I can't escape it.

The cop car is closer with every split-second and my brain's not coughing up the goods.

Throw a rock at the car? Why?

Duck down, lay low? I'd look even more conspicuous if spotted.

Wait for the officer to hop out of the car and get within biting distance, see if I can claim nose number two for the day? Low odds for survival, smashed in a locust swarm of lawmen.

Run?

Again? Well, it worked before . . .

I hear the bottle of rum smash to the concrete behind me and my legs are kicking doubletime. Crazy heat is searing in my gut— this is all too much for one day—and I want to stop and throw up, but it's a fair bet that even if the patrol car wasn't looking for me before, they are interested in me now. They are awfully suspicious of people who flee their presence. They make assumptions. Draw conclusions.

I'm running down a thin alleyway now, taking in deep lung-stretching loads of stale garbage stink, and I'm laughing like a kid. Oh boy, a chase! Only when I look over my left shoulder—Grandpa always told me I'd see Death coming for me over my left shoulder—all I see is the alleyway receding behind me. No cops. Maybe I am invisible, or maybe the cop was changing radio stations or looking at his fingernails or something else as I ran across the street. No trail.

No pursuit. *Deus ex machina* in my favor.

Especially since her house is only four blocks away.

I feel light in my shoes as my Mini-Thin engine goes into overdrive. I'm so close to a safe place, if she'll let me in. God, what an *If*.

Four blocks of footwork and three knocks on a pale red door connected to a cheap stucco apartment complex determine my fate. Will she or won't she let me in? Has she forgiven me?

The thin door creaks as it opens, and standing there in an old pair of Guess pajamas and an older pair of fuzzy white slippers is the sister I haven't seen for five years.

I'm speechless. My lower jaw has dropped open on its hinge and I can't move my diaphragm or expand my chest or vibrate my larynx or make plosive sounds with my lips or anything. What do I say?

"Come in, I guess," she says as she turns slowly back towards the couch and the bowl of popcorn on it. "I'm watching this episode of Real World for the fourth time, but it's not getting any better. Don't ask me for money 'cause I won't give you shit. I'm barely making it as is."

One quick look around her place pins a verification on the statement. There are Salvation Army blankets up instead of drapes, a broken-down futon at the center of the room, movie posters on the walls (Switchblade Sisters, Reform School Girls, Bound), cheap Target dishes, the anodized kind that stay almost ruthlessly cold, and stacked Ramen packets on the dusty countertop. Trailer park chic minus the porcelain unicorns and the "Hottest Men in Firefighting" calendar. Still, she let me in.

"What's up, Tyler?" she asks as she sits back down on the futon and tucks a thin afghan over her lap.

"Um . . ."

Long pause. Beat . . . beat . . . beat . . . beat. I can't just waltz in here after five years incognito and tell her I'm on the lam because I just bit off my friend's nose for no good reason. "I was just in the neighborhood . . . "

"Bullshit, Ty. Fucking bullshit." She's still not looking at me, her eyes stay on the television, not blinking. "Ty, look down at your shirt. You fucked up again, huh?"

My shirt is plastered to me, the collar loose with sweat, and the front is saturated with crusting blood. My chest is a red waterfall that smells like moonshine. She's right: I most definitely fucked up again.

"First of all, Ty, if you're crazy again I want you to stay right where you are and understand that if you try anything I will pepper spray you until you choke on your own vomit. Second, I've heard the police sirens, and if you think I'm going to harbor you, well, you're crazier than you ever were. Well? . . . Talk, Ty, I'm not in the mood for games . . . listen, stop mouth breathing and tell me something."

Shit, she's amped up and I'm slowed to a crawl. I'm terribly confused and I'm thinking they switched her Paxil to methamphetamine, 'cause I've never seen her this aggressive.

There used to be days when she wouldn't even get out of bed, she'd just lay there and stare at whatever was past the ceiling in her room.

"Sis, I'm scared."

"What'd you do?" she asks, but the undercurrent in her voice says she's sick of this already.

"I . . . uh . . . well . . . there was this smell like motor oil, and the little plant was sending electricity to me, and I . . . well, I'm fucking sorry now, so sorry . . . and I think he's okay . . . things . . . I mean . . . I know what I did was . . . I know that I am sorry . . . I'm sorry, I'm so sorry and I really mean it . . . I'm so . . . " and then it's all too much for me and for the first time in weeks I'm really feeling something, and my breath is hitching and my knees are going weak and I'm sobbing as I hit the cracked linoleum and curl up on my side, and then the story spills out in between sick, wet sobs and snotsniffles, and tears so hot they feel like rubbing alcohol on my face.

I tell her about Todd's nose, and then his lack of a nose, and I tell her about the smell, the motor oil, and the angry man, and GER-GEN, and the octopus eating the old man's head, and the booze, and the pills, and the panic, and somewhere in all of this mess I tell her that I miss her terribly, like every day, and that I miss the way she smells. She kind of laughs and cries at that at the same time, and now she's getting off the couch, moving towards me.

She's standing above me, looking down and mumbling something like, "Saturn's reign never ends, right?"

Saturn . . . .

It's her nickname for Dad. The first time I was in the hospital, she brought me a book of paintings by this Spanish guy, and on one of the pages there was this seriously fucked, black painting of the God Saturn chewing a big hole in his Son. Next to it was a Post-it Note that said, "Kind of reminds you of him, huh?" Ever since then, he's been Saturn.

Ever since then I've been playing his game. Trying to control myself, trying to deny what he did to me, trying to exist despite the scars on my brain that fucked up the wet-wiring.

Now she's crouching down over me and I *do* love the way she smells, like green apples, and I kind of want her to hold me, but I know she's going to blame him and talk about him now, and I'm sick of her treating our past like this great tragedy, because we are not a fucking heavy metal song, we are not a Goddamn Oprah Book-of-the-Month story, and we're not a made-for-TV-movie. We don't have to be weak and afflicted like those people, like those songs and stories, and now her arms are around me and I can tell that I'm shaking and she's rocking me just a little bit, just enough.

Something switches inside of me and my brain kicks out feedback and I'm smelling the dust embedded deep in the shag carpet in my bedroom, seeing the tiny droplets of blood that hung on the end of my eyelashes, hearing the sound of Dad snoring, passed out on the floor across the room, oblivious to what he has just done and already forgetting. I'm remembering the look on Mom's face when she came into the room and saw that the claw of Dad's hammer was buried in my skull.

What then? Doctor after doctor, surgical specialist, mental specialist, anger therapist, chemical dependency specialist, none of them explaining to me exactly how a Dad, a Buddy, can turn into Saturn and chomp down on his kid.

It's all noise now, right? He made his choices. I've tried to make mine.

Sis is kind of crying now, holding on to me. Maybe she's just shaking. She's so full of anger; I think maybe she took mine into storage when I got too crazy to deal with it. Yeah, maybe I am a heavy metal song.

So I'm curled up, and she pulls the afghan off the futon and drapes it over me, and I push my fingers through the little holes in the fabric and I try to make a cocoon, and I fall asleep there, with her running her fingers through my hair, the smell of green apples floating between us.

AND WHEN I WAKE up the first thing I see is blue and red flashing across my sister's plaster ceiling. I know she called them. Deep down I knew she would when I walked in the door. I'm not angry at her, she's just big on consequences, closure, whatever.

I'll go without conflict. They'll take me in and they'll call me a monster, and they won't be all that wrong.

They'll put me in the hospital. The staff will hear what I've done. They'll sweat fear when they stand near me. I'll try to prove to them that they're wrong.

Maybe I'll learn to control myself in there. I'll have the time. I'll practice. I'll try to focus.

For myself. For my sister. She'll visit. I know she will. Please.

There's a knock at the door.

I hope they'll let me take the afghan with me. It keeps away the cold.

I press her blanket to my face, inhaling deep with my eyes closed, so that my nose and throat and mind are filled with green apples, sweet to bursting and wonderful. Then I open my eyes, steady my hands, and unlock the front door.

The Sharp-Dressed Man
at the End of the Line

He was collecting roaches. They moved faster than he'd expected. They'd be within centimeters of Dean's fingers and suddenly speed left or right with quarterback maneuverability. Crafty fuckers. Even more survival driven than he gave them credit for.

Survival, Dean's modus operandi. He understood the cockroaches on that level. Both of them had a clearly established Goal One:

Do Not Die.

He left out muffins. They swarmed the muffins. Dean harvested the unsuspecting bugs by the handful.

He replaced his regular bulbs with UV black lights, so he could see, but the roaches didn't scatter like they would under normal apartment light.

In between roach round-ups, he watched television. He grimaced. He cringed. Every image on the screen was a fat, flashing sign that read WWIII.

The news showed Conflict with a capital C, international and senseless.

It caused Dean to sweat stress and stink up his flop pad, the worst in all of DC. Check the rotting floorboards, the dripping faucets. Noise-aholic neighbor bass and baby screams as the soundscape. Swinging bare-bulb ambience. Mildew and asbestos fighting for airspace. Punctured pipes leaking slow into linoleum cracks. Plastered pellets of roach shit as the common denominator.

Living cheap. Barely living.

He watched television. The President poked angry bears with sharp sticks.

We will not relent to this Axis of Assholes!

Take that Iraqi-Bear!

They're hoarding weapons and plannin' rape missions!

Yield before us Korea-Bear!

Commie baby-killers, pure and simple!

Oh, China-Bear, you'll rue the day!

The President was up in the polls. The populace—petrified and war weary, but strangely supportive, Dean included. He'd back a bully as long as El Presidente could guarantee a win. It was that possibility of a loss that spooked Dean to screeching simian defense levels. A loss, at this heavily armed and nuclear point in world history, meant Apocalypse.

Dean's answer—Cockroach Suit. Thousands of cockroaches hand stitched through the thorax, tightly sewn to a Penney's business suit bought on the cheap.

Dean's days and nights were occupied with the spreading of wings and the careful puncturing of his pathogenic pals with needle and thread. He positioned them all feet-out, so their mouths could still feed.

Dead roaches were of no use to Dean. The live ones carried the instinct.

The instinct had kept them alive for four hundred million years. Their bodies were natural radiation shock absorbers. They could live for ten days after being decapitated. Dean knew that in the event of Apocalypse, he'd be rolling with the right crew.

He knew they were training him for war, and for suffering. He'd already borne the brunt of their bacterial ballast. He'd coped with clostridium. He'd dealt with dysentery.

He was becoming impervious to disease, like them.

He kept and catalogued the roaches, separated into clusters of speedy Smokybrowns, ravenous Germans, and over-eating Americans.

Jars upon jars of the bugs were stored in his deep freezer. They slowed down in the chill. The cold goofed them like opium, kept them still.

It kept them from eating each other.

That insatiable appetite had been the primary problem with the first cockroach suit. Dean had left it out in the muggy tenement warmth at night, stored along with some chocolate cereal in a microwave-sized cardboard box. When he opened the box in the morning the cockroaches had not only eaten all the cereal, but had ravaged each other. His carefully crafted suit had gone cannibalistic.

He bought another suit. Dean didn't sweat his cash flow. Daddy Dean Sr.'s estate was still kicking out cash in steady intervals. The primary source of cash—royalties from the sale of Daddy Dean's Ivy League–approved books on entomology.

Daddy Dean Sr. had been a big time bug man and serious scholar until his car accident. A deer had run into the road. Daddy Dean Sr. swerved hard with his right hand on the wheel. His left hand gripped a cherry Slurpee with a thick red straw. Daddy Dean Sr.'s car hit an elm tree straight on. The dependable airbag exploded and jammed the fortified Slurpee straw straight into Daddy Dean Sr.'s left nostril and right on through to his frontal lobe.

Dean had shown up at the scene in time to see the cops detach the straw and blood-filled cup.

Dean had heard one cop on the accident scene call it a "straw-botomy."

Dean didn't think it was funny.

Dean didn't think a single fucking thing was funny for quite a while, and resolved to find happiness however he could.

For a long while that meant spending Daddy's textbook royalties on hallucinogens. The "straw-botomy" had taught him that the world made no sense anyway, so he traveled the world hunting head-trips. He tongued toads. He feasted on fungus. He inhaled ayahuasca. A bad encounter with a sodomizing shaman and some industrial strength desert peyote finally scared Dean straight.

Then he moved back to the states and began his survival training.

He knew the world wanted to erase him. He'd seen it in visions. He'd seen it in the eyes of the priapic shaman. He saw flash frames of his own father felled by a plastic straw.

Dean moved to the slums of DC. He wanted to move to a place that resisted and destroyed life. He knew there were survival secrets in the daily struggle.

He holed up and watched television. He watched El Presidente taunting nuclear-armed countries anxious to see if they could one-up Hiroshima.

Y'all ain't got the bomb, or maybe y'all just ain't got the balls to use it!

C'mon Korea-Bear, show us you got a pair!

Dean read books about roaches. He studied sewing and stitch types. He bought spools of thread and heat sterilized needles.

Dean developed his cockroach suit and watched it fail.

He cried and sucked up the sick, musty attar of roaches when his first suit dined on itself.

He cursed himself when the second suit crawled through a hole in the crumbling apartment drywall. Fifty seconds to piss. That's all he'd taken. That was all they'd needed. He heard his roach-riddled jacket and pants skittering around in the crawlspace above his kitchen.

Every time he failed, he felt as if Apocalypse was seconds away. He got weak, the blood flow to his head lagged. He thought he could hear the roar of approaching bombs overhead. He worked harder, his hands shaking with fear.

He ignored the doubt that crept into his skull and took up permanent residence.

Dean, don't you know the bomb is coming for you? You think some bugs and some cheap threads can stop a holocaust?

He ignored the fists that pounded on his door, the angry screams, the vulgar notes slipped through the crack of his mail slot.

The note last Tuesday read: Mister room 308, you are the cockroach man and ever since you came all up in here they've gone crazy. My little sister has to wear cotton balls in her ears to keep them roaches from digging into her head and laying eggs, like they did with Brian. You ain't right at all Mister room 308, and you ought to leave and take your roaches with you. I see them coming out from under your front door right now. My dad says if Brian has eggs in his brain, then you die. Go away. Love, Maysie.

The neighbors thought Dean was bad mojo. They threatened litigation. They threatened worse. Dean knew it was part of the world's plan to erase him. He kept working.

DEAN ACTUALLY SAW THE first bomb hit. He knew it was coming.

He knew from the silence. El Presidente had gone silent for three days. No more TV broadcasts promising patriotic retribution. No more shots on CNN of El Presidente grabbing his balls and shouting, "Eat this, Iran!"

El Presidente was quiet because he was hiding, somewhere, from the grief he saw coming America's way. El Presidente was crafty, even more survival driven than Dean had given him credit for.

In the calm before the atomic shit-storm, Dean finished his third cockroach suit.

It was perfect. A living tapestry of twitching legs and chittering mandibles. Add to the threads a pair of Kroeg blast goggles, a crash helmet, a refillable oxygen tank, and a thick pair of foil-lined tan work boots, and Dean was suited for survival.

When the first newscaster started crying on air, Dean geared up and walked from his apartment to the street. He didn't want to be inside that roach trap when the Earth started shaking.

Dean walked by apartments, heard the crying of the tenants. They could sense the bomb was coming. Their cries were weird and strangely complacent, the mewling of doomed animals with no options. Baby seals, waiting for the spiked bat to spread their skulls wide.

It made Dean sad. He cried and fogged up his goggles. He felt the suit writhing around his body, taking in his warmth, seething. He stayed in motion.

Dean made it into the street and turned to his left, not sure quite where to go, hoping the cockroaches' instinct would take over soon. Then he would just lay down on his belly or his back and let them carry him to survival, like a God.

The DC streets were packed with people looking up at the sky, waiting. Dean expected chaos and conflict. No one even gave him a second glance. They were waiting for the Big Delivery from above.

They got it, twenty seconds later.

The flash blinded Dean, even with the goggles and helmet on.

He crouched behind a cement stoop and heard the most cohesive and unified scream any dying species had ever let loose.

Then there was silence, and heat, terrible heat.

And, of course, darkness.

THE COCKROACHES CARRIED DEAN, like a God. He woke to dark clouds and electrical storms and drifting gray ash. His retinas were blast burnt, but functional.

He was alive.

That was the part he could not comprehend.

He was fucking alive.

The roaches were too, and they were moving quickly towards a perceived food source. Dean felt them moving, swift and single-minded, driven by constant hunger.

His hands were cold. Nuclear winter was just beginning and the air already approached frosty. He'd forgotten to buy gloves. He hunched his shoulders, pulled his hands inside the living suit. He relaxed and enjoyed the eerie quiet, and reveled in being alive. Being a survivor.

He moved without effort through the ash of nuclear winter. His suit surged beneath him as it crawled up onto a sidewalk. The legion of tiny legs pushed onward as Dean zoned out on the gray snowfall floating down from the sky.

He watched the sky darken. He saw thick red and green clouds of nuclear dust float above him. He saw an obelisk in the distance, stark and tarred jet black by the bomb blast.

It was the Washington Monument, just like he'd seen on TV There was something walking back and forth at the base of the monument. It moved like a human, but glowed bright yellow.

Dean let the suit carry him closer, and then stood up when he was within ten feet of the yellow shifting mass.

Dean lifted the visor of his helmet and de-fogged his goggles. He could see clearly after that, aside from the bright imprint of the blast that wouldn't leave his sight.

The peripatetic figure was a man. A man in a Twinkie suit. The thousands of Twinkies were half charred and oozing cream filling.

The man turned to face Dean.

The man's face was slack, and the eyes were empty of thought or feeling. Despite this lack of emotion, El Presidente was still the most recognizable man on Earth.

He looked at Dean and started to weep.

Dean opened his arms, offering a hug.

El Presidente stepped forward, and then hesitated. It was too late. The cockroach suit was upon him, a thousand mouths demanding to be fed.

Dean looked into El Presidente's eyes, caught dilated pupils, animal-level fear.

The eyes no longer promised Dean's destruction, as they had from the static screen of his television. The world's plan to erase

Dean had failed; it was vaporized to dust, silt in sick Strontium-19 winds.

The scarred sky above Dean grew darker, the air around him even colder. Dean shivered; El Presidente screamed.

Dean reached up and warmed his hands around El Presidente's throat. He felt the pulse under his hands drop to zero.

The weeping had ended, and the feasting had begun.

A Flood of Harriers

We're on the reservation now, so the blasting bass from the stereo goes into silent mode and the car drops to exactly whatever speed it says on the road signs. You come through here calm and quiet, especially if you look like me. The Kah-Tah-Nee rez is mostly Paiute and there isn't an Indian alive that's going to give the look of love to a ginger-haired white dude with a mohawk. Not on a sweat-river-down-your-back heat-blast of a day like this. Not in this place, where the meth and the booze have jacked-up and sludgebrained the populace.

The Kah-Tah-Nee rez is a charmer. Greatest frequency of drunk driving accidents—affirmative. Highest child mortality rates in the state—every year. Corrupt cops—big old check. Some punk kid like me caught a bullet to the face last year during a traffic stop. Spooked witnesses said the kid wouldn't kick up any bribe cash. Got uppity. Got his brains plastered to the tempered glass behind him. Cop caught a temporary suspension, then got pinned by the Feds for meth traffic while on *that* little vacation.

You drive the exact speed limit through here, hold your breath and pray to the Gods of Invisibility. *Dear Gods, Please let me and my lovely girlfriend Sage pass this gauntlet until we are among a group of people that our ancestors didn't attempt genocide against. Let no tire pop. Let my speed remain a smooth constant. Let my presence go unknown. Amen.* The impulse is to speed until you clear the rez, to rush towards the comforting sight of the next concrete Wal-Mart behemoth. But don't. It's not worth it. Picture bits of your own skull stuck in the upholstery, that nice tan bucket seat turned dark red.

Slow down. Enjoy the drive. Sage looks beautiful in the seat next to me. Five years together and she's still a stunner. She's reading a *Glamour* magazine so she can get angry at it. She's one of the new breed of feminists that likes to constantly decry the effects of the skinny, blonde, big-breasted, All-American Beauty Myth, while, of course, trying as hard as she can to look exactly like the girls in the magazines. Awareness, even awareness coupled with anger, isn't always power. Not that I'm complaining; I get nervous when her armpits start to show stubble. I tell her otherwise of course, because I admire her attempts at personal growth, but when it comes down to it I prefer the shaved-and-primped pornstar look. I don't really want to stick my dick in some idealistic, earthy Sasquatch.

"Look at this shit, Darren. They've got this girl posed, passed out in the gutter with her panties around her ankles. You want to tell me what this has to do with selling pumps? Seriously."

I could say something in response, about rape fantasy as a commodity and the saturation of shoe fetishism in American porn, but it's boring preaching to the choir. She and I both read the same AdBusters, go to the same town hall meetings, use the same compost pile, get the same e-mails from lefty groups pretending they aren't socialists. So I say nothing, just shake my head from left to right and purse my lips and huff a breath out through my nose to let her know that I'm with her in her parade of constant disgust.

I can't let her know, ever, that I jerked off to the ad before we packed the car up this morning. Sleaze presses my monkey-brain buttons. The cerebellum doesn't always offer a counter-move. Let her think I'm enlightened.

Sage slurps up the last of her 32 oz. iced cappuccino through a red plastic straw and turns to me with unexpected urgency.

"I have to use the bathroom."

"What? We just stopped back at the top of the pass, and you'd already drank most of your coffee by then."

"I'm not arguing with you about the size of my bladder. I just need to go. Bad. Whatever the next stop is."

"Shit, Sage, that's in about forty miles, outside of South Barker."

"What about one of the stores up ahead?"

"No. Remember, we don't stop here. Ever."

"We're going to have to, Darren. My bladder infection isn't all the way gone yet and I seriously need to go. Don't be a control freak."

"I don't stop at the rez."

"Why? Are you a racist? You afraid you're going to get scalped? Whatever your hang-up is, you need to can it and find me a bathroom."

I don't tell her my reasons. Never have before. Never needed to. She might peg me for the scared little white guy I am. Besides, not even counting today we've got about nine hours of driving tomorrow before we make it out to the Burning Man festival, and I want to keep this car clean of tension.

"Okay, I'll stop at the next restroom."

That earns me a series of soft kisses on the spot next to my right ear and a hand sliding up and down my thigh.

"Thank you, baby," she says. "Find it quick."

STATE PARK FACILITIES. SUNNY day. Lots of traffic passing by. Ramp for fishermen to slip their boats into the Sheenetz River. Two outhouses, one for men, the other, women. Looks clean enough. Why not?

My compact blue Ford sedan stirs up dust as I pull a quick right turn in to the rest stop. My bladder's starting to feel a bit full, too, and this stop will let me make the rest of today's drive in one haul.

Hop out and stretch. Let the slight, warm wind blow across my lower back and dry some of the sweat puddled there. When the lower half of my shirt touches my back again it feels cool and wet. Goosebumps, and the hairs on my arms are up.

Sage is putting makeup back into her purse, and then bringing it with her as she steps out of the car. She also stretches, giving me a good look at her long legs, barely encumbered by a short black skirt. The wind must have caught her, too, because now I can see her nipples through the thin white fabric of her tank top. I'm starting to wish that this little rest-stop had more trees so we could hide away for a moment and have a nice travel-fuck. She smiles at me like she's thinking the same thing, then ducks her head like she's shy. Too cute. The girl can press my buttons.

She starts to walk towards the bathroom and I finish my stretching with a wide, open-mouth yawn and look down at the river. The sun is bright off the water, white-silver, and the area downstream from the dock is dotted with dried brush. The opposite side of the river is walled in by a sheer, tan stretch of rock, high enough that a jump from it would guarantee shattered legs. At the far right border of the park I see an old, leafless tree with a trunk wide enough to cast a few feet of shade.

There's motion from inside that shade, then a voice, loud and deep across the park.

"Hey, girl! I want your ass! Now!" Then laughter. More shapes moving. Five shapes, all visibly in motion now, as if they'd been invisible in their stillness before, sitting beneath that tree. Waiting.

We should get back in the car. Now. Right fucking now.

I hear the women's bathroom door close behind Sage. Too late; the girl's on a mission. Not going to let a catcall bother her.

Focus on the dark space by the tree. There are five of them. All men. All seated or resting on the ground. Still laughing, watching me. Two are shirtless and wearing old blue jeans. One guy, lying on the ground towards the back of the shade, is massive. When he laughs his girth barely moves. His lungs and diaphragm must be so small under all that fat.

One of the shirtless guys stands up. He's looking right at me. This can't be sustained. This will lead to something. Act casual. Move your feet. Soon the men's bathroom door is behind me and I've latched it and there are enough flies buzzing around in here to block out the noise of the men laughing outside. I try to stay in motion. I piss quick through a fear-shrunken dick and then squirt a couple drips of anti-bacterial cleanser onto my hands and rub them together. Even in this heat, my fingertips have gone cold. My head feels like there's a wool hat of electricity over my skull and I can sense my heart is kicking double-time. You couldn't find a drop of spit in my mouth with a microscope.

There are men outside this small bathroom yelling that they want my gorgeous girlfriend's ass. The best odds say that they are Indians, and I'm a skinny white kid with a red mohawk. This is like being a Nazi and wearing a yarmulke into the heart of Israel.

The world has just gone real. The pleasant harmonic fuzz of daily life has been stomped to the concrete with atomic bomb speed. I'm fucked.

I hear Sage stand up in her bathroom and buckle her belt. Shit. *We're* fucked.

I unlock the bathroom door and grab the handle. For a split second I can't seem to push it open and at that moment I know that one of them, one of the men from the shade, is going to keep my door held tight and not let me out and the others are going to step into my girlfriend's stall when she opens her door and then they'll have her and they can lock themselves in with her and rape her and beat her down and cum on her and piss on her and I'll have to listen from inside this shitty bathroom, surrounded by a legion of flies, and I'll hear everything, every last moment, separated from her by a thin wall, and when they're done . . .

But then the door does open, as if the wind across its surface had given it a moment's extra weight, and I'm thanking God until I see that the man that was looking at me earlier is now headed my direction.

I stand in front of Sage's bathroom door. Five of them. *Goddam-nit*. How can I stop five of them? Only one is headed towards me. I'm shaking but trying not to let it show. Things are moving so fast that it seems my brain is a second behind, disconnected, not alto-gether worth having. Hard to think. Fight or flight? Never fought a day in my life and I can't run and leave sweet, delicate Sage here. What other options?

He's ten feet away now. The other four men in the shade are standing, expectant. Can I take this one guy if he starts swinging? Would the other four leave me be if I beat this guy? Right. The guy's definitely an Indian, dark skin marked in all directions by inch thick scars. Oily black hair smattered with dust. Lip scar from a cleft restructure. Moon-surface pock marks from cystic acne. The booze on his breath hits me at five feet away. This guy's a wreck, and he's not wearing shoes. The sight of his bare feet pulls the breath from my chest. Something about seeing his feet caked in dust.

At three feet away he speaks up. "Hey, man, I need to talk to you." He's talking loud enough for his friends to hear. I'm their entertainment.

"Okay, yeah." *Say as little as possible. Don't puff your chest out. Don't let this escalate. Be ready if he swings.*

"Sorry, man, but you can't have that here." His right hand points up at my head. His left hand hovers near a slim shape in his pocket. "People 'round here are crazy. They see you with that hair, you could get hurt." He's smiling a three-tooth smile, happy as hell to watch me twitch. "Not everybody's like me, man. People 'round here get crazy. You know that's a tribal haircut, right?"

"Right." I don't think telling him that I'm trying to go for a Mad Max/Travis Bickle look is going to mean shit to this guy. I'm a target, regardless of hairstyle. I could have stopped in here with a fully shaved head and he would have asked me if I was a Nazi. He's looking at me with one eye, his other floating slightly to the left, unfocused.

"You Scottish? You sound Scottish."

I must sound Scottish when I'm about to piss my pants, or maybe it's the red hair. For just a second I'm thinking that this is my way out, that I'll tell him I'm Scottish and we'll kick back with some beers and joke about how the English fucked both of us over and that'll be that. Brothers-in-arms. But what if I can't sustain an accent?

"No. I'm not Scottish." This response leads him to step closer towards me. His left hand slides into his pocket, towards the thin rectangular shape. His breath is heavy and thick in my nose now, like dumpster breeze on the wind. Old eggs, gallons of cheap, pissy lager. His focused eye is locked on mine.

"I'm not scared of you, man. I just left Reno, with the Paiutes there. Proud people. We made sacred shirts so I wasn't never afraid. We did the Ghost Dance. Got into some trouble, though, knowha-tImean?" He gestures to the inch thick scars on his body, what appear to be stab wounds interspersed among faded prison tats. A crucifix with the word "Wokova" across its horizontal arm. Another on his left shoulder reads "FBI" and beneath it "Full Blooded Indian." Doesn't he know Full Blooded Native American would be more PC?

He's covered in these marks, black ink and flesh wounds. He knows what it's like to fight. If something starts, I'm decimated.

The door clicks open behind me. Sage steps out, her makeup refreshed. Her innocence makes my heart ache. She's been dolling up for what could be our last day on Earth. The look she gives me says she's been listening to our conversation, though, and now she's ready to get the hell out of here. I slip her the car keys and am waiting for the guys to come rushing towards us.

The men in the shade whistle at her. Mr. FBI in front of me doesn't even look at her. All his attention's on me. He smiles again. "Pretty girl. What's she doing with a guy like you?"

I hear the passenger door close behind me and knowing that Sage is in the car gives me a moment's relief. She isn't locking the doors though. Doesn't she know she's in danger? Or is she being brave and leaving it open for me? Shouldn't someone else be pulling into this rest stop soon?

"Cat got your tongue? Rude, man. Rude. Listen, don't stop here again. My friends are about to go crazy on you. But I told them I wanted to talk to you first. I got this watch I need to sell."

Should I reach for my wallet? Could be my quickest shot at getting out of here. I tell him I could use a new watch, and he tells me that he'll have to give it to me later but I can buy it right now. I don't ask him the price. I know what it is.

I hand him all the cash in my wallet, three hundred in twenties.

As he takes the money with his right hand his left slides from his pocket. Before I can retract my arm he's grabbed my hand and he's slashing across the top of my forearm with a dull silver box opener. The pain is sharp and immediate and the sensation of the blade touching bone turns my stomach.

He's still got my hand and he pulls me in close and spits on my face. His saliva is hot and it's in my right eye and trickling to the corner of my mouth. He's whispering to me in my left ear and in my right I can hear the men in the shade laughing and shouting.

His breath feels damp on my face. *"You NEVER come back through here. Ever. This is our land, stupid white bitch. This is our place."*

Blood is running in a steady stream from my arm to the dust below. Muddy spatter is hitting the front of my sneakers. Sage, thank God, is still in the car. I can hear her screams through the glass.

Mr. FBI's hands are on my chest now, pushing me back and down and I'm turning even as I hit the dirt, to scramble back to the car and get in and lock it and bail out of this place we never should have been.

Sage has already got the key in the ignition, and she hits the auto-lock just as my door closes. I start the engine and begin to pull out of the lot in reverse. Going forward would steer me by the shade tree and that's not a chance I can take.

Mr. FBI is standing behind my car now, box opener in one hand and my cash wadded in the other. Sage sees the gash in my arm and her screams gain volume. I can't take her freaking out right now. I yell back, "Quiet! I've got to get out of here!" Mr. FBI is smiling at me, laughing. I start to back up and he kicks my bumper. I feel the kick through the seat of my car.

I start to back up again and now he's dancing.

We did the Ghost Dance.

He's chanting something and inscribing small circles in the dirt with his feet. As quickly as the dance began, he's done and steps to the side. He's letting me go.

The exit to the place is on a slight incline and my right tire catches the soft shoulder, almost spinning my car into a drop that would pull us end over end to the river below. Back to where they are.

Sage is crying now. *OhmyGod, ohmyGod, ohmyGod . . .*

My arm is still dripping, and I can see dust in the wound. The dust of that place.

This is the beginning of our vacation.

WHEN YOU LOSE YOUR friends here, at the Burning Man festival, you lose them for days. The desert shifts time around you. The dust storms, the wind, the drugs, the sense of having drifted into a separate reality, all of these things break down the way your brain used to function. By the end of your first night you've seen an all-male gangbang, watched two dwarves get married at the foot of a giant temple, snorted enough Charlie to make Bob Evans jealous, fondled a theremin dressed as an alien, and fallen asleep at the foot of a door to nowhere. This all before you see your first sunrise.

No surprise that the place is tough on relationships.

Sage was pretty shaken up in the first place, and no matter how much I tried to get her to relax, the Kah-Tah-Nee rez scenario keeps her freaked out. Paranoid. I'm the one with seventeen stitches. I'm the one who can still feel the spit on my face (*Looks like he's got Phantom Saliva Syndrome, Doc*). I'm the one who had to ask his parents to wire extra travel cash. But Sage is the one making this into her deal. Her trauma.

And we did not come here for trauma. We came to party. But she could barely party anyway, with her "friend of Bill W." bullshit and her twelve steps and her insistence that we stop and meditate every hour and absorb the peace of the desert. I'm not here to get centered. I'm here to escape into the chaos.

So that's what I bought. One big fistful of chaos.

I've never seen mushrooms like this. The guy that sold them to me said his name was Scheme. I told him that was a tragically dodgy name for a drug dealer. He told me thirty bucks could buy me a ticket to outer space. Said the 'shrooms came from the Moapa reservation and were used mainly for religious ceremonies. The idea of my drug money eventually trickling back to the Indian population pissed me off, but I've seriously never seen mushrooms like this, so small with such a bright purple tint. Besides, they burn The Man down tonight, and there's no way I'm going to be within shouting distance of sober for that social call.

It's about three hours till the big wooden Man gets blazed and I want to be peaking when he topples over into his own funeral pyre. I've got no girlfriend obligations, no friends to slow me down, a CamelBak full of filtered water, a dust mask, and warm clothes on.

Sage put clean bandages on my arm tonight, moments before she decided to take off with her new yoga friends, Dale and Kristin. She was getting ready to leave our tent and I leaned in to kiss her. She pulled away.

"What?" She's been hyper-hesitant towards me since our bad time at the rest stop. I can't figure her out.

She speaks, carefully, like she's been thinking about this for our whole vacation. "Well . . . I'm having a strange feeling about you now, like something changed since you got hurt. You looked so scared. You just didn't look like the guy I thought I knew. And I feel like luck or God or whatever is all that got us out of that place. I don't think you could have protected me." She breathed out heavily like she was about to tell me I had terminal cancer. "I just don't feel safe with you anymore."

Sage kissed me on the forehead like I was some lost puppy about to get the gas chamber treatment, and then she stepped out of the tent and zipped it up behind her. If she would have stayed I'd have told her that I don't feel safe anymore either.

I'll try and find her at the center of The Burn tonight. We can straighten things out.

But first, I've got some mushrooms just dying to be ingested. I dig into the Ziploc bag and pull them all out, all the little bright purple stems and caps. Best to eat them quickly, the whole batch at once. They tend to taste like the shit they're grown on.

I'm chewing, and they've definitely got an earthy taste, but it's one I can't quite place, or at least I don't want to, because the flavor most reminds me of the dust I huffed down when Mr. FBI cut me and pushed me to the ground.

Stranger still, the wound in my arm begins to throb as I swallow the last bite of fungus. But the throb isn't my heartbeat. The rhythm is not my own.

THE DRUMS CAN EAT your blood. The drums can eat your blood. They move in circles. Sing words I can't understand. Try to melt into the dirt. Try to crawl inside. We are swallowing everything. This whole desert runs on gasoline. We are not separate. All plunder. All rape. We are reptiles. We will eat your children. Keep your drums. Keep them away. Have a blanket, let it soak into you, join the stitches and I'll skin you alive. Unravel. Consume. Swallow.

Try to breathe. This dust storm can't last. I'm surrounded. Can you hear them? Where's Sage? She's shrinking away. Gone. I'm cold. I'm naked. Why am I naked? Thirsty. The Man is burning somewhere; I can see the flash of the blaze through the dust, light gone soft in the storm filter. They're around me. Every direction. I can't keep them away. I can't make them BE QUIET!

This dust is ancient. A wall one thousand feet high, pointing at the moon. He appears like a cloud. The dead are alive again. We were one but you ate us to nothing. Wokova, your dance will bring the flood. Your armor will make us safe. We are all around you. Pull you back through yellow-black. We'll keep you alive till sunrise and eat your tongue to steal your lies.

Dancing in circles all around me. The sky is opening up and the spears are raining down. They will eat my heart. The drums are finding their way home. I can't stop throwing up. I bit my way through my stitches to try and set the drums free. My blood is still pulsing on the ground. Tiny eyes in the soil. Watching. Waiting. Shit. Help me. Sage? If I'm still naked when the sun rises I will be burned black. Burnt to dust. Floating. Breathe me out.

The land will return. The water will be made of flesh. Wokova is coming. The Earth will breathe again. Wokova is risen. Balance will return. The drums can eat your blood. The drums can eat your blood. The drums . . .

YOU CAN TRY TO imagine it. You can picture what it must feel like to walk naked back to your camp covered in the dust of the playa, with a bloody arm and your own vomit dried on your chest. You would know how hard it would be to get the well-meaning hippies to leave you alone, to not drag you back to a med tent. Or you could imagine the fear that you see on the faces of people who came here for bliss, the people whose trips you are utterly devastating with your wrecked appearance. You can grasp all that.

You might even be able to understand what it's like to hear drums that can't be real coursing through your bloodstream. You might be able to picture the phantom blurs of bodies dancing in circles around you as you shamble home. Could be a trick of the light, right?

But is there any way to truly understand what it's like to unzip the flap to your tent and find the girl you love lying there dead? To understand that she's gorgeous and naked there, with her legs spread, so much so that you're instantly aroused despite the fact that her eyes are wide open and staring at nothing and there's old vomit pooled in her mouth and caked in her flowing hair? When you smell the booze on her breath, the stink of the alcohol that she'd sworn off by oath and will so many years ago, would you know that she'd found something to make her feel safe again? And would you be surprised to find you can only think one word?

Would you ever understand what it's like to be there at the foot of the dead, bathed in new sun, whispering the word "Wokova" like a holy prayer?

.45S COME CHEAP. I'M just glad that Scott's brother still lived in Aston. His place was an easy stop on the way back towards Kah-Tah-Nee. Even when I was little, Scott's brother Dean always had crooked guns. No numbers. Said he bought them at truck stops from cranked-out drivers doing a little extra traffic on their long hauls. Didn't say much more than that.

Even now, when I show up at his place still covered in dust and withering away inside of a gray velour track suit, he isn't the talkative type. He notices that my sleeve is crusted to my arm with blood and say he knows a doctor who can fix things without reporting them. I shrug it off. What can I tell him?

I'd see your doc, Dean, but this open wound is the only thing keeping me from hearing the drums. In fact, it was healing up and I cracked the scab open this morning, just outside of Merced on I-5. Didn't want to see the shapes dancing around my car anymore so I took my house key and raked the wound until the blood started flowing again.

Nope. I just keep quiet and buy the gun and feel its oil soaking into my skin.

I'm confused by Dean's question as I leave.

"Hey, Darren, don't you need to buy any bullets for that?"

I keep quiet.

THE SIGN TELLS ME I'm now entering the Kah-Tah-Nee reservation and I start to cry. Last time I saw a similar sign Sage was sitting there next to me, sipping on her coffee, planting sweet kisses in the soft spot by my ear. Now she's gone, cooking away in a little tent in the desert until the wind spreads the smell of her and other campers come calling.

And I'm back here, smelling gun oil in my nervous sweat and hearing the drums inside my blood. The wound has scabbed over again and the drumming is so loud I'm having a hard time staying focused on the road. I can try and think in the space between the drums, but I keep losing the plot and these words keep repeating in the place of logical thought.

Wokova.

Balance.

Revenge.

Fifteen miles. Seven. Almost there. These drums are smashing around in my head. I feel heat on my lips and chin and realize I'm bleeding from both nostrils. Bloodshot eyes stare back at me through a vertigo haze that makes me feel like the world is on permanent tilt.

My body is in the grasp of tremors, shaking to this rhythm that was never mine. The sun drifts behind a mountainous ridge and dusk floats down, spreading gray light across the Sheenetz River. I can see the rest stop. My pulse is the sound of long-dead tribesmen calling down the flood.

THEY ARE STILL HERE. The men in the shade. But now they aren't laughing. Can they hear the drums too? Apparently Mr. FBI is their permanent mouthpiece for tribal affairs, because he's stepping forward with his box cutter in hand and saying, "Man, you get in an accident or something? You deaf? I told you not to come back to our place."

The drums are so loud now. Can they see me shaking? With the sun gone there is no more shade, just dim light and dark shapes. I feel a drop of blood slide off my chin. The four-hundred-pounder shouts out from beside the tree.

"You lose your pussy somewhere, little man?"

I raise the gun up with my ravaged arm. They register it quickly and appear more angry than scared. I level off at Mr. FBI and he doesn't flinch. I'm not the first sick white man to aim a gun at him. He's resigned to it. He looks straight at me with his one focused eye.

"Pull the trigger, man. Because when you do, my friends will fucking kill you, and I'll be free."

The dancers are around me now. They're surrounding Mr. FBI and I, and they seem real. The drums get louder, too loud, and I grind my teeth together and I can feel the enamel cracking, my teeth splitting down the middle and now there's this pain that accompanies each beat of the drum, this soaring red fire that courses up my gut every time another invisible hand falls to a skin pulled tight, and there's only one way to make this stop before it tears me to shreds.

Wokova. Balance. Revenge.

They watch me as I lift the hand that isn't holding the gun and plunge the fingers into the wound on my forearm. I'm scraping. I'm digging. Get the sound OUT.

The wound opens and instead of dripping to the ground the blood sprays out fast, too fast, and too much of it, forming this thin mist that spreads quickly through the air.

We are all in it now. The dancers. The Indians. Whoever I've become. We are all standing in this red mist, breathing in the drums. We are breathing my blood, our lungs pulling a lost pulse from the sky.

Wokova. Balance. Revenge.

REVENGE.

I aim at Mr. FBI's head and pull the trigger on the .45. His good eye goes wide as the hammer falls on nothing.

Click.

I pull the trigger five more times, letting each empty click echo through the sound of the drums.

Revenge is here. And it is theirs.

They are upon me in seconds, all of them. The sound of the drums, the mist we are breathing in, the sight of the gun, all of it has brought forth an old rage. Not anger and booze and cheap, easy hate.

Rage.

Box cutters become talons. Fists become great stones. Their ancestors dance around us while they consume me. My teeth crack against smooth river rock. They float away, broken bits of white bone flowing over red clay. A fist grabs the front of my dusty mohawk.

Claws enter my scalp at the top of my forehead and then I feel fingers sliding under my skin and pulling up, pulling back. I can feel them sawing it free and my head drops down to the river stones as the men raise my scalp in the sky. They drink the blood that drips from the shank of skin and hair. They are chanting a name. Wokova. Bringing a flood to cleanse the Earth.

Mr. FBI is chewing at the back of my neck, tearing at the skin with his few remaining teeth.

They are becoming as hungry as we are.

And I can see by the light of the new moon that the waters of the old river are rising fast.

States of Glass

The Caller ID reads "Unknown" but the man on my phone says he's with the Thurston County Coroner's Office in Washington. I know precisely zero people up North so I peg the call as a prank or a particularly grim dialing error.

Darry is travelling on business, but I spoke with him this morning. He was fine.

Mistakes like this happen every day, right?

I can smell my breath on the phone, stale hints of cinnamon toast and mimosas light on the orange juice. The voice on the other end continues to intrude into my lazy afternoon, verifying my name is Elloise Broderick, and the sunshine coming in through the kitchen window suddenly feels too hot on my skin. That heat and the tone of the voice create a flash-fever in my belly that spreads quickly to my fingertips. I can imagine flowers wilting next to that warmth, petals curling, dropping.

Delirium. The blood in my head whirlpools down, a tornado spinning out of existence, rendering me transparent. So when the voice on the phone says, "I'm sorry to inform you that your husband has been in a fatal traffic accident," it's easy to imagine that the "you" being addressed is someone else, maybe someone standing directly behind me, someone older, someone who has three kids and a half-paid mortgage.

Not that the statement regarding the death of that other husband will hurt that person less. But it would seem, at least, appropriate. More real. Because my husband's not dead. Can't be. I've only had him two years since last October. The expiration date for a guy like him is so far off that I can't even conceive of it.

"You" could, though. The "you" being addressed on the phone has had her share of life, with its troubles, even its deaths. She isn't the one with weekend bar-hopping plans and a yellow plastic cell phone in her hand that feels sweaty and toy-small. She isn't the one getting nauseous, eyeing the distance to the kitchen sink because her belly might evacuate its contents. "You" understands mortality, may even have found some strange peace accord.

Mistakes like this, I'm sure they happen all the time. That's why I ask the misguided voice on the phone if I can see the body.

Static, then a hesitant, "Yes . . . actually we are required to have someone, family or friend, identify the body, to satisfy coronial procedure. But you may not want to be the one who does this. The accident was high velocity, and the body . . . "

Then he's telling me about the condition of this body that's not Darry's; how useless the dental records will be in the absence of, you know, teeth. He details the projected speed of impact, the rain on the roadway, the delayed response from authorities that allowed physical evidence to be dispersed by passing traffic.

Even finger-printing is a lost option. The poor bastard that they think is Darry tried to shield his face on impact. His delicate, thick-veined hands are as much a part of the interstate landscape as his well-bleached enamel.

Crow's breakfast, all of it.

His teeth now tucked in SUV tire treads, chewing up pavement.

If he didn't have his mind on the road before, well . . .

I'd caught a bad case of gallows humor during my short-lived stint at the Windy Arbor elder care facility. An old man named Percy Heathrow caught me weeping in a storage closet, sorry little red-faced me unable to handle the sight of all these intentionally forgotten people slogging away their last years. He called me over. I came forward, chugging back snot and wiping the corners of my eyes with the inside of balled fists. He didn't say anything, but his knobby hands floated down to his waistline and lifted up his shirt. I thought I was about to get perved on. Instead I saw a fresh colostomy bag hanging from the side of his belly, "SHIT HAPPENS" written on the plastic in black felt-tip.

That got me through the week; that moment where Percy and I were in on the cosmic joke. Since then my humor's veered obsidian black. So somehow my face harbors a misplaced smile even as this coroner dumps details.

The kind of wreck Darry's been in is called a "rear under-ride." This is what happens when a car hits the back of a semi-trailer and keeps going. The Freehoff trailer Darry didn't brake in time for acted like a guillotine on tires. Darry's death would have been instantaneous.

Because it's not really Darry we're talking about, I laugh quietly at this part. The voice on the phone said "instantaneous" like auto-dealers say "zero down," like it's a blessing. Like this guy they think is Darry died so quick, he might just come back.

This information is conveyed in the programmed, caring polite-speak of someone who talks death all day. It's me applying the realities, putting sauce on the steak. I remember a semi-snuff video Darry had me watch with him, how at the moment this hapless Russian girl got hit by a train she turned from a moving, breathing person to a flying sack of tissue and bones and nothing else. I've seen that side of death. I'm de-sanitizing this whole affair. Easier work for the brain than coming to grips.

"There are a few tattoos, Mrs. Broderick, that we believe could assist in the identification process."

I pictured Darry, home from getting his second tattoo, showing off the still-bleeding black cursive lines between his shoulder blades. There it is, stuck under his skin, my name marking him forever, more than any ring—Elloise. I'd run my fingers through the soft, warm ointment coating it and felt the abraded ridges where his skin had been torn by needles. This feeling, I think of it later, months later, while I'm masturbating. It helps me finish.

I prefer those tattoos that look like Japanese tapestries—dragons and whirlpools, ornately-scaled fish. But I couldn't argue with the intensity of seeing my name trapped under his skin.

His first tattoo, some random black tribal band encircling his left arm, he had that before we met. The kind of mark that binds you to the Tribe of Other Dudes Who Think That Shit Looks Cool.

His phrase for it was, "Purely aesthetic."

My response—"But it *looks* stupid."

We never spoke on it again. Verboten, you could tell from the silence following my comment.

Yes, I know his tattoos.

I ask for the address of the morgue before the voice can say anything else about identifying ink. The address is in Olympia.

Darry's "Introduction to Data Marketing" conference was in Olympia too, downtown, just off the water. Maybe I'd visit him at his hotel *after* I told the people at the morgue that I'm sorry I couldn't be of assistance. Wish them the best of luck, offer telegrammed sympathies to "you."

They'll want to apologize for the worry they've caused me.

They're used to apologizing, I'm sure. Mistakes like this . . .

Sweat beads along my hairline. If it runs I'll get hairspray in my eyes, like some cosmetic company test rabbit. My stomach is not altogether in the right place now. It's plastic-wrap tight around a belly full of nothing, relocating acid to the back of my throat.

The phone call has had the necessary effects.

It's the *unnecessary* effects that have me so goddamn confused.

Moments after I hang up the phone I get this feeling— warm, sweet molasses spreading down the inside of me from underneath my belly-button. That's the start. Then fullness, a subtle pressure as I expand against the fabric of my underwear. Then my heartbeat heads south, steady, filling me up, exposing my nerve endings.

The phone call's natural response should be crying, right? Even with my textbook denial there should be tears at the rims of my eyes, waiting to run down my cheeks.

No tears. And I need to get off.

I try to rationalize. This sudden urge is a biological sidekick to mortality. It has nothing to do with Darry. I'm not a whore, not sick. We oppose death by fucking. It's our weapon.

But Darry can't *ever* know how the false news of his death has triggered this need . . .

He can't know how much his death makes me want to fuck. More precisely, how I have never before, not in the recorded history of Elloise, so desperately wanted *to be fucked*.

These responses, my denial, my instant want . . . I can see them for what they are, but I can't shake them. So I stay in motion. I start packing bags for the drive up to Oly.

The new focus—grabbing my toothbrush, deciding which gas station will have the best mocha for the road, not looking in the mirror, not getting my vibrator out of the closet, picking my favorite towel because I never like hotel towels, wondering how long my sandals can go without falling apart, remembering that Darry is still alive, remembering that mistakes like this are commonplace, getting the gummies out of the corners of my eyes, putting fresh saline solution in my contacts case, not calling Darry's gorgeous friend Peter, not even thinking about how big Peter's hands are, not even letting this stream of thought go any further . . .

STOP!

Deal with the problem.

I flop onto our bed and catch a quick whiff of Darry's sweaty sleeping-boy smell, soaked into our lumpy old goose-down comforter. I'm so used to Darry's smell that my nose won't pick up the scent for long. An accepted part of my life. No need to process.

I undo the top button on my pants. I can't separate the buckle of my belt quick enough. Reason has vacated this moment.

My fingers do their work, tracing the paths of familiar sense memory, making my back arch and my stomach tighten. I can't remember the last time I was this wet.

I can't remember the last time I felt this good.

Slow circles turn to pressure. I close my eyes and there's Darry's friend Peter, watching me, lying next to me, sliding one of his huge hands up and down my belly. I can feel the calluses on his hands, an accumulated roughness that Darry's data marketing job would never give him.

I'm close to coming and Peter turns into the checker at the grocery store, the one with the jet-black hair and blue eyes, the one that told me about the detergent coupon. His breath still smells like black licorice.

Behind my closed eyes, far from my desperate hand, parades of men are waiting for their turn with me.

Hips are lifted, calves are squeezing tight. So close. My body drops back into the comforter and stirs up another wave of boy-smell.

I smell *my* boy. My Darry.

I can't come.

The wave crashes that quickly.

Fucking Darry.

I try again, try to climb the peak, but now I'm numb. I'm only touching myself now, meat on meat, no sacred shock of nerves. Just a sudden guilt, virus-quick through my system, flushing me with heat. Staring at the ceiling with my right hand cupped against pulsing warmth. Thinking about the last thing I want to acknowledge.

Darry and I have been together so many times in this bed. Too many times, I guess. That's why I've needed more lately—my fantasies, the images that I've transposed onto Darry's body while he's inside of me.

I don't think he's caught on. Even with me always turning the lights off beforehand, and asking him not to make noise, and asking him to come in from behind. Even with all my delicate fantasy preparations—these little tricks that allow me to screw another man when I'm married and faithful to a fault—he hasn't seemed to notice.

The thing making it easy for me to ignore who he is while he's inside of me—his weakness—is that he loves me too much. I guess his love is *my* weakness, too, because the love itself—his fingers running through my hair at night, his hand soothing my sore belly after I developed my first ulcer—is wonderful. His type of true, warm affection is more suffocating and alluring than any hotel fling or office tryst.

The idea that this lust, even now creeping back through my skin, is suddenly upon me because Darry's dead and now I've got a chance to be with other men . . . it worries me because it feels true. And knowing that it's wrong hasn't given me power over it.

If he is dead, I'm sick. Sick and alone.

I'm thinking too much. I sigh a long, shaky sigh and can feel myself on the verge of tears now, but I don't know if I'd be crying for Darry or myself. I just know I hate the delicacy of trembling air leaving my chest.

In five more minutes I'm in my car, headed north on I-5.

Even as my right leg becomes fatigued to shaking from the two hundred mile drive, I take comfort in the inappropriateness of my situation; in the fact that I've received this misguided message. It'll make for a crazy story at the least. I wonder how Darry will respond when I tell him that the rear end of a semi-truck tore off his head.

He'll want details, of course. To flesh out the morbid fantasy of his own brutal, blood-and-diesel demise. I'll tell him about this drive—how I flinched at every bit of sulfur-smelling road-kill that littered the roadside, at every tuft of skunk hair shifting in the wind of traffic. How the bright red flashing brake-lights of each semi-truck I passed were fists squeezing my heart.

Tonight, as we're curled up in bed together, I'll lay out the whole absurd affair for him. And he'll laugh. That's the easy thing to do. I'll feel the familiar heat of his breath on my neck, rub my head against his chest, and we'll both acknowledge this strange truth:

For a moment, he was dead.

This is what the world, excepting us, had believed.

THE CORONER'S NAME IS Brad Fuller, and he has hands that could casually palm a basketball. Or a human skull, which must be a more common occurrence for him. He's tall and butterfly symmetrical. Strong forehead. Wide jaw. Alpha all the way. He smells like nothing because he works in a place that goes to great lengths to smell like nothing, provided you don't take a deep whiff. Brad's younger looking than I expected from his professional demeanor on the phone, and I wonder if he's even past his third decade.

I'm smiling at him and extending my hand, saying, "Nice to meet you, Brad." I want to feel the size of his hand over mine. He seems a little off-center, unsure of how to respond to my casual greeting.

"Good to meet you, Mrs. Broderick."

Even hearing myself addressed as Darry's other half doesn't save me from the feelings that have returned to my belly. Brad Fuller is politely dressed in a dark blue suit that I'd like to peel away from his skin.

The fact that I'm standing in the clinical foyer of an Olympia morgue does not make me want Brad any less.

It should. I know this as a basic truth. But it doesn't.

The desires that I'd managed to repress on the long drive up are soaring through my skin now, crashing into my borders, speeding up every breath.

I'm not letting go of Brad's hand.

"Mrs. Broderick?"

"Oh, sorry." I release my grip, feel the heat from his fingers slide off the thin skin on the back of my hand. "My first name's Elloise."

"Are you expecting any other family members to arrive before we view the body?"

"Um, no. It's just me. Darry's mom lives in Tennessee, and his Dad's passed on. So it's just me."

"Okay. We can proceed unless you'd like a moment for yourself."

"Aren't you closing soon?"

"Only technically. In our line of work, we can't assign any set hours to our responsibilities. So take your time if you need to. Chantel at the front desk has already prepared the required paperwork."

My pulse picks up, faster now, this time because of the confidence Brad Fuller has that I'm the right person to identify this body. He's willing to go through with this charade.

I can do this. I'm not afraid. Go in there, give my negative identification, and head across town to Darry's hotel. Surprise him with the best sex of his life. Behind my eyes, I'll be seeing Brad Fuller. Darry won't care. He won't know, and I'll make him feel so good.

"No, I'm ready to go now."

"Alright then . . . I'd like to let you know in advance, that once you've made the identification, you can request to spend time with the body, if you want to. If you believe that this is something you want, you just let me know and we can facilitate it. In this case, Darry's body will need to remain covered, due to the extent . . ."

"I won't want to spend time with the body."

"Okay. I'll take that into consideration. But you can still let me know, once you've seen him."

Darry's body. What the hell am I doing here? And I just checked out Brad's ass. Strong, if a bit high up on his back. I'd love to feel it, love to wrap my hands around it and pull him into me over and over again. If there was ever an apex of wrong place/wrong time, I'm shooting for it. Drowning in compulsion, surrounded by the dead, fantasizing about this stranger in a sharp suit.

I should be hungry, but I'm not. Should be sad, but I'm not. Should be scared . . .

I am scared. I stood by my car for twenty minutes before entering the morgue, and now I'm headed into what Brad's told me is the viewing room.

The viewing area is a carpeted closet with a window separating it from a tiled room. Two cheap chairs, a 10 gallon trash can with a fresh plastic bag in it, a small wooden table adorned with tissues and fake light blue flowers, and a wall-mounted microphone round out the décor.

Brad is in here with me, and his forehead shines with sweat even though the room sits at that clinical un-temperature. The sweat reads as discomfort. This is the part of the job he hates.

He flips a switch by the microphone and says, "Go ahead, Dale."

Dale, looking uncomfortable in a gray Sears bargain-bin suit too tight for his many pounds, wheels a polished silver cart into the room. An opaque black bag is resting on top. Dale is sweating, too, with moisture beading on his polished, bald head as he struggles to push the cart in a straight line to the center of the room. No one is looking forward to this.

The body on the cart, it's much shorter than my Darry. I take comfort in that.

The comfort lasts maybe half a second. I remember the words "under-ride."

Dale unzips the body bag and reaches into it with one hand, his fingers twitching like latex-coated spider legs.

I DID NOT WANT to spend time with the body. I didn't want to stand next to it, or touch it, or hold it.

I did not want to spend another second in that low-ceilinged, piece-of-shit morgue.

I did not want to spend another moment looking at that tattoo of my name—Elloise—with nothing but torn flesh and empty space above it.

I know I didn't cry, although you could ask me until the end of time what look was on my face and I couldn't give you an honest answer. Can a face show nothing?

Paperwork was easy. I left Darry's mother's phone number with them so she could handle their questions about what to do with his body. I signed another sheet that let me have his effects, which turned out to be a wallet and some breath mints. His car keys were still in the wreckage.

I grabbed Brad's business card while at the front desk.

Through the whole process, I just sighed. Constant, shaking sighs—contents under pressure. No tears, and I still wanted to get off.

I'm sick and I've pinned a confirmation on alone. The widow, throbbing and numb.

So now I'm solo and sitting shocked in Room 202 at the Valu-Rest hotel off I-5. The key to the room was in Darry's wallet. It's one of those plastic cards that pops in and out of the lock and greenlights your entrance.

Darry had already been here a day. His toothpaste tube was uncapped, and a towel was sitting in a wet lump on the floor of the bathroom. One twin bed remained unmade—the Do Not Disturb sign was on display when I arrived—and his open suitcase rested on the other, the clothes from inside sprawled across the bedspread. I always admired Darry's tidiness at home so I'm a bit shocked by the disarray here.

By the bed stand there's a half-gone cup of tap water and Darry's alarm clock from home. He never trusted hotel alarm clocks. Press the over-sized snooze button on one of those and you miss the meeting you traveled so far to attend.

I can't ignore the thought—Darry should have hit snooze just one more time.

My mind flashes on Percy and SHIT HAPPENS but not even a twinge of smile follows.

Television makes me anxious. Not an option. I want distraction.

What would I do if today were a normal day? How much better would it feel to be at home now, in bed, drinking an iced coffee and reading one of Darry's Nabokov books and waiting for him to call?

But Darry won't be calling. Darry doesn't exist anymore. Jesus.

How alone am I now?

How hard do I have to deny this entire day to make it disappear?

I don't know. I don't. Stop thinking. Stay in motion.

I use the bathroom and smell Darry's musky cologne amidst the stronger smell of mildewing towels and the fermenting, hair-clogged tub drain.

It's easy to picture Darry running his morning routine, applying a spritz of cologne to each side of his neck before heading out for work.

Instead I picture rubber-gloved hands trembling under the weight of dead flesh, pressing into too-white skin beneath the black-ink scrawl of my name.

I picture myself, doing ninety down the interstate, looking for my own under-ride.

This is not the way. I may be sick, but I don't have to be alone. There's an army of men out there, lining up for me. They don't know it yet, but I'm available. And I want them all. Right now it might take a legion to fill me whole.

I'm a goddamned widow. Which isn't right. It isn't the way my life is supposed to be.

A mistake like this has happened to me.

Darry's clothes are quickly shoved off the made bed—I can't bring myself to touch the one he slept in—and I have a seat by the phone.

Eleven digits, a nine and Brad Fuller's cell phone number.

His voice comes through after the third ring. "Hello?"

Then, "Who is this?"

I almost hang up. Then I remember the width of his jaw, his broad shoulders.

"Brad, this is Elloise. Elloise, from earlier in the day. I need someone to talk to. I'm all alone, and I just . . . I'm thinking the wrong things and I can't . . . "

"Do you have any family in the area, even that you can talk to on the phone?"

"Nobody."

He's hesitating, looking for an out. This call is going beyond the boundaries of his job. I use his words against him.

"'In our line of work, we can't assign any set hours to our responsibilities.' You said that, right?"

"Well, yes I did, but . . . "

"Please, Brad, please come over. I can't sleep and I can't think straight and I'm afraid I might hurt myself."

He asks where I am. I tell him. He's ten minutes away, headed my direction.

I'm not wearing underwear, just a thin blue T-shirt and a pair of faded, soft khakis. My skin feels too hot, so I turn on the A/C and cool and wait.

I'M CLOSE ENOUGH TO smell him now. No longer overwhelmed by the morgue, I can really take him in.

His cologne—Drakkar backed with a hint of formaldehyde, giving me fetal pig flashbacks. He's been chewing on breath mints, some sort of spearmint.

My perfume—Arden's Sunflowers, thinned by salty sweat, slightly undercut by the smell of sex on my right hand, which I hope he can detect.

He tries to talk to me from the doorway but I turn and walk into the room, sitting on the bed and leaving an obvious space for him next to me. He hesitates, but follows.

It's his responsibility to be sure I'm okay.

His right hand is holding a thin slip of something papery that looks almost like a grocery receipt against the span of his fingers.

Those hands . . . the idea of his hands underneath my shirt, wrapped around my ribs, forcing me down onto him, it's flooding through my brain and I can barely remember his name.

"Mrs. Broderick . . . "

"Elloise, please."

"Elloise, I brought you a short pamphlet about the grieving process that I think might help you to understand how you're feeling right now."

I doubt this pamphlet can tell me why I'm ready to tear the shirt off the man who showed me my husband's corpse today. Even if the person writing it understood, they wouldn't write about what I'm feeling in there. There are truths about this that will never make pamphlet-grade. But I don't want to understand this experience. I just want to smash it away.

"Brad, will you sit down by me?"

He sets the pamphlet down on the coffee-table to the side of the television hutch and has a seat.

Before he can say anything I shift my body right up next to his and put my head on his shoulder. He doesn't move away. I start to hitch my body and blow puffs of breath from my nose like I'm crying.

It works. He's got his arm around me now, and my body sinks into his. I let my left breast push against his ribs. My T-shirt's so thin he can't avoid feeling my nipple harden. He doesn't move away.

My left hand moves toward his neck, fingers drifting into his hairline. My right hand drops down and brushes the inside of his thigh.

With my head positioned like this I can actually watch him get stiff. Pavlov should have worked with men instead of dogs. They train easier.

Then his left hand reaches down and lifts up my chin.

His lips do not hesitate and mine are already open. This was a simple threshold to cross. Need is need. This is what people do. People that see death do this even more. A show of will, screaming at the ocean.

Soon we've got our shirts off and I'm kissing his chest when he picks me up and tries to set me down in the *other* bed.

The one Darry slept in last night.

I scream. Like I'm being stabbed. Like the knife is twisting and pulling back out at wrong angles.

I can't. I can't touch that bed. It's the last place *he* slept. It's the last place that I can picture Darry alive and peaceful and happy.

Reeling from my scream, Brad almost drops me. I probably blasted him deaf in his left ear. He sets me down and backs away.

"Jesus, Elloise. What's going on?"

Good question. And one with zero decent answers. I just shake my head from side to side, not acting upset anymore, but genuinely confused.

I mean, if I really love Darry, why is Brad the Coroner shirt-less in my hotel room? What makes touching Darry's bed so wrong? Haven't I already proven how little Darry meant to me?

"Brad, my head's all twisted up, and I don't want you to go away, but I'd understand. I'm probably not a healthy person to be around, but I think I need someone to talk to, I mean, I'm sure I do. This has been the most messed-up day of my life . . . I'm not acting like myself and I'm not sure that I'd recognize who I am right now if I looked in the mirror. I can't . . . I mean, I'm just going to take a shower for a little bit. Try to calm down. You're welcome to stay . . . "

Before I finish the sentence he drops onto the bed where Darry's luggage used to sit and picks up the remote control.

He's still hard, biding his time. When he asks, "Are you sure you're okay to take a shower?" it seems like a courteous afterthought. Then I realize he's probably afraid I'm going to carve a y-section down my forearms.

"Yeah, I just need to relax for a moment. Sorry, this is weird. I'll be back in a sec."

I lock the bathroom door behind me, knowing the sound of the bolt clicking over will keep him around, wondering if I'm ever coming back out or if he'll be seeing me on his slab tomorrow.

The shower runs hot, near-scalding, to where the steam is hard to breathe. My face pushes into the water until the full force of the shower is focused on the spot where my hairline starts, dead-center. A wish floats through my mind, that the water would turn to white light and bore into my head and wash this whole day away. The wish goes ungranted, leaving me with the steady, pulsing streams of heat coursing down my face.

I wash myself with the credit card–sized bar of hotel soap that Darry had already unwrapped. The thought of his hands holding the same soap, rubbing it against his body, his warm, moving body, I can't bear it.

I block it out and turn the water temp up even hotter, to where my skin is turning beet-red on contact. The little fan in the ceiling can't keep up with the steam. There's a desert-hot fog bank in this bathroom I should never have known.

I sit down in the tub and curl up at the back of it, letting the water blast against my shins and the top of my feet. Somehow, I sleep for a couple of minutes like this.

I pop up out of my cat nap and for a second don't remember where I am. Then I see the little soap in the corner of the tub and try to fall back asleep.

No chance. Now I'm just bone-wet, and too hot, and ready to move past the reality of this day. Maybe Brad wants to lick me dry . . . .

What? No, that doesn't sound right. Who am I now, without Darry? I've got to get my head straight.

I grasp the shower curtain in my hand, the new hotel plastic squeaking against my skin. I pull the curtain back and almost scream for a second time tonight.

The steam on the mirror is not a steady sheet of moisture.

There are lines where the condensation is thinner. These are lines I recognize from a hundred mornings with Darry, evenly drawn letters on the mirror spelling out these words:

I Love Elloise.

Pavlov should have studied men. Darry's been writing the same thing on our bathroom mirror ever since we moved in together. He always left for work before me, always took a hot shower, always wrote this message.

Even hundreds of miles away, he wrote these words.

Even hundreds of miles away, I'm sure he meant them.

It's too much.

I wrap myself in a towel and rush out of the bathroom, steam twirling behind me. Then I'm yelling at Brad, who's watching music videos, probably unaware that he's stroking his crotch with the palm of his left hand.

"Get out. Get out. Go, please. Please get out of here."

"Are you okay?"

"No, but I don't want you here. I can't have you here right now. This isn't your place!" I hate my voice when it shakes like this.

"Listen, Elloise, you're obviously distraught. Maybe it's better if I stay here, just for the night, to make sure . . . "

He still wants to get laid. If he really cared he wouldn't have initiated that kiss, and right now he would be making eye contact, and he sure wouldn't still have his left hand on his dick.

"Fuck you, Brad. Get out."

He's putting his shirt on and moving toward the door. He stops and turns back toward me with his eyebrows scrunched together like he's never been so confused in his life. I know the look. I don't want to hear his voice.

"Go, Brad."

"I'm going, but I just want you to know . . . "

"Go." I don't want to hear this dejected little coroner telling me that I'm sick, or that I'm confused, or crazy, or anything. I just want to be alone. "Get out of here, Brad."

The spoiled bastard, he slams the door so hard that the corporate-approved watercolor painting by the entry falls off the wall. The frame breaks and there's shattered glass on the carpet.

I'm not cleaning it up. I hit the POWER button on the remote control by the bed stand and the television winks out.

When I feel truly lost, truly afraid, I try to fall asleep as quickly as possible. I have to do this now.

My towel drops to the floor. The A/C gives me instant goosebumps.

The bed Darry slept in last night is cold too, but I get in and pull the covers up to my shoulders and hope my body will warm the fabric.

The smell of Darry's skin is on the sheets, but each time I inhale it feels like the scent is fading.

I'm breathing him away.

And down below, between my legs, I can still feel my pulse.

I let my fingers seek out my heartbeat. I open myself up under the disheveled sheets and feel drips of water running from my skin to the bed beneath me.

I close my eyes, and now all I can see is Darry.

Thoughts of warm ointment, a still bleeding tattoo, and I'm moaning.

When I'm finished, I can feel tears tightening the skin of my face as they dry. The whole time, while my hips rolled and I remembered every sweet and every rough way Darry had ever touched me, I was crying and didn't know it.

I roll out of bed, slowly, and I've got hollow bones. I step around the shattered glass on the way to the bathroom.

I run the shower and the sink as hot as I can and fill the room with steam, sheathing the mirror and every other surface in tiny droplets of water.

Then there's just my finger, tracing trails on glass for longer than I'll ever remember.

The Sleep of Judges

I.

Birthday parties at Pizza Playhouse were hell, but Julie was a great kid and Roger knew he'd do just about anything for her. At least their hosts had kept the pitchers of cheap beer flowing, and in the end that had been the only way to tolerate the keening screams of the children and the repetitive parental small talk. It definitely didn't help that Roger and his wife Claire ended up at a party table with Abe Pearson, who wouldn't shut up about the fence he'd built by hand on his family's property. Fucking perfect Abe—who had four equally perfect little boys and a thriving dental practice and a real charmer of a wife—couldn't stop talking about how he'd got a permit and cut down every tree he wanted to use for the project, and milled the boards, and pounded in every post for a half acre, all by himself.

"Saved a bunch of money, I think, and it felt good to really work the project from beginning to end and watch it come to life. But I'll tell you there were some sore mornings where I thought about calling in help. And my hands, well . . . " and then Abe held up both of his palms to show off a topographic map of scars and calluses. "You probably know how that is from working over at Cumberton, right Roger?"

"I'm not on the mill floor, actually. I work scheduling admin and help with our safety program. But most of our guys wear gloves."

"Oh, they're missing out. Sure, it's tough on you at first, but working with your bare hands you get a real sense of the wood, you know."

Roger drained half his frosty mug of beer in one gulp.

Claire reached out and lightly set her hand on the side of Abe's arm. "Looks like fence building's a good workout, at least. What do you think, Rog? *We* could use a new fence."

"Sure," Abe said, before Roger could even respond. "I could even help you get started, bud. Give you a couple tips and save you a few of my dumb mistakes."

"Oh, that'd be great!" said Claire. "Last time I asked Rog to build me something I got a planter bed with no bottom and the gophers destroyed our garden." She laughed, then looked over at Roger with a smile and winked. Her hand was still on Abe's arm.

Roger drained the other half of his mug and slammed it down on the table. Abe and Claire jumped. "Yep. That planter sucked. I guess I didn't get a sense of the goddamned wood."

He stood up, not sure if he felt more embarrassed or angry, and excused himself to go grab another piece of cake.

Failing to locate any extra dessert—the kids had wiped out the entire chocolate-layered thing at locust-speed—he found a full pitcher of beer and poured himself another. He finally looked back over at Claire, who had moved to another table and was using a tiny plastic brush from the party gift bag to style Julie's hair, and he realized that this was the same thing as ever—Claire was the fun, flirty, social one who tried to make something worthwhile out of these parties and that's all it was and she was such a great mom. But still . . . . *fucking Abe and his precious hand-made fence and Claire laughing at him with her hand on his huge arm.*

Another beer disappeared, and then it was finally time to go.

The ride home was quiet—Julie was in a cake coma, and Claire stared ahead at the road. Roger was still thinking about how he could build a fucking amazing fence if he wanted to, if that was really what he wanted to devote his time to. But he didn't *need* to do that, because he did a million other things for his family, and they knew that.

They loved him.

Regardless, every time he thought he'd calmed down, he pictured Claire's hand on Abe's arm again, and found himself wrapped up tight in the same bitter, halfway jealous vibes.

He drained his water bottle on the drive home in an attempt to dilute the effects of his overindulgence at the party. Still, when Roger arrived at their house he was slightly more buzzed than he probably should have been, and he made it all the way past the living room and into the kitchen before his beer-lagged brain acknowledged the massive hole in the drywall where their flat-screen TV had been ripped away.

Fucking goddamn.

We got robbed.

Panic. It hit instantly, alongside the heat-flush of a heart leaping into double-time.

They could still be here. They could still be in our house.

He turned toward Claire and little Julie, thankful they were exhausted and hadn't yet made it up the walkway to the front door, which was still wide open. Claire had a batch of tin foil-wrapped pizza in her left hand and their sugar-crashed kiddo cradled on her other arm, half-asleep against her.

Not safe. They're not safe.

Roger quickly took several long, urgent strides across the living room and out the door, covering the distance to his family, doing his best to look composed.

"You have to go, babe. Now."

"What? I'm tired . . . "

"Now." He leaned in and whispered. "We got robbed. Get back in the car. Take Julie down to your mom's place. I'll call when you guys can come back."

"Are you fucking with me?" Her eyes flashed, alert but suspicious. "Is this about that party thing? You're just kidding around to freak me out, right?"

Roger instantly regretted all the pranks he'd played on Julie over the years. He needed her to take him seriously at times like this, when there could be people with guns inside their house, somewhere, right that moment.

"I'm not kidding. GO!" He yelled it. Too stern. A well of anger was boiling up inside him, mixing with fear, causing him to shake.

"Daddy, what's wrong?"

Shit.

"Nothing, Jules. There's a little problem with the house." They were moving back toward the car at least, heading in the right direction, even though it wasn't fast enough for him. Roger imagined a man in a ski mask charging out over their foyer, hatchet in hand, ready to slaughter them all. He put his hand on the small of Claire's back to speed her along. "You're going to head to grandma's for a special sleepover and I'll call you when the house is all fixed up."

Claire played along. "Surprise, baby. It's a sleepover party."

"A sleepover. Can I bring Mr. Grubbins?"

"No, honey." Roger opened the back door to load Julie into her car seat. "We can't go into the house right now."

"But I *need* Mr. Grubb . . . "

Roger couldn't stand the idea of dealing with a tantrum over a plush blue owl while someone might be escaping their backyard at that very moment with a laptop containing all of their unencrypted financial data. He went with a cheap counter-move.

"Check it out, Jules. I've still got some of the Skittles you bought with your game tickets. You want tropical or regulars?" He tightened her seat belt while she pondered the question. Claire started the ignition and gave him a *"Seriously, more sugar?"* look that he did his best to brush off.

It's like she's already forgotten our house has been robbed. Who cares about the goddamn sugar?

He was wise enough to say nothing. He kissed Julie on the forehead, slid her some candy, and gave her a hug. "Have fun at the sleepover, baby." He turned to Claire. "You'll call and let me know you guys made it, yeah?"

"Of course." She sounded pissed, like this was his fault.

"And I'll call you once I have this figured out. I'll let you know when it's safe."

Safe. Cute word—felt like an absurdity over Roger's lips, but it seemed to give Claire a sense this was really happening. Her face softened.

"Okay. Are *you* safe, though? Why don't you get in and we'll call 911 on the way and then they can let us know once they send somebody out?"

She doesn't think I can handle this myself. Why? Because I can't build a planter? Jesus. That's bullshit. She needs to know I can take care of us.

Roger looked back at the house. He pictured strange men crawling in through the windows and across the bed where he slept with his wife and he had a sense of all that had been taken from his family. He wanted to look Claire in the eyes and say, "I've got this, babe. I'm going to head in and secure the place, and if anybody's still in there I'll fuck 'em up."

But she might not believe me. She needs to believe me. I can show her. I'll handle this.

So he lied: "I'll wait out front for help. I promise. It'll be fine."

And Claire believed him, and drove off into the night, leaving Roger with their broken home and the fresh wounds inflicted by strangers who'd claimed it as their own.

ROGER COUNTED TO THREE hundred—enough time to ensure Claire wasn't pulling back around the block—and then walked through the front door.

He crept over to their kitchen and pulled their largest knife from the wood block.

You know how to use that, pal? Or you just want to hand some career crimi-nal an easier way to kill your dumb ass? Maybe Claire and Julie can come back and find your head's been sawed off and stuffed in the dishwasher? Don't be stupid. Get out. Call the cops.

Roger held the blade out in front of him and did his best to not notice the way the steel blade vibrated along with his jackhammer-ing heart.

You should yell something. Let them know you're here. They'll go running. Do it for Claire. She trusted you, and now you're back in the house playing Rambo like you're not someone's dad. Jesus.

Roger sensed a new electricity in the air. The part of him that had a long history of diving deep on bad impulses was enjoying the idea of conflict. Something to make him feel vital, and strong. He imagined himself confronting a thief, driving his blade into the man's guts and looking into his eyes as he bled out.

They shouldn't have fucked with me. They shouldn't have threatened my family.

The part of him that cared about making coffee for Claire in the morning and braiding his daughter's hair thought: *You're only gassing yourself up because you know the robbers are already gone. What are you trying to prove?* But that idea was quickly washed away by a haze of adrenaline and beer and forward motion.

The rear of the house was well lit, the bedroom doors wide open.

Did we leave it like that, or did they? How long were they here? Are they even gone?

Roger was five feet away from the master bedroom, silently approaching, steeling himself to rush in, sweat beading across his forehead, when his cell phone rang.

Shit.

It rang again. And this time he wasn't the only one who heard the jangling tones.

Something thumped against the rear wall of the house with enough size and strength to make the floorboards under Rog-er's feet tremble and send shockwaves through his bones. A paint-ing of two nesting doves fell from the wall. The glass in the frame shattered—Roger was looking at the shards in disbelief when he heard the sound coming from his bedroom. He felt it in his chest first, then his ears, as the rumble moved from its subsonic state to full warning.

Something was in the house, and it was massive, and it was *growling* at Roger.

The knife was forgotten, dropped to the hardwoods. The anger drained to nothing.

Instinct took control and Roger's brain was re-wired with only one purpose:

Escape.

He was all the way to the street in front of his house when some kind of reason returned, and it was then that he heard a more human sound in the night air.

Laughter. Sounded like a young man. Close. Maybe in Roger's backyard.

Wherever the man was, he sure as hell thought the situation was hilarious. Robbing this dumb family. Scaring the husband into a cardiac arrest with some kind of sound effects.

One big laugh.

They're playing with you, old man. Rush back there. Bust that punk's nose and pin him until the cops show.

But the feeling of the growling animal was still a tremor deep in his marrow, and Roger found he could not go back into the house.

"911. WHAT'S YOUR EMERGENCY?"

"Somebody robbed us. They took a TV at least. Probably more."

And they might be huge. Or some kind of animal. But I can't say that or you'll ditch this as a crank call.

"Thank you, sir. Your location?"

"1450 SE Lily Court."

"Are you at the house currently?"

"Yes. In the driveway."

"Okay, Roger, is anyone else with you?"

Roger blinked, and pulled the phone from his ear to look at it. *Did I tell her my name?* His ears were ringing. He couldn't remember. *Don't be dense, they can probably pull it up on their caller ID system.*

"No," he finally answered. "My wife and daughter are headed to the in-laws."

"Okay. That's good, sir. Do you have any reason to believe someone else might still be in the residence?"

"I . . . I'm not sure. I only saw the living room, really, and noticed the TV missing."

Static crackled over the line. Roger felt a sharp pain behind his forehead, pressure behind his ears, building to nearly intolerable levels.

What now? Wasn't my house getting jacked and me getting scared like some little bitch enough? Is this what a heart attack feels like?

"Sir, do . . . might be . . . enter the house . . . kill them a . . . grab . . . shovel and . . . pieces?"

"Come again? I'm sorry." *What the hell? Am I going to stroke out right here? I'm losing it.*

"A man knows . . . must be done . . . ."

And then, as quickly as the pain came, it faded. The white noise which saturated his hearing cleared, the sound of ocean water draining from his ears at the beach.

"I wanted to know if you have somewhere you can go until police arrive?" the voice on the other end said clearly. "We do not advise you remain at or enter the property. Nothing you own is worth risking your life. Do you have a neighbor you might visit?"

Roger tried to think, but it was like the gears in his mind wouldn't lock together. *Three years at this house and I still can't remember a single neighbor's name.*

"No, I . . . uh. Sorry. I'm freaking out, I think." Roger saw a flash of light, short and bright, from the periphery above his right shoulder.

Someone on the roof, shining a flashlight around?

"Hold on, miss, I think I saw . . . "

"Sir? We've got an officer in your area. He's being dispatched to your property. Do you have a vehicle on site that you can enter and lock?"

"Yeah. My truck's right here."

"Okay, let me know when you're inside."

Roger couldn't stand the idea of being cooped up in the cab of his truck. Hell, he was breathing so fast he felt the night air around him running thin.

He opened and closed the door of the truck, holding the phone out for the 911 operator to hear it creak and latch.

"This isn't a game, sir."

"I know."

"I'm only looking out for your safety."

"I know."

"Still sounds like you're outside. I can hear crickets. Wind on the receiver. Your dress shirt flapping in the breeze."

"No, I'm in the . . ." *Wait, how does she know what kind of shirt I'm wearing?*

"Okay, the officer is reporting he's a block out. He'll be with you in a moment."

And with that there was a click on the line. Roger turned from his house to see an unmarked patrol car parked across the street.

THE OFFICER'S LED FLASHLIGHT was so bright that Roger could barely see him until he was a few feet away. Casual dress. Must be an undercover. Or maybe he took the call after going off shift. Happened to be in the neighborhood. Something like that.

"You the owner? Called about a break-in?"

"Yup."

The cop holstered his flashlight and pulled out a notepad.

"First name Roger. Last name?"

"Stephenson."

"F or PH, sir?"

"PH."

"Very good. Thank you. I'm Officer Hayhurst. Can you tell me a little bit about this situation?"

"Sure. My wife and daughter and I got back from a kid's party . . ."

"Round what time, you think?"

"Maybe nine-thirty-ish. It's kind of a blur."

"You been drinking tonight?"

What? What's that have to do with anything?

"I had a couple of beers at the party. Maybe one an hour or so."

"Sure. Have to if you want to make it through one of those damn things."

What's this have to do with anything? What about the robbery?

Roger squinted at Officer Hayhurst and waited for him to continue.

"Only asking because I had a case last week, the guy comes home blitzed, I mean three sheets, trashes his own house for whatever reason, breaks his ankle stumbling down the stairs into his garage and passes out. Then he wakes up, calls us, thinking somebody knocked him out and rifled his house. We show up, ask him what they might have taken, or what he'd have that they'd want to steal, and he gets shifty and tries to give us the boot. While I'm trying to calm him down, my partner looks in the guy's bonus room and finds a couple of pounds of partially wrapped mushrooms—I'm talking the Schedule I type—and there you go."

"There you go."

"We booked him for it and logged the contraband, but it still felt like a colossal waste of time. So, when I get calls this time of night, I start to look for how much alcohol might be a factor in the situation."

"That makes sense. But I didn't get drunk and rob my own house. I mean, I was driving home with my five-year-old and my wife in the car."

"You'd be surprised, sir. We pull over plenty of parents who thought they were sober and still blow a point one zero."

"I'm sure. That's very sad." Roger thought back to when he was five, flying around the big back seat of a Ford Galaxie while his dad swerved and took slugs off the bottle of Crow he kept stashed in the dash. A different era.

Officer Hayhurst's eyes narrowed. He was making some kind of decision.

"So, you returned around nine thirty p.m. to find the property disturbed?"

"Yes. When I went inside I noticed that the TV was missing. I got Claire and Julie out of here and then called you."

And then I went inside thinking I might kill whoever busted in, but I got spooked when I realized there might be a giant in my bedroom and I was about to shit my pants when something growled at me and then someone was laughing and I called 911 and maybe started having some kind of seizure or psychic breakdown and now I'm here with you and you're not helping one fucking microscopic iota. So that's about that, pal.

"Do you have any reason to believe the perpetrators might still be in your house?"

"No. Might have been here when we first arrived but I think they would have heard us and left by now."

But there also might have been someone on the roof, shining something at me and filling my head with noise. I break out that little fun fact and you'll have me puffing into your breathalyzer, right?

"Okay, Roger. I'm going to head in and clear your property, and then I'll invite you in and we can go over the next steps. Is there anything inside the house—dogs, security devices, things of that nature—that I should be aware of?"

"There's . . . um . . . no. No dog. Nothing I can think of."

Maybe a kitchen knife in the hallway, but you can't tie that to me. Can I be prosecuted for self-endangerment?

"Good then. Back in a moment."

Roger nodded and looked up to the sky and listened to the sound of police helicopters hovering over the city in search of the kind of people who laughed when a man ran in terror from his own home.

"Well, they definitely made a mess of things. But they're gone. You can come on in."

Roger had never had a man with a gun tell him he was allowed to enter his own home. Had never needed *anyone's* permission to enter his own home before. Something about it made him shiver.

Officer Hayhurst gestured to the gaping hole in the drywall where the television and its mount had been ripped clean away.

"That surprises me, honestly. They're not grabbing TVs much anymore, now that the price point came down and they got more trackable. Obviously, they didn't have the time to unscrew it from the wall. Did you have that thing hooked into a stud?"

"Yeah." Roger had wanted to mount it dead center on the wall, but Claire was paranoid about the thing falling on Julie's head during an earthquake, so he'd made sure it was secured to the frame of the house even though the asymmetry set his brain to twitching when he noticed.

"Strong guy, to rip that right out of the wall."

"You think the robber was a male?"

"Most of 'em are. And in this case, actually, you're dealing with a burglar. A robber steals from people using force. A burglar steals from properties. Easy way to remember it is to think of the Hamburglar. He was sneaky. Creeping around, stealing burgers. Already dressed in jail duds, which was dumb now that I think about it. But you didn't see him pistol-whipping Ronald and jacking his fries. He did that, he'd be the Hamrobber."

"Duly noted." *Fuck this guy.*

"Main other places you want to check are the master bedroom and the office. They usually don't bother with kids' rooms and the kitchen. They stay away from the front of the house in general, especially if their exit point is out the back. Nobody wants to get trapped."

They walked down the central hallway. Hayhurst pointed to the knife on the floor.

"That's weird to me. Sometimes they grab a nice set of knives, but they usually nab the whole block. Can't help but picture the intruder waiting for you with that, trying to decide if they were going to run or fight. Looks like you got lucky."

"Lucky?"

"Well, all things considered."

"So, you see anything missing in here?"

They turned left into the office.

Missing: laptop, computer speakers.

Opened and tossed: the file cabinet. *Did they get the checkbook? Tax records?*

He pictured the thieves collating his routing and checking numbers and Social Security numbers and birth certificates and credit card numbers and everything they'd need to make his family's finances an unholy mess for decades to come.

Those numbers have too much meaning. We're screwed.

Toppled, probably just for fun: the bookshelf. Technical manuals and military thrillers and comic books everywhere.

And there, on the center of his desk, surrounded by the dust outlining where his laptop used to exist, was a framed black and white photo of him and Julie, taken last Father's Day.

Over the top of the image, scrawled on the glass in fast, violent strokes, a large red X across both of their faces.

"Fuck."

"Now Roger, I want you to know that we're going to take that seriously, as it could be construed as a threat, but I also have to tell you that I've seen thousands of burglaries and I can't tell you how many times they leave behind a little something to mess with the victims. You seem like a down-to-earth guy, so if you'll pardon my French, I can tell you I've seen much worse. Family photos shit on. Wife's unmentionables laid out on the bed with come all over them. Housecat strangled and stuffed in with the kid's plush animals. Awful. Some types, it isn't enough to take a family's property. They want your sense of security too. They're either too juvenile to guess at the kind of damage this sort of thing does, or worse, they don't care at all. It's fun to them."

Roger remembered the laughter echoing from his backyard.

"Let's move to the next room."

The reading lamp in Julie's back corner was on, shedding soft light on dayglow kid posters and pony bedding. Nothing appeared to be disturbed. Roger flipped the switch for the brighter overhead lamp and paced the room looking for anything amiss, skin crawling at the thought of some asshole in what was supposed to be his daughter's idyllic space.

"Looks fine."

"Yeah, I don't think they came in here. Quick check in the bedroom and then we'll go around back and see if they left anything behind for us."

Hayhurst went in first and walked to Claire's dresser, pointing to the open jewelry box on top.

Roger scanned the box. It was in total disorder, but he didn't know enough about Claire's jewelry to determine if anything was missing.

"Maybe check the little black boxes. Burglar's been at this any length of time, they can tell right away what's costume jewelry and what's going to get them something at pawn."

Three black boxes.

Not a thing left inside. Her whole diamond set, gone.

Son of a bitch. He rarely had enough money to get something nice for Claire of his own accord, and now they'd taken five anniversaries worth of scrapping and scrimping and they were probably already on their way to trading them for one tenth their value in drug money. Goddamn it.

"Yeah. Looks like they were pretty well targeted. You're going to want to check that drawer too." Hayhurst pointed down to the lowest drawer, where Roger kept his boxers and socks. It was already open, the contents tornadoed. He squatted next to the drawer.

"Why?"

"Guns. Drugs. Your best jewels. That's mainly what they're looking for. Small, valuable shit. Easy to abscond with. Easy to use or trade. And the odds say they can find at least one of those things in a man's sock drawer. You tell me why that is, because I don't know. But this definitely looks professional. Normally, this close to the bus line, I might guess a bored teenager did it, but the longer I look around your house, the more this seems too pro for your average teen or tweaker."

A pro job. The idea gave Roger zero comfort. *Had they been watching us? For how long? Had my computer been hacked? Had they seen my response to the party evite? Could it have been one of the parents who didn't come to the party? Who else would have known we'd be out . . .*

"Do you own any guns that might have been stolen? It's very important that we get as much info about firearms as we can."

"No. No guns. I grew up with them, but my wife . . . " Roger shrugged. Claire saw guns as death incarnate, a physical manifestation of fear, and the need for them a kind of moral weakness.

"Say no more. My wife's the same. I try to not even let her see my service pistol. That's good news though. One less stolen gun on the streets." Hayhurst walked around the king-sized bed at the center of the room and pointed to the open window. "And over here we have the point of entry. Looks like they pulled the screen, applied a little pressure to the glass, and slid the window to the side. You can even see a footprint here where they stepped on your bed coming in. Tracked some grass with them." Hayhurst clicked on his flashlight and leaned out the window. "Yeah—very close to the ground here. Easy to hop in once it's open. No security latches?"

Roger couldn't think of a response that didn't make him feel either dumb or defensive or both. The truth was that he'd fucked up. He'd barely thought of the windows, of how accessible they were, of how easily secured they could have been. He'd thought their new place was, somehow, safe. He'd done nothing and now his family had been endangered. Who knew how this would impact Julie, or how Claire would look at him now? It was his job to protect them and he'd failed.

Fuck.

I'll fix it though. I can fix this myself.

The cop cleared his throat, waiting on Roger's response.

"No. Nothing. No security, aside from the deadbolt on the front door. We thought . . . this kind of thing isn't supposed to happen in this neighborhood. That's why we moved out here after dealing with all the bullshit in the Northeast."

Hayhurst's eyes took on a strange dull softness then. He looked right at Roger, then past him.

"Hey, Roger." The cop's voice had taken on an odd monotone. "That's magical thinking. There is no glass which can't be shattered, no lock which can't be broken, no life which can't be taken should someone else possess both hunger and the will to feed it."

What?

The cop's disturbing lack of affect reminded Roger of the strange voice he'd heard on the 911 call. *Is he even really saying this?*

Then, just as quickly as his demeanor had changed, Hayhurst smiled, and the light returned to his eyes. "Yeah, I'm surprised too," he said, as if he hadn't already replied. "This neighborhood has very low crime. I can't remember the last time I was called out here, honestly."

Roger decided—especially with his sobriety already in question—to let the moment pass.

It's all the adrenaline. My head's just a mess right now.

The officer crossed the room and pulled out a smaller flashlight which emitted a soft purple light. He shone it on the jewelry box while running what looked like a tiny shave brush over the surface.

"That's what I expected—jack shit for prints. Burglary's a hell of a tough case to crack, most of the time. Last year we only caught folks in about twelve percent of cases, and most of those were tweakers too dumb to recognize tagged or LoJacked gear. I mean, if you *have to* get into a career in crime, burglary's probably the safest bet you've got."

Roger stared at the cop and wondered if he had ever passed any form of sensitivity training. Hayhurst spotted his bewilderment.

"Sorry, man. Facts are facts. Anyway, let's check your medicine cabinets and then take a look around back."

THEY SCANNED BOTH BATHROOMS and their cabinets and Roger ran an internal monologue matching meds to maladies. All was accounted for, aside from a small bottle of Valium which he occasionally used when his lower back went out. But Roger said nothing of the pilfered blue V's, as he used them to treat a pain caused by the risk and impetuousness of his youth, and Hayhurst might ask too many questions about mistakes in Roger's past he felt lucky to have escaped.

THEIR OUTDOOR ADVENTURE CONSISTED primarily of Hayhurst pointing out many of the house's additional unsecured areas—"This place is a burglar's dream, Roger. You could hide in a yard like this all day and strip the house at your leisure with a truck in the alley."—and then acknowledging that the rained-on grass would yield no useful shoe prints.

It wasn't until they stopped scanning the exit route and Hayhurst brought the flashlight up to the outside surface of the bedroom window that they found their first real clue.

There, in the caked dust on the window glass, they saw the shape of the two massive hands which had so easily pushed the window out of the way.

Hayhurst lifted his own gloved hands up to the window. The outline of the fingers on the glass was easily an inch wider and two inches longer than the officer's.

And most notably, the imprint of the left hand appeared to be missing its pinkie finger.

"Will you look at that, Roger? *Big* guy! And that missing digit means we just might find out who burgled your house after all. Let me dust for prints."

But Roger—whose mind was awash in red X's and low growls and flat voices telling him about hunger—wasn't so sure that even solid evidence and well-applied laws offered any kind of comfort anymore.

"Nope. Gloved up. No prints. Pros for sure. Not that this was a hard nut to crack, mind you. Truth is you made it easy for them. You were *so* easily penetrated." It almost sounded like Hayhurst was admiring them. "Not your fault, not really. These days it's not as clear cut as it used to be. Back in my father's day a man knew where he stood. You prepared and you protected. You kept a shotgun near your bed if trouble came calling, and you knew it was on you to provide your wife and child with a sense of security. You get that, right?"

Hayhurst's earlier comment was still echoing in his head—*You were so easily penetrated.* Something about the way the cop said it sat in Roger's guts and made him feel like he was shrinking away and furious at the same time. He crossed his arms over his chest and wondered what it would feel like to drive a fist into Hayhurst's nose.

"Yeah, I can tell you know what I'm talking about, Roger. You'll do the right thing, going forward. Maybe you could use a new fence back here. Something more serious than that chicken wire. City code will let you go up to six feet now, plus trellis on top. Anyway, let's head in."

IN THE END OFFICER Hayhurst left him with only a floppy, computer-printed business card with his police department info on the front and a case number jotted on the back.

"That case number's really all I can give you at this point. I got a photo of each room and the vandalized picture in your office. Besides that, all I found was a partial print that's probably yours."

"Probably."

"Well, like I said, this guy or guys, it was a pro deal. And even if that partial is theirs, it doesn't work like you see on the CSI. I'm not sending out a tech for what appears to be a standard-issue jewel theft. So what you do now is take inventory of what you lost and call the insurance company first thing in the morning. They'll make it right. And remember, they have no way to verify how much cash was or wasn't stolen from your property. So be certain to search through your house and figure out how much cash was stolen. It was probably quite a bit."

"What?"

"I would never officially advise you to falsely report cash losses. But I can tell you that by the time this all sets in, you are going to find yourself spending a lot of money securing this joint. Trust me. So let the insurance company make that right, too. Take care, Mr. Stephenson."

There was a moment of silence after Roger closed the front door of the house. He was exhausted. He leaned his forehead against the cool of the door and wished that he could close his eyes and when he opened them he'd find out it was all just a bad dream, that everything was the way it had been before they'd left for the party. But that was bullshit, so he considered another option: set fire to the place. It wasn't theirs any longer—the moment intruders opened the window and stepped inside it had ceased to be his family's home. Even if he tidied up and offered reassurances, his family would always remember this night. How the only ones he yelled at that night were the ones he should have protected. How some stranger had walked through their home and taken everything they'd wanted. So he'd soak the damned place in gasoline and spark a match and watch all proof of the invasion turn to ashes, then drive two cities over to be with Claire and Julie and start afresh.

This never happened. I did all the right things.

But then his phone rang, and the world wasn't a place which allowed such fantasies, and the screen said "CLAIRE" so he had to answer it and start lying to her about how everything was going to be okay.

II.

HE DECIDED TO TELL Claire as little as possible about the evening.

Yes, we were burgled.

I'm sorry, but they got your jewels. The diamonds. All of them. Sorry, babe.

I'll bring some clothes and supplies out to your mom's house tomorrow afternoon. I need you and Julie to stay there for a few days until I get things cleaned up and safe around here.

No, the officer says it was a standard-issue crime. In and out.

They did get the laptop.

I know. I know. It sucks. But I'm pretty sure I have most of our pictures and videos on a back-up drive. Or in that cloud account I keep forgetting to cancel.

No, they don't have any of *those* videos. Those are only on the camera card. I never moved them to the hard drive. *I swear.*

No, you make sure Julie gets to school and then head to work. I'll call in tomorrow, stay home and deal with all of it. Insurance. Banks. Credit agencies. Get this place locked down.

I know, babe. It's a fucking mess. It's going to be okay though. I'll handle it.

I promise.

Love you too.

You guys get some rest, okay? I'm taking care of everything.

I'll make it right.

HE WONDERED WHAT WOULD have happened if he'd told her every-thing. What if she knew about the strange voices and the ink-slashed photo and had some sense of who might have been in their home? He imagined she'd demand that they put the house on the market and move somewhere, anywhere, else.

But he'd hidden the truth, and the doubt and concern in her voice doubled his resolve.

"Are you okay?"

"Are you sure you can handle all this?"

It ate at him. What did she think of him now?

She's just worried. She loves me.

Or, maybe she doesn't think I can fix this.

He'd cleared his throat halfway through the call and shifted his voice into a lower register. He would show her he was the kind of guy who could handle any trouble that came his way.

But are you, Rog?

Are you really?

DESPITE A FLOOD OF adrenaline from the night's events, Roger knew the right thing to do was to get some rest and start as fresh as he could at daybreak. But when he walked back to his bedroom and felt the air blowing in through the open window and saw the huge footprint canyon in the middle of his wife's pillow, he knew that this was a place which would offer no sleep until set right.

So: TRIAGE.

What was the worst of it? What had to be addressed to quell the rage and frustration he felt pressurizing in his chest?

He thought back to Oakland, when things had gone bad there. You had to work fast to reshape reality before it became the thing that swallowed you whole.

Roger hit the kitchen and brewed a whole pot of jet-black coffee.

Get some rest?

Nope. Not tonight.

First: undoing the things he didn't want Claire to ever know. A Windex wipe down for their rear window erased the outline of the printless four-fingered hand. Screen reinserted, window closed.

But nothing locking that window in place. God, we were so vulnerable.

The comforter and pillows went in the laundry. If Claire ever found out the burglar had stepped on her pillow, she'd throw it in the fire before sleeping on it again.

The X'ed out picture frame was stuck in a trash can two houses over, and the photo of him and Julie tucked away in a family album. Couldn't risk Claire asking about the absence of the frame or spotting it in their own trash.

Roger would have to ensure any and all follow-up cop conversations rolled through him.

The knife he'd been unable to wield found its home in the chopping block.

The worst and most unsettling evidence of the burglary addressed, Roger worked the rest of the night on restoring order, feeling like a lonely ant tasked with rebuilding an entire hill after some kid had kicked it to pieces for cheap thrills.

He dusted his desk to de-emphasize the absence of their computer. He pushed his bookshelf back up and tried to remember in what order he'd organized his books, back when they'd first moved in. He hit the hole in the living room wall with a patch-and-paint kit, and since there was more coffee in the pot he drained that and then stayed in motion until sunrise so that he could perfect the illusion that nothing bad had ever happened here.

HE HADN'T FALLEN ASLEEP so much as he'd just stopped being conscious right there in his chair at the kitchen table. He woke to a puddle of drool on the dark wood table and too-bright sunlight beaming in through the sliding glass doors to their patio.

The table had become the central workstation for Operation: Un-Fuck This. Roger reoriented himself, poring over the insurance docs and jewelry receipts and current bank statements and even the laptop manual, where he'd actually had the rare foresight to jot down the serial number. He checked his phone and saw nothing from Claire and hoped that she was about her usual routine. That gave him nine more hours to lock things down.

He used his phone to shoot an email to his supervisor at the mill. They were still a month out from quarter end, so if Roger had to be gone, now was the time. He'd miss a few droning meetings about the implementation plans for the new safety regs. That was fine by him.

"Stomach flu knocked me sideways. Trust me, you don't want me there. Might be sick for a day or two. Lance has access to my Q3 folder for the morning reports."

Roger had figured out a while back that a stomach flu was the best illness to fake when you needed an excuse to take a day off. Everybody sympathized and nobody asked questions, for fear that they might get answers involving shit and/or vomit. Plus, if you stayed out for a fake cold, you had to spend that whole first day back putting on theatrics, making little dry coughs and sniffling back imaginary snot. The flu would get him to the weekend without having to worry about anything other than the house and how this was going to affect his family.

Even after all the clean-up, she might still think it's blowback from Oakland. But it's not. It can't be. That was sealed up tight. Anybody who would give a damn is still in jail.

And normally those thoughts would have given Roger comfort—it *was* true, he knew it in his bones. No matter how much Claire fretted, it would be pure paranoia at play. Oakland was behind them, so long ago, and even if it wasn't, then at least he knew what kind of folks he was dealing with. This, though . . . he had no idea. And even in the light of day and the heat of work, he still found himself plagued by cold sweats and a fluttering heart.

I'm exhausted—that's all. I'll get the house together, get one night of good sleep, and then things won't all seem so out of joint.

He nodded his head at the thought, trying to drive the affirmation down, to make it feel true.

HE'D HAD NO IDEA how hard it would be to leave the house.

I need to leave to pick up supplies and get the place locked down. But if I leave and it's still unsecured they might strike again, and this time they'll take everything. They know the layout now. They think I'm a mark.

They'd been watching this place, right?

They'd hit us at night, when we'd have normally been home. Your average burglar shows up during working hours because they know everyone is off on their grind. But we were hit at prime time. They had to have been watching. Waiting.

They could be out there right now.

So Roger walked the perimeter of the house three times with an aluminum baseball bat slung over his shoulder. He poked around in the bushes and high hedgerows that surrounded his backyard and made it so thief friendly.

He walked the street in front of their house, the bat now slung at his hip. He covered the whole block, doing his best to memorize the neighbors' cars and minivans so it'd be easier to identify any intruders.

The street was sedate. Only squirrels, birds, and Roger and his bat were in motion.

It's morning. They're working. I could rob all these places right now. Hell, the guy across the street left his fucking garage door open again. I could walk right in and help myself to some pie and jewelry.

Spotting nothing obvious or out of the ordinary, Roger returned to the house, turned on every light, and then locked the front door and started to leave.

Wait. What if they are watching? Once they see me drive off . . .

BY THE TIME HE had the hammer and nails in hand, he knew this was what Claire had been nervous about. That this would turn him manic. That his more questionable impulses would surface.

He put up the hand-printed note anyway, nailed it to the forest green siding beneath their bedroom window.

HEY, FUCKFACE,

FIRST OF ALL, NOW YOU KNOW THERE'S NOTH-ING LEFT INSIDE BUT AN OLD-ASS TV, SOME MIS-MATCHED DISHES, AND SOME PLUSH TOYS. SO STAY THE FUCK OUT.

SECOND, HOW DO YOU KNOW I REALLY LEFT? HOW DO YOU KNOW I'M NOT THE KIND OF GUY WHO PARKS FIVE BLOCKS AWAY AND THEN SNEAKS HOME TO WAIT FOR YOU TO COME BACK IN? HOW DO YOU KNOW I'M NOT IN THERE RIGHT NOW, WAITING BEHIND THAT CLOSED BATHROOM DOOR, HOLDING ON TO A HUGE KNIFE?

MAYBE I WANT YOU TO COME IN. MAYBE I WANT YOU ON MY PRIVATE PROPERTY SO I CAN ASSERT A FEW OF MY RIGHTS. THAT MIGHT BE ALL I WANT IN THE WORLD. TO HAVE A LITTLE FUN WITH YOU BEFORE THE COPS COME TO HAUL YOUR DUMB TWEAKER ASS OFF TO A TWENTY YEAR JAIL TERM.

YOU DON'T KNOW WHO YOU'RE DEALING WITH.
SO THINK ABOUT IT, BUDDY. IS IT WORTH IT?
SINCERELY,
THE OWNER

P.S. BRING THE LAPTOP BACK. IT'S LOJACKED. PUT IT
ON THE FRONT PORCH BEFORE THEY CATCH YOU
WITH IT.

Roger pictured Claire coming home to find that note. Another
wave of sweat popped on his skin.

HE DROVE THREE SLOW laps around his block before he finally felt
comfortable driving away from the house. Saw nothing which caused
alarm. It was a quiet neighborhood. He'd loved it, until last night.
He resolved to do everything he could to make it so he could love it
again someday.

Every second he was away, someone was robbing the house.

THAT'S HOW IT FELT.

He drove accordingly. If he happened to run a red or two, he
put his hand up in front of his face in case the intersection had one
of those automated photo ticket systems. He rode a few bumpers to
induce a sense of fucking urgency. Speed limits were suggestions for
people who weren't trying to protect their homes from giant four-fingered professional thieves.

He hit the home supply and electronic stores in turbo mode.
His cart tilted to two wheels when he rounded corners. He almost
clipped a gray-haired old lady who was indecisive about which prun-
ing shears she wanted.

Why is everyone in goddamned slow motion?
Fatted fucking cows, man. It's like they can't see it.
Something's coming. I can feel it.

It didn't feel like mania to Roger. It felt like clarity.

It felt like purpose.

I can make things right.

HE EXPECTED TO FIND the house gutted upon his return, instead of locked tight and smelling like burnt coffee.

Shit. I left the burner on.

Time to lock it all down: toolbox opened on the table, drill on the charger. Credit card receipts and open boxes strewn across the control center/kitchen table.

Room by room. Every window got a vibration alarm. Anybody who tried to enter from the outside would get hit with enough decibels to drive them deaf in less than two minutes. Every window got a security dowel and sliding aluminum lock latch. Every window got metal screws across the top of the frame, every three inches, so there was no possibility of lifting the pane out unless you removed them from the inside.

New front door and garage deadbolts and knobs installed.

The sliding glass door got quadruple-redundant lock systems. Side gate got a lock you couldn't drill through unless you owned a diamond tip.

Rear fencing was fortified with three upward-extending feet of chicken wire. He'd bought the cheap kind because it cut his finger when he was trying to make a decision on which roll to buy. He'd almost asked the clerk if they had razor-wire, but decided that was beyond the pale. Plus, that would give Claire a sense of how he felt, which was how she *shouldn't* feel. This was *his* problem.

He ripped up his little warning note. The rear window it had been protecting was now a barely-openable sheet of glass rigged up to wail like a banshee if a fluttering leaf accidentally brushed its surface. He felt better about that.

Roger noticed that it would be easy to escape from his backyard to a side alley through one of the neighbor's unfenced yards. That was unacceptable. There should be no easy point of access.

Where's Abe Pearson and his amazing fence-building skills when you need him?

But Abe Pearson was a goodie-two-shoes—hell, a *dentist*. Roger thought himself from scrappier stock. He went old school, constructing a four-foot-high bramble patch outside that stretch of his fencing, stacking cut blackberry stalks and thorny rose branches until his arms were covered in tiny seeping cuts.

If I bleed, they bleed.

CLAIRE WAS STILL SPOOKED. He could hear it in her voice. It was easy to talk her into staying another night at her parents' house.

"How's it going there?"

"Good. Good. I think we'll be all set for you guys to come back tomorrow."

"You want me to call at Julie's bedtime tonight?"

"Hell yes. I miss you guys. It's too quiet here. I'm used to having some music playing through the TV . . . "

"Yeah. Thank you for taking care of this."

"Of course."

"And you're taking care of you too, right? Getting some sleep?"

"Definitely. I mean, not a lot. It still feels kind of weird here. It's going to take some time."

"But you're okay?"

He looked around at the chaos of the dining room, the unaddressed paperwork, his arms smeared with clotted droplets of blood and metal shavings.

"Yeah. Of course. I'm good. I've got this."

"Okay. Love you, babe."

"Love you too."

By seven that night he had their exact same model of television installed in the living room, and a slightly newer laptop running in the office. High On Fire was blasting from the TV speakers in the living room; Roger found the sound a comforting replacement for his own frantic breathing and constant room-to-room footfalls, even though at one point the vocals reminded him of something he was trying to forget from the night before—that *growling*—and he had to turn down the volume.

On the way back from his second outing of high-speed shopping and credit card limit testing, he noticed, for the first time ever, that there were little signs mounted on the lamp posts around his block.

"Protected by Neighborhood Watch."

Some job they'd done.

He decided it was time to reinvigorate the watch and rouse it from the fucking coma which had allowed his house—and *their* neighborhood—to be infiltrated. They needed to know that they had failed, and they needed to start keeping an eye out for the next invasion. Roger wolfed a batch of microwave chicken tikka masala and tried to calm down his all-day coffee binge with some beer. Then he opened up a new document on the laptop.

Dear Neighbors,

I regret to inform you that our house at 1450 SE Lily Court suffered a break-in yesterday evening, somewhere between 4:30pm and 9:00pm. Several pieces of jewelry and electronics were stolen. Our family is unharmed, so we're very thankful for that blessing. However, we're now feeling much less safe in a neighborhood that we've loved for a long time, and we certainly wouldn't wish for you to feel the same. In the event that these burglars have decided to target this neighborhood, I recommend you take a look at the security of your household. And I know it's considered rude for this area, but it might be wise to start leaving exterior lights on through the evening.

Also, as this occurrence managed to slip right under the nose of our normally vigilant neighborhood watch, perhaps we should step up our game and really keep an eye out for anything strange (whether that's unfamiliar vehicles on our block or questionable, lingering pedestrians, or even solicitors who ask too many questions about the inside of your home).

Hope all is well with you, and my apologies for whatever my filing this police report might do to our property values. Ha Ha!

Best wishes,

Roger Stephenson

He printed fifty and distributed them to every mailbox—or failing that, doorstep—in a six block radius. He noticed how many houses were dark, looked uninhabited. He noticed how easy it would be to break in to almost all of them.

"There is no glass which can't be shattered, no lock which can't be broken. No life which can't be taken."

Jesus. What was wrong with that guy?

He contemplated filing a complaint about Officer Hayhurst, but knew "He Made Me Generally Uneasy" wasn't something they'd put Internal Affairs on right away.

He saw no one else on the streets. But on the way home there was a rustling in the bushes in front of him and suddenly a tiny black rabbit shot out and darted across the street, finding cover behind an above-ground garden hutch.

Roger didn't actually leap into the air, but inside it felt as if he had.

The incident made him notice two things. The first was that he was scared in a way he couldn't spend too much time thinking about. The second was that his instinct, immediately, had been to kill that rabbit.

MOUNTING THE SECURITY CAMERA was the last step, and then he promised himself he'd call it a night.

The eaves where he wanted to tuck the camera were up much higher than his bedroom window, and night had already fallen so he had to work with a headlamp on, but he was determined. After struggling to find even footing in the wet soil below, he finally got to the top of the wobbling ladder and found a way he could shift his weight that kept at least three of the feet below firmly planted.

A huge brown mama spider hovered near a bright white cluster of eggs. Was she waiting to nurture them, or was she exhausted and hoping to eat a few babies on their birthday? He didn't care, cancelled his normal laissez-faire policy toward spiders, and crushed the lot of them under the knuckles of his leather work glove.

He'd nearly bought the fake version of the exterior camera at the electronics store, thinking it would save an additional eighty dollar dent to their credit balance, and that the *appearance* of surveillance would be enough to make a burglar think twice. Then he remembered the laughter which had come from his backyard the night before.

Someone else was treating this like a game. Someone clever enough to leave no prosecutable trail. Someone who wanted to severely agitate and confuse Roger as a bonus.

He bought the real camera. Even splurged for an upscale edition which could broadcast to both his laptop and a concealed hard drive near the device.

The mounting went easy, aside from Roger's exhaustion-based hand-tremors and one quest through the wet evening grass for a dropped screw. Then he drilled a slightly larger hole through the siding into the attic and ran the camera lines into the house.

He hadn't been in the attic since they bought the place, years ago, when he'd decided to save on handyman charges and box some improperly insulated electric splices by himself. He didn't remember much from that adventure, other than wishing he'd worn a mask after stirring up all the insulation, and regretting the moment when he un-hunched just enough to drive the point of a rusty roofing nail into his back. The moment after that nail went in he pictured Oprah in his mind, yelling, "*You're all getting . . . TETANUS SHOTS!*"

He wasn't a fan of the attic, but he was ready with a headlamp and dust mask this time, so up he went. He'd have an electric eye beaming down on his backyard by midnight. Anybody made it past the brambles and the sharp elevated fencing and the drill-proof locks, they'd be right there under Big Brother's gaze, exposed for the bullshit creepers they were.

The attic: exposed beams and insulation, trapped heat and tubing and years of suspect electrical modifications. Spiders ruled the far corners, and the old wood framing seeped sap which looked like blooms of mold or clusters of frozen blood droplets. The ceilings in the house were high and the attic was squat, which meant that Roger had to slide or crawl to get anywhere. At some point in the life of the house someone had run plywood across a couple of pathways, but not enough to get Roger over to the rear of the property so he could finish bringing in the camera wires. That meant there'd be a long section where he'd have to do a combination push-up/crawl under the rafters until he made it all the way back, his hands and feet balanced on the attic beams.

The only way out is through. Let's get to it.

He stayed low, shaking with fatigue, and did his best to dodge splinters, nails, and plumes of lung-seeking insulation. Spider webs and long tendrils of drifting dust clung to his sweaty face. For a second he thought he saw a spider about to drop from his headlamp to his nose, and in the effort to brush it away he slammed a shoulder into the drywall beneath him.

Great! Fucking great! Yeah, honey, I got the property secured, but I also fell through the ceiling trying to wave away a spider. Hope you don't mind the insulation in the bed. We can pretend this is the skylight you always wanted.

When he finally made his way back to the newly drilled hole and threaded in the remainder of the camera line, he found it was actually quite easy to hook up the dedicated hard drive and tap into the electric line.

He almost had the camera wired in when he heard something on the roof.

There was a slow scrape, followed by something slamming down.

Drag . . . THUMP. Drag . . . THUMP. Drag . . . THUMP.

The final thump fell on the roof above his head. Fragments of sap and insulation drifted down onto his hair. Roger froze.

He was still trying to decide between remaining entirely immobile and speed-crawling out of the attic to pursue whoever was on his property, when he heard the unmistakable sound of a man's laughter.

What?

And then a white light was born behind his eyes and there was pressure and pain and then nothing at all.

HE WOKE IN THE dark with dusty insulation coating his mouth. The taste reminded him of when he'd helped demolish an old barn on his Grandpa Dave's property, after he'd passed and they were prepping his property for sale. Everyone had been crying that day, but Roger was young and had barely known the old man, and was mainly excited they'd given him a sledgehammer and the right to use it. They didn't worry about things like black mold back then. They got the job done. But in retrospect it made sense to Roger that he'd had a chest cold for about three months after they tore down that rotten old barn.

Without light to orient him, Roger spent a moment thinking he was in his bed. Only after something crawled across the back of his neck did he realize he was still in the attic.

Christ!

He slapped the back of his neck and felt an immediate, sharp jab as something crunched under his glove.

Should have brushed it off, idiot! You just slapped yourself into a nice old spider bite. Great. And my lamp's out. I have to get back to the garage and grab a flashlight. Finish this wiring. Then I HAVE to go to bed. I'm cooked.

Roger turned around and started to crouch-crawl toward the dim, distant light coming from the attic access point in his office.

Damn. I wish this fucking thing . . .

He slapped the side of his headlamp once, then twice, and something in the jostling set the batteries straight and light came flooding out across the sea of insulation before him.

It was then that he saw the bodies.

Dozens of dead birds. Tiny, desiccated. Some with their talons turned toward the sky, others curled in on themselves. Some with eyes missing. Some with eyes dried and hollow but still shining back as the light struck them. A field of them, each a few inches apart from the other, their corpses floating on insulation, entwined in the fiberglass.

He heard a rustling sound behind him and turned his lamp to see another tiny bird struggling to lift its body and fly away with its one remaining good wing.

Roger felt the bite on the back of his neck.

Not a bite. It pecked me as I crushed it.

But how did all these birds get in? And why didn't I see . . .

Roger almost finished the question but knew that there was no reason to be pursued here. Something wrong was happening—staring at it wouldn't aid survival but might induce some kind of paralysis.

Wait. Wasn't there something on the roof?

No. That's insane. Jesus, man. Get your shit straight.

Got to clean up this die-off before it smells. I'll look for the hole in the siding where they got in later. Then finish the camera hook-up. Claire and Julie are coming back! And I could really use another beer.

He did his best not to think again for the rest of the night, to let motion remove reflection, and so he cleaned the wound on his neck and gathered all of the corpses in the attic in a white plastic work bucket and set it out on the patio. And once he'd finally powered up the security camera and ensured it was running properly, he headed back out to the patio to grab the bucket of dead birds.

He lifted the rusty metallic lid to the fire pit in their backyard and dumped in the bodies, watching loose feathers drift down onto the pile of ash-covered dead. Then he sprayed them with an entire bottle of lighter fluid and dropped a match and tended the blaze long enough to ensure that all of the tiny hollow bones were rendered to nothing.

Once the pyre was embers, Roger turned and walked back to the office and deleted the last two hours of security footage because none of this had ever happened, and that was fine.

III.

"I KNOW, I KNOW. I miss you guys too. There's a little more work to this than I expected. You guys camp out for one more night and then we'll have all weekend to hang out."

And I need a little more distance between you and the last two days, so you don't look at Daddy and see he's losing his mind. One more day and we'll be alright.

In the end Claire acquiesced, though she was slow to make the call and Roger was certain she was worried about him now. But he'd promised to drive down with Mr. Grubbins and Julie's favorite blanket to join them for dinner, so he knew if he could spruce up by then he would set Claire at ease. He'd shave the beginnings of the wolfman beard creeping up his cheeks, take a much-needed shower, and wear a nice long sleeve shirt to cover up his lacerated arms.

Things would be good.

ACCOUNTS CLOSED—NO SUSPICIOUS TRANSACTIONS identified, thank god. New accounts opened, cards issued. New checks ordered— "Have them shipped to the branch and give me a call when they show up." Social Security Number, birthday, and mother's maiden name provided over and over again to a variety of bored call center employees. Equifax/Transunion/Experian notified to place a permanent "Fraud Alert" on their systems to shut down attempts at identity theft. Credit monitoring account established and hard copies of all reports pulled and reviewed. Passwords changed for eighty-three goddamn internet accounts.

There was not enough coffee and music and sunshine in the world to make that morning feel like anything other than some kind of modern circle in Dante's Inferno.

"And here we see the poorest of souls, guilty of the sin of being burgled."

"But how is this a sin? Shouldn't it be the thieves who suffer so?"

"No, this is what is owed to these souls, who imagined a fanciful kind of safety was owed to them and chose to live in a tapestry of lies which denied the

true balance of the world. These are souls who ignored the evils of our kind and by doing so allowed it to flourish."

"And to verify I'm speaking with the correct person, sir, could you please provide your Social Security Number?"

"And to verify I'm speaking with the correct person, sir, could you please lean toward your webcam for a brief retinal scan?"

"And to verify I'm speaking with the correct person, sir, could you please write your earliest shameful memory on fine vellum and send it to me via certified mail?"

"And to verify I'm speaking with the correct person, sir . . . "

ROGER WAS FINALLY SITTING down to what he was certain would be a long and arduous call with his insurance company when he heard a knock at the front door.

He sped to the foyer—ready to explain the meaning of his NO SOLICITING sign to those mouth-breathing CenturyLink reps for the third goddamn time—and was surprised to find a diminutive, old-timey cowboy on his stoop.

The man stood all of five-and-a-half feet, even with brown leather boots on, and was wearing a golden belt buckle so big it could have been a buffet plate. His perfectly-waxed white moustache came to a sharpened-pencil point on each side and stood in stark contrast to the deep leather wrinkles which gave his face a look of permanent concern.

The man removed his cowboy hat and held it to his chest.

"Sorry to bother you, Roger. My name's Clem Tillson. I'm a neighbor of yours from a few blocks over on 17th. I got your little note on my doorstep this morning and I have some concerns."

Roger looked at him and waited for the concerns to begin.

Damn it! Did I just invite every retiree in the neighborhood over for a stop-and-chat? I can't deal with that shit right now.

"Shoot, Roger. It's cold out here. I can tell from your face you think I might be in my dotage and looking to run my mouth. That ain't it. I promise. We need to talk about this, and I'm hoping you might be the sort of fella'd be kind enough to offer me a beer and your ears for a spell."

Something about the look on the old man's face told Roger he was sincere, and the smell of Brylcreem from his slicked-back gray mop reminded him of his own grandfather. Aside from that, the sound of Clem's voice—clear and unencumbered by the hisses and clicks of a call being recorded for quality control purposes—made Roger feel human and a little less than crazy for the first time in days. Maybe it'd be good for him to take a little break. He'd earned it.

"Sure, Clem. Come on in."

"NOT TO SOUND UNGRATEFUL, but you happen to have any Budweiser? Or Milwaukee's Best? This fancy stuff tends to write me a one way ticket to Nap Town." Clem handed his smoked porter back to Roger.

"Mirror Pond's the lightest thing I got. It's a regular ale."

"Sounds about right."

Roger popped the tops off two ales and handed one to Clem. He slid a batch of insurance docs toward the center of the table and offered the old man a seat at the end.

"Great family space you have here."

"Yeah. This table is old school. It's giant. I've got an extra leaf for it out in the garage. I think it's from 1918, but who knows? My wife finds this kind of stuff at the Goodwill. She's got a sixth sense about bargains."

"You happen to have a coaster? Wouldn't want to leave a beer ring on your wood."

"Oh, sure." Roger had a stash of promotional coasters from beer festivals stored above the fridge. Coaster off the top promised that Hammertown's Double IPA would deliver a Lethal Dose of Hops. He handed Clem the cardboard disc and then sat down at the table.

"Thanks, pard."

"You're welcome."

Pard?

The room went quiet. Clem tapped the base of his beer on his coaster a few times and took a deep breath. Roger looked over at his insurance docs and imagined the hours he still needed to spend on the phone. "You said you have some concerns?"

"Sure. Sure I do. Only thing is, when you get to be an older fella, you kinda learn to pick what they call an 'angle of attack' when you have something important to say. Otherwise people have a real easy time writing you off."

"Yeah, that's too bad. I think we'd be better off if we would . . ."

"Listen to your elders? No, that ain't true either. Trust me, I've got plenty of friends my age that haven't had a new thing worth saying for years now. That's why we mostly fish and drink and sit there quiet. Maybe play some cribbage. No, don't listen to me because I'm old. Listen to me because I used to be the county sheriff, and I understand a particular malady that's gripped this area for too long."

"I'm all ears, Clem."

"Well . . . there's a house. It's right over by me, on 17th, across from my place and down two, right next to that big beige foursquare McMansion thing they built last year, that don't fit the look of the neighborhood at all."

"Okay."

"And I need you to know that this house, and the folks who live there . . . well, pardon my language, but if this side of town had an official 'Department of Fucked Up Shit,' then the headquarters would be right damn there."

Great. Gramps has some old beef with his neighbors and now he's trying to drag me into it.

"Clem, what's any of that have to do with me? You think the people who live there are the ones who broke into my house?"

"I do."

"Did you see something? This could be great! Did you see them carrying stuff into their house on the night of the burglary? Maybe a really big TV that looked like the one over there in the living room?"

"Nope. Didn't see a thing like that. But a couple of nights ago it was a full moon, wasn't it?"

No wonder this guy's making me feel sane. He's fucking Looney Tunes senile.
"A full moon? I, uh . . ."

"Roger, I can see I'm losing you. Maybe I chose the wrong angle here. So forget the moon thing. And did I mention their tunnels?"

"No."

"Okay. Well imagine I never said that either. Damn. It's never easy to talk about this."

"What are we even talking about?"

"We're talking about a house where I see people go in, but never, ever come out. Or I see people leave and they come back wearing the same clothes but not the same face. And some nights there's a purple shimmer over the place—"

"Clem, I'm sorry, but I'm going to have to ask you to go now. I've still got a lot of clean-up left to do around the house."

"Night they busted in, you get any kind of weird headaches or earaches?"

Roger had almost forgotten the way the pressure had built in his head the previous night, how it had been followed by phantom conversations, and the appearance of those bodies in the attic. He couldn't hide the truth on his face. He flinched. Clem's eyes lit up.

"I knew it! I'm telling you, Roger, I'm not crazy. They have ways. We watch those sonofabitches all the time and they're always changing how things work."

"'We'?"

"Oh, ah . . . royal we, I guess." Clem held his beer out and looked at the label. "This is definitely hitting me faster than a Bud." But Roger couldn't help but notice that the old man's eyes were sharp and his speech never slurred.

"Maybe I should call back the cops. You want to talk to them—maybe leave out the stuff about the moon and tunnels—and tell them you think you know who hit my place? It's possible that they were the ones that broke in, and if the cops pay them a visit, maybe we can put this whole thing to rest."

"I wish. I *wish*. I gave up calling the cops on them a while back. Even my old friends on the force were getting impatient with me.

Getting old's the worst. But I've suspected it's them whenever a house in our area gets robbed. There's a nasty smell that comes from their place too. Like blood sizzling on a hot plate."

Roger wondered how Clem would even recognize that smell, then remembered he'd once been a sheriff and decided not to venture the question.

"I think they're making drugs in there too and venting it right out of the damn side through the dryer exhaust. They don't even try to hide because *nothing sticks*. I managed to record enough footage of comings and goings to help get a search warrant drafted. They found all kinds of chemicals, but nothing that made sense. Nothing that'd make the street drugs you'd expect. Then, after there was that rash of dog killings—maybe that was before your time out here—I worked with some other folks in the neighborhood, Susie Jenkins who's a realtor and Dan Rostrum who's a banker, to see if we could do some kind of workaround and get the house foreclosed. Hell, they'd nailed Dan's dog Chester to the tree in his front yard . . . no eyes . . . nothing left inside that poor mutt . . . "

"Holy shit."

"*Un*holy shit, you ask me. But again, nothing stuck. Get this—*nobody* owns that property. Not really. Somebody owned it once, sure." Clem pointed at nothing with the neck of his beer bottle, as if to say, *This is the only reasonable fact I can state.* "But after the banking crash, the original deed of trust got passed from bank to bank and then whichever one was supposed to have had it last couldn't even find a scanned copy in their files. Not even the damn county can find their version. Somebody services their property tax with cash once a year, so we can't get 'em that way, and there's no viable documentation to force a regular foreclosure. City even says they have some kind of damn 'squatter's rights.' Since when does a dug-in tick have fucking rights?"

Clem set down his beer with a hollow clunk. He'd drained it. Roger offered him another.

"No. That's kind of you, but I'm good. One more beer for me will turn into all the beers for the rest of the day. Took me eighty-some years but I finally learned to accept that about myself. Besides, I need to be clear in what I'm telling you next. I need you to really listen to me."

Roger leaned forward and made eye contact. He was still unsettled that Clem knew about his strange fugue state headaches. And he hated to admit it, but the more he listened, the more he could reconcile the last few days with the world around him.

"Something about your note . . . forgive my saying so, but you sure seemed scared, and angry, and right away I thought to myself, 'They're playing with him.'"

Roger remembered the laughter he'd heard on the night of the burglary, the feeling that someone was enjoying his terrified reaction as he'd fled the house. Still, Officer Hayhurst said that some criminals did extra shit like that for kicks. It didn't mean he was part of some ongoing harassment.

"How do you know it's them? Couldn't it be a standard-issue crime? They got my wife's best jewels."

"First, that kind of thing really *doesn't* happen all the way out here. I mean, this is the city in name only—most of your regular criminal element can't deal with the inconvenience of getting all the way to the boonies. Why do you think I chose to retire out here? Cops know where the pits are, and where things are mostly nice. No, this little enclave, it's a good place. Aside from that one house. Second, though, I responded to thousands of burglaries in my day and I know this wasn't your regular old bash-and-dash because now I've seen your face. That's what I had to come over to confirm. You *really* want to tell me this feels normal to you?"

Roger's lips sealed tight. He thought of the dead birds in his attic. *Had that even happened?* His brow furrowed and he took a deep breath and shook his head from side to side:

No. No. No.

"Okay. So you *are* hearing me."

"I have to, Clem. Listen . . . I think they're threatening my family. They messed with a picture of my daughter and I. And everything that happened the night of the burglary felt . . . wrong. There was a handprint left behind, and it was missing a pinkie."

Clem's eyebrows raised at that, but he said nothing.

"Okay then. Thank you for being honest with me. This is good. Because if I know they're targeting you, and you believe me about that, then maybe you have a chance to do the right thing."

"What's the right thing?"

"Nothing at all."

"That's cute, Clem. Maybe ale really isn't for you."

"Not joking. Not drunk. Never cute, young man. Now you look me right in my fucking eyes." There was a new electricity emanating from the old man. He was still sitting in his chair but he'd tensed up, coiled and wiry. Looked ready to beat his message into Roger if he had to. "They're interested in you. Why? I don't know. Never understood how they pick their targets. But this is bad, truly *bad*, and I'm sorry to you and your family that you've wandered into this. I've watched this happen before. Watched them target someone in this neighborhood and drive them fast as they could in the wrong directions. I've seen people, good people, walk into that house and never come back out. Not really come back out anyways. And that's not going to happen to you. You're not going to give them what they want."

"But what do they want?"

"Hell if I know. I gave up on trying to understand the devil a long time ago. You just gotta steer clear. They'll try to use your anger, or your curiosity, against you. How do you think human beings found out which foods were poisonous and which ain't? How many poor fellas died clutching their guts on the way to that know-how? The cost ain't always worth it. So I'm *telling* you—that house, and the people who live there, the whole damn situation is as poisonous as they come. You don't need to know what you're dealing with. You only need to get away."

"We only bought this place three years ago. Claire will never . . ."

"She will. Lots of folks feel like moving after a break-in anyway. It's natural. Start there. Or, hell, we're close to the interstate . . . tell her you're worried about the air quality. Don't know your wife, or what would sway her. That's on you."

"Moving's out of the question. This is crazy. Assuming what you're saying is true, or even a little bit of it is, there has to be something else this neighborhood can do to drive them out. What if we got the whole community together? Like every last one of us, and we had a town hall meeting, and we focus on the fact that there's a house right under our noses where the tenants might be involved in theft and drug manufacturing and animal mutilation, to say the least."

"I tried that, a couple of times. The folks around here are mostly retired, and not just from working. Loads of 'em gave up giving a shit about anything that don't directly affect them. Hell, I've tried most things I can think of, aside from setting that damn house on fire."

"But I feel like—"

"Stop feeling here, Roger. *Think.* Think about you and your wife and your child, and get out of here."

Roger's exhaustion and confusion finally set in. He slumped his head into his open palms.

"Fuck. This is crazy."

"I'm sorry. I've pushed you too fast. But I think you're hearing me, and I hope you'll make the right decision. I know this is a lot to absorb. Nobody wants to be uprooted, especially if they feel like they're being a coward. But you have to understand that you won't be running away. You'll be running toward a real future."

"I'm no coward, Clem."

"Never said you were."

Roger remembered Officer Hayhurst: *You were so easily penetrated.*

These men didn't understand that Roger could handle things when the chips were down. It could be that running away wasn't the answer at all. Maybe there was only one real method for dealing with criminal assholes like the ones this tiny old man had come to warn him about.

Roger straightened his shoulders and leaned toward Clem. "You mentioned setting the place on fire. And that's *insane*, I know it, but what if . . . maybe there's some way, hypothetically . . . maybe we get a group of like-minded guys together late one night and we pay that house a visit and make it really clear that those bastards can't live there anymore."

Clem held Roger's gaze for a moment and frowned.

"Shit. They're already drawing you in." Clem ran a hand over his slicked back gray hair and sighed for a moment before looking back at Roger. "I know we just met, but . . . I worked with the law long enough to get a read on folks, and I don't think you're the kind of hard man that runs around at midnight issuing threats."

Roger crossed his arms over his chest. "You don't know me, Clem."

"No, but I've talked to you long enough. What I'm saying isn't meant to insult. World needs more kindhearted men. Lord knows we've got more than our share of macho morons bashing around. Besides, the kind of ugliness you're talking about is just what they want. The violence. The conflict. Devils love a good game. They *love* to get you outside your own head. So, no, Roger, there aren't going to be any old-fashioned lynchings down at Doc Frankenstein's place."

Roger stared at Clem, then past him.

Telling me to stand down. It wasn't his goddamn house that got broken into. It's not his wife waiting in another city to hear that everything is safe again. You want to help me, old man? Help me take care of the motherfuckers who did this to my life.

"Christ, Rog. I've seen that look in your eyes before. Don't go thinking some moral upper hand gives your anger any more power. I had a friend, once, had that look in his eyes all the time. I don't like to talk about what happened to him, but I think it's clear you need to hear his story. Can you stop mad-dogging me first?"

The old man smiled and held his palms up, facing Roger.

Fuck. I'm acting like an asshole. This guy, crazy or not, is just trying to help.

Roger laughed and shook his head. "Clem . . . I'm sorry. It's been really intense, the last couple of days."

"Fair enough. Fair enough. And thanks. So . . . my friend. Name of J. P. Schumacher. Good guy, solid as they come. If they had a factory for righteous dudes, Jason P. Schumacher would have been the prototype. I knew him when we were brothers on the force, back when we all called him 'Spud' 'cause he brought a baked potato for lunch every day."

"Clem . . . "

"Forgive me. It's how an old man's memory works, plowing through the garbage to find the rest. Anyway, he worked vice with me for a while before he took another tack—got married, had a kid, went back to school and pursued a judgeship. He said the bench was better for him. That once he had a family he couldn't handle some of the shit we saw out on the streets. But the truth was that even behind the bench it all still stuck in his craw. He'd never learned to let it go, or drink it away at least. And then he had a case that went sideways in his court and a fuck-up in the chain of evidence puts some repeat kiddie fucker back on the street."

"Goddamn."

"Yeah . . . . So one evening a week later J. P. decided that court was still in session. Bought a pistol, put down the short eyes like a rabid dog."

Roger nodded. Fuck. Yes.

"You're thinking he made the right call. Part of me feels that way too. But the moment he decided to pull that trigger he signed his own death warrant. He exposed himself *and* his family to something he didn't fully understand. Turns out the pedo had been mobbed up and running a film line for a crew out of Ukraine. Now Ol' 'Spud' had put a kink in their money. He fucked up their production sched-ule. So what do you think they did in return?"

"They killed him, yeah? But at least he got one of those bastards off the streets."

"Oh, they killed him. After everything else. After raping his wife in front of him and stomping in her face. After force-feeding him shards of glass and trussing him and running a white-hot fire poker up his ass."

"But they didn't get his daughter?"

"Well, we never found her. So maybe they introduced her to their film business. Which means maybe they killed her once she no longer proved useful, or maybe she overdosed on the shit they use to keep those kids docile. Either way, she was in hell. Might still be there for all we know. And all because J. P. Schumacher thought the righteousness of his anger was a shield. He charged into a world he couldn't understand, and it destroyed everything he loved."

Clem stood up, letting out a low moan as he rose. He lifted his cowboy hat from the table, and slid it onto his head.

"I'm so sorry to be the bearer of bad news, Roger. I hope that later in your life you'll be able to look back and thank me for it. You choose to stay, you try to fight them, try to force some kind of order . . . it won't stick. Okay? They don't have the same laws. Not so sure they have any laws at all. The only truth that matters is that you need to get you and your family as far from here as you can."

Roger's head had fallen back into his hands. Clem patted him on the back.

"Yeah. I know, buddy. It's a shitter, no doubt. And thanks again for the beer. I'll show myself out."

IV.

CRAZY OLD COWBOY.

He thought it and did his best to believe it, to no avail. Fact was, the things Clem told him put Roger's feet back on solid ground for the first time since he'd discovered the crime.

You call what you're on right now 'solid ground'? You're just happy to find some doddering old man as crazy as you are. How do you know this isn't some form of mass psychosis? Maybe the stained-glass factory a few blocks away let off a bunch of toxic plumes again . . .

Clem's little talk had eaten up Roger's chance to call the insurance company, and he'd barely had time to shave and give himself a whore's bath with a washcloth before bolting out the door to deliver Julie's plush toy and blanket. He'd slicked back his hair with a wet comb and hoped the wind through the open truck window would help it dry before he saw the girls.

God, I miss them.

He wanted to be fully present for Claire and Julie by the time he arrived, but he couldn't help obsessing on things Clem had said.

"You're not going to give them what they want."

But what could they want from him?

Clem mentioned drug manufacturing. Was there even the *slightest* chance that someone in that house knew about Roger's time in Oakland? How dumb and reckless he'd been, and how much he'd risked for . . . what?

Money?

Partly that. Partly the thrill. Knowing he was doing the wrong thing. Knowing he didn't even need to be trafficking—his college tuition had already been covered and with his work-study job and credit cards he could have managed everything else. But Claire liked fancy restaurants and cruises and how he had a big new truck when most college boys were still driving the busted old sedans they got when they turned sixteen. And her friends loved how he kept an open tab and bought round after round of champagne when they were at the club. It had been easy to win Claire's interest and her friends' endorsement, and he truly adored her.

But he didn't tell her, until much later, about coming through LAX with a thirty-year-sentence worth of ecstasy jammed up his ass. She barely knew about the time a regular buy turned sour and he found out he was capable of violence when threatened (though even the memory of him and Bobby S. kicking Kenny Liedke's curled-up body and bloodied face turned his stomach and crept into his dreams). And he certainly never told her about the long, terrifying shipment run he made to Utah and back, how he'd never buckled his seatbelt once because he knew that if he heard sirens he'd have to take his own life in a fiery car crash. He couldn't stand the idea of being caught—he knew the gravity of what he was doing and he sure as shit knew that his reasons for doing it were childish at best. What shame, to have your devil-may-care attitude turn into a devil on your back? He'd rather have died than face his parents and say, "You raised me right and I still did all this dumb shit and I barely even know why."

Then he and Bobby S. got robbed and beat by a batch of kids with hatchets, and Roger suffered a cracked vertebrae. Doctors told him he narrowly avoided paralysis. Shortly after that Wilson straight-up *disappeared* and Roger knew it was time to cut and run and never look back. He dodged a multi-pack meetup that turned out to be a bust, but everyone who got clipped was higher up in the operation than him, so he couldn't imagine them bothering to roll on his name. But he *could* imagine them thinking he'd been the one who rolled. That night he told Claire that he was in trouble and she told him that she wasn't some naïve Kansas farm girl and that she'd long-guessed what he was up to. In fact, she kind of liked it. That he was crazy.

He'd bailed north and couch-surfed with friends. Grabbed an easy gig as a lab courier and waited for the other shoe to drop. Claire finished her semester and moved up to join him in a little apartment he'd scored for them on the outskirts of town.

He felt so lucky to discover that she still loved him when he wasn't crazy. That she'd agree to marry him when he was just another schmo with a nine-to-five.

Roger had been waiting a long time for his past to finally catch up with him, but it felt more distant each year and eventually he guessed that the statute of limitations had passed on the ugliness of his early twenties and he decided he was ready to be a father.

Claire was six months pregnant when Roger's parents had died in a terrible RV accident outside of Sedona. It crushed him. But he secretly felt a sense of relief: They'd never found out. No matter what happened from then on, they would never know.

Then Julie was born and it shifted the hands of the clock forward, past the time when he was ashamed, past the time where all he could do was grieve, forward to a time where he realized that his past was behind him, and he could be pretty much anyone he wanted to be.

And now, for some reason, it was possible that someone was trying to drag him back to that old, bad place.

*Why? Is this really some game? Couldn't it be that somebody actually wanted
a fast way to come up on a TV and some jewelry?*

"Night they busted in, you get any kind of weird headaches or earaches?"

*How could Clem have known about that? And why did everything he said
feel so true?*

Roger needed more time to figure things out.

He made the blanket and plush drop off at the in-laws in time—
he had to blink back tears when Julie pushed right past the Mr.
Scrubbins toy he was holding out and jumped into his arms—and
let Claire know that he wouldn't be able to join them for dinner.

"You're sure?"

"I'll grab a burrito on the way back."

"No, not just about dinner. You sure you should be headed back
there? Maybe a night with us would be good for you. You look kind
of . . . *rough.*" She smiled, but it was slight. "Or maybe we should
pack in and come home with you."

"No!" He'd nearly yelled at her. Damn it.

Well done, buddy.

"Oh . . . okay."

"No, I'm sorry. Don't know why I said it like that. I really want
the place to be dialed when you guys come back, and the dining
room is still a blowout. I have to call insurance in the morning.
Besides, I thought I might surprise Julie and have a big LEGO set
waiting for her in her room. Something nice to help her feel comfortable coming back."

"Oh, she'd love that."

"Yeah. So give me one more night to take care of everything and
we'll all hang out tomorrow. I promise."

"Okay." Her smile widened. "You sure you don't have your mis-
tress over? We've been gone a *long* time." She always joked with him
about infidelity. It felt like a show of power from her—he figured she
knew deep down he was like a rescue dog she'd saved and that he'd
be forever faithful.

"Damn it, you've got me figured. She flew in from Brazil and we still have half the Kama Sutra to work through before you can come back."

"Well, better get back to it, chief. I know what you're really up to anyway. The bank called me today to authorize a bunch of your changes. Said I had to sign off since I'm the primary on the account. Hold on, Julie has something she wanted to give you."

Roger crouched to see what she had in her hands. Some kind of abstract LEGO creation. She made these tiny things all the time and declared them to be fascinating, complex contraptions.

"It's a Robber Die-erator, daddy. This is the sensor, see, this little yellow part, and it shoots out lasers and if any robbers come in and the sensor sees them then they get lasered in half and they die. So they can't take away our things anymore! Do you love it?"

"I do, Jules. It's awesome. Thank you so much!"

"You take it home with you, okay? It'll keep you safe!"

"That's perfect. I'll put it right in my pocket."

He spent another ten minutes trying to say goodbye without really being able to leave. Finally, Claire's mom shouted out to the condo parking lot that dinner was ready, and he had to let them go. Once she confirmed that Julie was back inside Claire ran over to Roger and grabbed him and gave him a long, slow kiss. She looked him in the eyes as she pulled away and said, "Thank you for doing all this, baby. You're the best." And in that moment he felt like that was true—that he was doing right by her, despite the cost. He felt like a good man.

HE WAS HALFWAY HOME, doing his best to focus on the shiny, rain-slicked road, when he hit a rut and his rear tires exploded.

The truck fish-tailed. Roger tried to compensate and apply the brakes slowly enough to keep from heading into a spin. The rear of the truck made an awful grinding noise that vibrated his teeth as he slowed. Then he veered right too early, and only narrowly avoided the chariot spikes of a neighboring semi-truck's front tires as he swerved back into the middle lane. Once the behemoth passed he managed to hobble to a narrow shoulder and bring the truck to a stop. Even with the windows closed he could smell the noxious smoke of metal on asphalt.

Fucking Christ, you're kidding me!

One tire and he would have slapped on the spare and gimped home. Two, though, meant he was immobilized. He put in a call to AAA and let them know his make and model and that he would need two fresh tires.

Twenty minutes later help arrived and had the rear of the truck jacked up. The Incident Response driver was busy removing the blown-out remnants of rubber when he called Roger over.

"Any chance you work construction, pal?"

The man held up a swatch from one of the busted radials. In the headlights of the rescue truck, it was easy to spot all the screws embedded in the rubber.

Motherfuckers.

"Actually, both tires are like this. Whatever day crew you're paying for site clean-up, you might want to dock their pay or give 'em some better magnet sticks."

"I don't work construction."

"Oh. You do any house projects recently?"

"No."

"Well, who knows then? I chucked those junkers in the back of your truck, for whatever they're worth. Your front tires looked clear for screws, far as I could see. Those new ones'll get you back on the road but you might want to park somewhere different tonight until you get a chance to check your driveway."

"Sure. Thank you. You need me to sign anything?"

"No. We're all good. Drive safe."

Roger got back in the truck, furious.

"Devils love a good game. They love to get you outside your head."

He pounded the steering wheel with clenched fists until he could see straight.

They almost killed me.

He composed himself. Started the engine. Found his water bottle lodged under his seat. Looked to the floor mat in front of the passenger seat at something scattered there. Hit the dome lights.

The Robber Die-erator. It'd flown from his jacket pocket and crashed to the floor, bright plastic pieces in disarray.

"You take it home with you, okay? It'll keep you safe!"

He had no idea how to put it back together.

SURE ENOUGH, THERE WAS a profusion of tiny silver screws glinting back at Roger from the lower half of his driveway. He parked next to the curb between his and the neighbor's house and got out for a closer look.

The screws were sharp and short and it looked like a whole contractor's box had been emptied behind his truck.

It's attempted murder, if you think about it. This is insane. Claire and Julie can't come back as long as things are like this. It's bad enough they're doing this shit to me. I'll lose my mind if they try anything with the girls.

Roger entered the house, relieved to find the interior hadn't been gutted—*Think of the positives!*—and grabbed a push broom and red metal dustpan.

I'm keeping all of those screws. That's evidence. This is a case now.

Some other part of his mind said, *This isn't a case. It's a game you shouldn't play. They're trying to get to you. Clem's right. You want to end up like J. P. Schumacher?*

He took pictures of the evidence with his phone before he swept and bagged it. Then he pulled the truck into its spot, slumped into the house, ate a half-cooked frozen burrito while standing in the kitchen, and staggered to bed.

He was surprised at how quickly he passed out. The room was stuffier than he wanted it to be, but with Roger's upgrades it now took an act of congress to actually get the windows open, so instead he simply threw off one of the comforters and slid into a much-needed sleep.

EXCEPT: THERE CAME A knock at the front door.

A single knock, thunderous, threatening to crack the wooden door from its frame.

Roger jolted awake, run through with a shock of adrenaline.

It's them.

This is how it's always going to be here, from now on, every single night. Any noise will be the end of the world. Everything will be them.

He ran to the front door, stopping only to grab his baseball bat from the dining room. Then he cursed himself for not installing a peephole. He couldn't throw the door open, not without knowing who was behind it and why their knock might have shaken the house through its frame.

He hopped the sectional couch in the living room and peeked through the slats of the front window shade.

Nothing. Nobody.

He waited, half-expecting a sudden piercing headache to flare up.

Nothing.

Was it the wind? A tree branch that finally fractured and slammed the front door on its way down? Kids out night-knocking for cheap thrills?

Clem really got to you. Maybe he's right, and there's a purple light floating around the neighborhood, hoping to claim the first poor soul that answers its knock. Or maybe it's one of his face-changing squatters trying to provoke you to do the wrong thing. Or maybe it's fucking Santa Claus, lost and looking for directions back to the North Pole. Christ, Rog, you've officially lost it.

Or maybe you were just dreaming. Did you ever stop to think of that? Go back to bed.

So he did.

EXCEPT: THE ALARM ON his truck went off.

Goddamn it!

He checked the clock on his bed stand. He'd only been out forty minutes.

Within seconds he had on his jeans and long-sleeved shirt. He slid into a pair of canvas slip-ons in the foyer, grabbed his truck keys and his bat, and charged out into the driveway, heedless of the tremulous knock which had fallen on the front door a short time ago.

His truck headlights flashed on and off. The alarm whooped until he could figure out which worn button on his key fob actually shut off the damn thing.

All the doors were closed. All the windows were intact.

Roger was still wondering what had triggered the alarm when he heard someone charge over the hedgerow in his neighbor's yard and bolt out into the street.

He didn't have to think, because it was night and someone had been terrorizing him and he had a bat in his hands. Claire had told him he was the best and that made him feel strong, like he was ready to put an end to things. He gave chase.

The figure was tall, lean, clad in white pants and a long black hoodie. And they were fast. Roger hadn't run in months, and he felt the beginnings of a beer belly jostle as he pounded the pavement. If he couldn't close the distance, he hoped he could at least keep them in his sightline to see where they went.

They made it to the end of 14th and the would-be truck-jacker gave no sign of slowing.

He's turning left, toward 17th. Maybe I can catch him out front of the house by Clem's and give him enough of a scare to make those fuckers back off.

They crested the peak of the street. The road dropped down into a valley and Roger tried to take longer strides, to find some way to let gravity help him catch this son of a bitch and put an end to the whole mess.

It was no use. Whoever it was, they were too fast.

Roger yelled, "Hey, asshole!" hoping the distraction might slow them, or provoke whoever it was into turning around. No use. As if spooked by the sound, the figure suddenly veered right and hopped a neighbor's fence on 16th.

Damn. Damn. Damn.

Roger made it to the fence, but knew he wouldn't follow. He wasn't about to risk entering someone else's property and getting shot for the trespass. He didn't even know if he had the energy left to hop it.

Was this all some kind of a trap? Is that what they wanted? For me to chase them all the way out here?

There was a foul smell coming from the fence where they'd cleared it in a single easy vault. Roger stepped closer and squinted, and that's when he saw the dark handprints left behind.

The smudged prints were shining in the moonlight. They were shifting, dripping slowly downward. Blood? Black oil?

Roger watched the prints slug trail their way down the wood fence for a moment, disturbed by the musky animal scent that hit his nose.

He looked toward 17th, wondering if the one he'd pursued had made it back to the so-called house of horrors. *I've got to show these prints to Clem tomorrow.*

Except when Roger looked back to the fence the fluid was already fading. It almost appeared that it had seeped into the wood. The fence made a cracking noise, as if it were expanding ever so slightly as it absorbed the evidence.

"They don't even try to hide because nothing sticks."

Roger looked up at the sky and took a deep breath, then another. He was exhausted, or knew he should be at least, but he felt something. An urge to see more. To not give up the chase just yet. Maybe he could find a way to finish this.

Let's go see that house.

ONCE HE WAS ON 17th, he didn't even need to use Clem's description to find the place. Clem's house was obvious: the squat white ranch, with an old hooptie Buick sitting out front, sporting a bumper sticker which read "Support Your Local Police." Right across the street was the new and aggressively mundane beige foursquare Clem had complained about, looming over the neighboring houses.

And *there*, somehow smaller and darker than the surrounding houses, was the house at the center of the old man's stories.

At the very least, Clem was right about one thing: the building had an aura, though to Roger the purple shimmer Clem had described looked more like a mist of ultraviolet light hanging over the place, wavering like the fumes from a pit of toxic waste. Made his eyes water.

How are people not seeing this? Or are they ignoring it? Or am I imagining it because these fuckers won't let me catch a wink and Clem gave me some world class heebie jeebies?

Even without the shimmer, there were other things *off* about the house. Someone had used what appeared to be white sand or borax to draw a series of lines and circles all over the black roof shingles. Maybe it was only moss killer, but there was something about the shapes and intersecting lines that made Roger's eyes vibrate from side to side and lose resolution. He found he couldn't look straight at the place for the disorientation.

The yard itself was too perfect and clean. Grass only, a pattern without variation. Was it AstroTurf? Nobody did that here. The grass grew like crazy. But nothing *lived* in this yard. There wasn't a single growing thing to be maintained or tended. It was more the appearance of a yard than an actual human space.

The windows were dark, but it was the dead of night, so he couldn't fault them for that. Still, the vibe of the place was actively hostile. The house sat low, as if hunched, ready to spring. The breeze shifted in Roger's direction and he caught another whiff of that strange animal smell. Made him think of the time they'd had to pull a dead squirrel from their chimney. Smoke and rot.

"Ain't too pretty, is it?"

JESUS!

Roger jumped out of his bones and stopped just short of windmilling around with the baseball bat at skull level.

Clem was behind him, his white hair in disarray and swaying above his head, his shriveled body covered by light blue pajamas decorated with covered wagons. Old leather flip flops on his feet. The left side of his moustache was bent down at a right angle.

"I been checking on the place every hour or so. Wife got me a phone with a fancy alarm in it. I can keep it under my pillow and it vibrates me awake without bothering her. Once I talked to you today, I had a feeling I might still find you here tonight."

"I think you might be right about this house, Clem. They spiked my tires tonight and I almost got smeared across the interstate by a semi. And I chased a guy over here but he jumped a fence and left behind some kind of disappearing oil print."

"Huh . . . never heard of them doing that before, but like I said, they're always changing how things work. They don't seem to take our reality too seriously. I hear 'em laughing sometimes. They got an *awful* laugh."

"'Our reality'? What does that even mean? What are they, Clem?"

"Stop asking, Rog. Go home. Lock your doors, wait for daylight. Stop playing their game. Book your family one of those nice long-term suites a town over and get your realtor on the horn. Please. I'm tired. I can't keep doing this." The old man brushed his hands together in each direction. "I'm washing my mitts of this whole travesty soon. Don't make me watch them take you. Go home."

With that he turned and walked slowly back toward his house, his flip flops smacking his heels and the road in turn. Roger decided to follow him, see him in and then go home. Whether Clem was crazy or not, his kindness meant something and he didn't want to keep him out and worried in the cold.

"Night, Clem."

"Head straight home now, pardner. Don't stop for nothin'."

It was good advice. Roger followed it and made it back, hoping to finally sleep through till morning.

EXCEPT: THE DOG IN the alley wouldn't stop barking.

He tried to let it go. Let the dog bark itself out. Let him finally get some goddamn sleep. He might actually call their realtor tomorrow.

Something about that house, about the way he felt *they* were playing with him . . .

The barking grew louder. It felt like it was closer now, or coming in through an open window.

Cocksucking fucking dog. Somebody wake up and bring his mangy ass back in the house.

Nobody cared about the dog. The bark was incessant.

No sleep would be forthcoming.

Now I can't wait to move. Shitty dog owners are the worst.

The barking intensified. Panicked. Hoarse. The dog whined loudly between the rounds of frantic barking.

"Hell, they'd nailed Dan's dog Chester to the tree in his front yard."

Roger couldn't sleep. And no matter what was going on, he couldn't listen to the dog suffer if something terrible was happening. He didn't have it in him to sit through that.

He slopped into his clothes—so tired, so fatigued—grabbed his bat, and walked out the front door. He almost forgot to lock the front door behind him and had to turn back to snap the deadbolt into place.

The dog's barking was riotously loud out in the open air.

How am I the only one hearing this?

He walked toward the unpaved alley that ran by the right side of his house, where the sound was coming from. But right as he stepped into the alley, his foot crunched on gravel, and the barking came to a sudden stop.

Roger looked over his shoulder toward the center of the alley. There was a man standing still under the single streetlamp illuminating the dark stretch, facing him. The guy was huge, not like the one he'd chased earlier, and wearing the same outfit—black hoodie and white pants.

He tightened his grip on the baseball bat, and walked closer.

"Hey, you see a dog running around here?"

The man said nothing. He stood unmoving under the lamplight, staring straight at Roger and saying nothing.

It wasn't until Roger got within ten feet of him that his eyes properly adjusted and he noticed something that couldn't be real. It looked like the man's eyes were . . . missing.

No, not missing. They *shimmered* in the light. His eyes were pools of black liquid, held inside the man's face by the corroded purple light which rimmed them.

Roger stopped and began to choke up on the bat when the man smiled, opened his mouth, and began barking.

Roger turned and ran, never once looking back, gauging the distance between him and the man only by the terrible tortured dog yowling which trailed. He had his key pulled and ready before he reached the front steps, and he swore he could feel the hot breath of the man fall across his neck as he slid through the entrance and slammed the door behind him.

And then, of course, he heard laughter. It sounded like it came from one man, then many, just outside his door.

"They got an awful *laugh."*

Clem was right—it was a terrible sound, and it echoed in Roger's mind long after leaving his ears. Only once the maddening noise had ceased and the early sun began to crest did Roger manage to fall asleep with his back still pressed against the door, doing what he could to keep out whatever that had been on the other side.

V.

Fuck this. We're moving.

All Roger had to do was figure out a way to sell Claire on the whole venture without scaring her and Julie to the high heavens and/ or getting himself institutionalized. Roger couldn't spend another night living near the house on 17th. Whoever or whatever were living there, they had his number and he knew they weren't going to let things go.

He put a call in to Claire and told her he'd be coming to stay the weekend with her and Julie, assuming her mom and dad didn't mind having guests a few more nights.

"I've been here for too long, dealing with the burglary. I think it'd be good to have some time away with you guys. Maybe have some pizza and root beer floats and all that." *And then I'll have a very long, strange conversation with you at night about how we're going to sell our house and I'll be the only one going back there, and only during daylight hours, and I'll have to hope you still love my kind of crazy, at least a little bit.*

"That sounds great, babe. We're missing you pretty bad. Julie's asking a lot of questions about the burglary. She wants to know who was in our house, and how we know they won't come back in. She thinks they're after her toys, which is cute, but still . . . it kind of breaks my heart."

"Yeah. Shit . . . I'll bring the laptop tonight, look up how to talk to kids about dealing with something like this. I'm sure I can find some advice."

"Sounds good. Hey . . . what did the insurance company say? Do you know how much they're going to reimburse us for?"

Shit! I've been so busy with . . . everything. She can't know I haven't even called them yet.

"Still waiting to hear back on the claim. I'm sure they'll call soon."

"Good. Thank you so much for taking care of all this. I can't wait to see you. And when we get this mess straightened out, you and I need a *serious* date, mister."

"Oh my god. Yes. I'm barely feeling human these days. Can't wait to see you guys either."

"Okay then. Finish up and get over here."

"I will, I will. I promise. I love you."

"Love you too. See you soon!"

Roger held out his phone to thumb the End Call symbol when he heard Claire's voice start up again.

"Oh, hey, wait, babe . . . are you there?"

"Yeah."

"This is a little weird . . . I almost forgot to tell you. The other thing I was thinking for tonight was that it might be cool if we could have a slumber party and all crash together. Julie's been having these really intense nightmares. Last night she woke up screaming and she said, 'They got him.' And I asked her who and she said, 'Daddy.' Then she said something like, 'The dog man got daddy in his van and he's taking him to where they kill the doggies nobody wants.'"

"What the fuck?"

"Yeah. So I think she could *really* use some time with you. And if she stays like this at night, we might want to talk to her school and see if they recommend anybody for counseling."

Roger could barely hear her last sentence, his head flush with the surge of blood brought by new panic. *What were the odds she'd see that in her dreams? Are they manipulating her too? How did they find her?*

"Did she mention any kind of funny lights or pressure headaches or . . ." He failed to hide the alarm in his voice.

"Roger, what's wrong? What are you talking about?"

It's my fault. They want me and now they might be messing with Julie. Even once we get moved, my kid's going to have to go into counseling because of this. How are they doing this to us? Will they be able to follow us? What if Clem is wrong? What if moving changes nothing?

Roger held the phone away from his face and tried to take a calming breath before responding, but was still betrayed by a shaking in his voice. "Nothing, babe. Nothing, I swear. Just exhausted. I had some bad dreams last night too."

"You sound weird. Are you sure we shouldn't come your way and help out?"

"NO! How many times . . ."

"Jesus. You don't get to fucking yell at me, Roger. This is hard on me, too."

"I know. I *know*. I'm sorry. I just need to attack a few more things and I'll be headed your way, I swear. But I need to go."

Claire said, "Okay, fine. Go then. Get it done and come back to us. We need you more than that damn house right now." And with that she ended the call.

Roger sat down his phone with shaking hands and felt anger thrumming through his body in a way he'd never before known.

The dog man got daddy . . .

He pictured a hooded figure crouched on the roof of his in-law's house, shining something down, invading his daughter's dreams.

"You were so easily penetrated."

His jaw clenched, teeth grinding. His hands balled into fists.

"Stop feeling here, Roger. Think. Think about you and your wife and your child, and get out of here."

He pictured J. P. Schumacher—impaled on a burning steel rod, screaming through a mouthful of glass, knowing before his death that he'd killed his family.

"He charged into a world he couldn't understand, and it destroyed everything he loved."

Roger slowed his breathing and unclenched his fists and he thought: No. This is over. Daylight is wasting. My family is waiting. It's time to finish up and get the hell out of here. They'll never even know I saved all of our lives. They'll never believe me.

He pictured himself later that night at the "slumber party" in his in-laws' guest room, Claire passed out on one side of the bed, Julie sleeping peacefully between them, and he knew that none of his other concerns mattered. Not really. He'd keep a clear head, he'd close out the last details, and he'd be the man they needed him to be.

HE SURVEYED THE HOUSE, dialing down a mental list of what absolutely had to be done before he could leave.

He grabbed and bagged a handful of Julie's favorite books and plush toys.

He packed a suitcase with photos—their wedding album, Julie's Baby Book—in case anything prevented him from returning.

He shaved as fast as he could and put on the aftershave that Julie had used her Tooth Fairy money to buy him for Father's Day.

He filled a thermos with coffee to offset his sleep-deprivation, and was headed for the front door when he spotted the spread of documents on the kitchen table.

The insurance.

Fuck.

The fact that Roger had dealt with spontaneously-generating bird corpses and barking humans with black oil eyes in the last week didn't negate the fact that he still *had to* call the goddamn insurance company. Both those awful realities existed and somehow the latter felt more surreal to him. Despite the absurdity, it demanded his attention—especially if he was going to pay off the credit card binge he went on to get the house squared away. And they needed to look financially solvent if they were going to start home shopping as quickly as he wanted. And Claire thought it was already taken care of. And he didn't want to do it later—Claire and Julie didn't need to hear any more details about the burglary than absolutely necessary.

So: the insurance.

He jumped through the standard hoops, gave their agent all the info he had. She let him know that even though she was his actual agent, he'd be receiving a follow-up call from someone at the adjustment center and they'd go into greater depth regarding the items stolen and their respective values. She told him she was truly sorry for the loss his family had suffered and he guessed from her cool, even tone that she spent much of her day being "truly sorry."

What he had not guessed was how quickly he would receive the follow-up call from the claims adjustor.

"Mr. Stephenson, we seem to have a bit of an issue with the info you provided. Would you mind giving me the case number and the name of the officer you dealt with again?"

Even as he flipped Officer Hayhurst's weathered card over in his fingers and recited the info, the shitstorm of the last few days told him where this was headed.

"Yes, that's the information you gave us the first time. This is a bit strange, sir. We're having difficulty locating an officer in your city with that name, and the police department told us the number you gave is three digits short of being an actual case number. We're going to keep this claim moving, for your family's sake, but it would be very helpful if you could go back over all your records and maybe speak with the local police department to get this information clarified for us. As is, this is a bit strange. But it's common for victims to have some confusion after an event like this."

Some confusion. How about a full-fledged mental breakdown?

Roger knew there would be no clarified info forthcoming.

Had he been playing this awful game from the very goddamn moment they arrived home?

The 911 call? How did they intercept that signal? What were they using on me from the roof? Is that why they knew my name?

Hayhurst was no officer. Between the post-party buzz and the post-burglary adrenaline, I let a giant flashlight and a handful of cop props fool me entirely.

These motherfuckers. Treating me like a goddamned puppet.

As if on cue, a single solid knock rang out from the front door.

He sprinted across the room to look out on the landing from the living room window. No one there.

They've never messed with me in the light of day. Maybe I'm hearing things because of the sleep dep.

Roger opened the front door. There was something on the welcoming mat: a single opened envelope. Extended auto warranty junk mail. Nothing special about it, but the post office never would have put his mail on the doorstep. So it was them, taunting him. Always them. He looked up towards the end of his driveway.

Don't open the mailbox. They're fucking with you, daylight or not. Remember what Clem said—they're always changing the way things work. So get in your truck, and only come back to this place with a few armed friends from the mill, and only if you absolutely have to.

But he had to know, to get some sense of what they might do next. If they'd really already figured out how to find his family then moving was no guarantee anyway. Maybe there was some way to bring their fucked up game to an absolute end.

He walked to the end of his driveway, head on swivel, scanning for movement.

There *was* something in the mailbox: the photograph from his family album. Him and Julie. Father's Day a few years back. Only the picture wasn't the same anymore. Julie's eyes were swirled out with purple-black ink. Above their heads was a note:

YOUR OFFERING HAS BEEN ACCEPTED

His phone vibrated. A new text: Home soon. Jules needed a few more things from the house and we couldn't wait to see you.

The time signature on the message looked like it was sent forty-five minutes ago, which meant Claire would already be home.

How was that possible?

Is that even really from Claire?

Roger glanced back down at the vandalized photo and found he couldn't bear the sight of what they'd done to his daughter's eyes. He started to crumple the photo and that's when he noticed the writing on the back.

HEY BIG GUY
WE HAVE THEM NOW
& THEY ARE *BEAUTIFUL*
& *SO SOFT*

The message fell from Roger's hands.

NO.

He rushed into the house and grabbed the same massive kitchen knife he'd armed himself with on the night of the burglary. Within moments he was running down the street toward 17th with murder on his mind.

THE BACK DOOR WAS open.

There were many things about that house which might have stopped a reasonable man from entering. The off-putting smell. The disconcerting softness of the ground once you took a single step onto the property. But for Roger, the only time he hesitated was when the knob to the back door turned smoothly in his hand.

For only a moment he thought, "This is what they want," but then the rage was back and it was all he could see, blinding him and driving him forward.

WE HAVE THEM NOW

No. This ends today. No matter what.

The back door opened on a staircase descending into a day-light basement. Roger stepped in and let the door glide shut behind him, keeping tension on the interior knob to ensure he gently slid it into place without any clicks. He descended the stairs, stepping slowly and lightly, waiting to hear a creak from the worn wooden steps.

Light fell through the basement from narrow rectangular windows above the too-soft soil. It was the same daylight Roger was used to, but down here it took on a liquid wavering—something was eating away at the light from its periphery.

He kept his eyes wide for motion, looking for white pants and black hoodies. Nothing. In the far corner of the basement there was a single plugged-in hot plate with a beaker sitting on it. The beaker housed a thick yellow fluid, though for one second Roger thought he saw a flash of something black unfurling against the surface of the glass, like a sea snake loosening its coils.

There was a set of carpeted stairs at the far end of the basement, next to some kind of primitive mural drawn mostly in black on the white-painted wood paneling. As he approached the stairs the image became clear: a great wolf floating in the blackness of space, head low as if approaching prey. In its line of sight was a small blue-green orb you'd be hard-pressed to see as anything but the planet Earth. Black drool hung from the maw of the beast.

The closer Roger got to the painting, the more eyes bloomed across the head of the wolf. When it was right by his side he could feel that it was nothing but endless sight and great hunger.

Something about the image transfixed him—he wasn't sure he could escape it. It felt . . . alive. He walked slowly up the stairs with the corner of his eye pinned to the wolf, waiting for it to move beyond the wall. Only when he reached the top floor did he let his gaze drop.

Roger rounded the corner and found himself in a small kitchen. Dated 70s décor. Cross-stitched art on the wall—Bless This Mess. A low, insectile buzz came from the fridge, its door slightly open, the sickly-sweet smell of soured pork floating out into the room. Another smell too—salty ocean rot that reminded him of the imploded anglerfish his Uncle Dutch had dragged from the deep sea. Roger remembered asking why its seeping eyes had popped. Dutch told him, "It was never meant to live up here, with us. It can't take the pressure."

The thin light from the fridge started to expand across the cracked linoleum floor. Roger scrambled through the kitchen and into the adjacent hallway.

The ambient sounds of the house dropped away, leaving Roger alone in the long corridor with only the sound of his thundering heart and short, sharp breaths. He pushed forward, knife held before him, wondering if he'd walked twenty steps, or two. The hallway seemed to have no end. He continued on, trying to ignore the sickening way time was stretching, wondering if his heart was beating too slowly or too quickly, until he suddenly had the sensation of pushing through a thin invisible membrane into sound and heat.

His vision blurred, then refocused: he was in a cozy, if poorly-lit, living room. The shades were drawn. There was a couch facing a wall with a grand fireplace, and his own TV, the one they'd stolen, mounted above it.

There was a man in the corner, seated in a plush tan recliner, his face barely illuminated by the glowing screen of Roger's laptop.

"Hey, Rog." The man looked up, bringing his empty blacked-out eye-pools to meet his gaze.

"WHERE ARE THEY?"

"Easy, killer! *Easy*. They are exactly where they should be, as are you. If you want to see them again, you need to set down that knife and have a seat and listen."

"Fuck you."

"Okay, sure. Fuck me. We can take that path. Honestly, I'm just happy you're here. I mean, I can't believe you showed. I actually bet against you. Clem's been on a hot streak lately. I think people take him more seriously now that he's so fucking old. Gives more gravity to his little story about 'poor old Judge Schumacher.' He still telling that gem? Didn't work on me, obviously, but he's gotten better since then."

Roger's vision blurred again. Something about this house, the man's voice . . . he could barely focus. He pictured Julie and Claire, bound and crying somewhere in this nest of devils, turning away from the empty-eyed men staring at them.

THEY ARE *BEAUTIFUL*

His vision returned. He pushed the knife out ahead of him and stepped toward the man in the chair. "My wife. My daughter. NOW!"

"You'll be with them soon enough, though I'm not sure how happy *they'll* be to see you. But slow your roll, Roger, and listen to me. All I've been trying to say is that I'm glad you're here. We've *definitely* got some work for you."

"What?"

"Yeah, that's your go-to, isn't it? Just confusion. What I'm saying is: We . . . have . . . work . . . for . . . you. It's pretty clear. The pill angle is starting to play. It's such an easy ritual—they buy, they swallow, we're in—and I think they're finally manufacturing that shit properly. We need somebody local to help with distribution. Somebody who knows how to keep product moving. Keep people interested. Somebody who'll push a condom full of toxic chemicals up their ass for a few extra bucks. That kind of guy. And a gentleman we used to know in prison down south told us you're exactly who we're looking for."

Oakland. I was never clean.

"Obviously you're not quite ready to work for us yet, which is why we have to go through all these old steps to bring you into the fold. All this ceremony. Speaking of which, I suppose we should get on with it."

"I'll never fucking work for you guys. You're insane. Now give me my fucking family before I chop off your goddamned head."

"Yeah, yeah. Heard it before, bud, and from scarier guys than you. But you're the one who's here now and I can tell from your face that it's time to begin. So I was hoping you'd take a look at *this* with me."

The man rotated the laptop around on his lap and grinned.

On the screen: a photo of Claire and Julie. Christmas last year, smiling in front of the tree.

THEY ARE *BEAUTIFUL*

& *SO SOFT*

"Maybe, Dad, you can help me figure out which one of these dumb cunts I'm going to fuck first, once you set them to our frequency."

And then Roger broke at last, and the ritual played out as it always had.

Reason was destroyed.

Hatred was ascendant.

And the man in the chair began to laugh even as Roger brought the knife down into his neck and his face and his jet-black eyes over and over again.

VI.

CLEM FOLLOWED ROGER HOME. He might have misted up a little as he trailed the man, but he held back the tears—that wasn't what a man did, and this wasn't his first time at the rodeo. But he really thought Roger had *heard* him, damn it all . . .

Clem had an unmarked pistol holstered on his right hip—enough to take care of Roger—and another gun tucked against his calf, its cool yellow plastic loaded with bright blue rounds in case those fuckers from the house tried to run interference. This was his mess to clean up, and he always did his job, no matter how much it was starting to hurt.

Though he did have half a mind to call HQ tonight and let her know he was ready to take out the house. The war was getting nastier—they'd come for Roger in the middle of the damn day, when Clem had least expected. He was ready to be done with the mission and its daily tragedies. Shoot, he *had* the explosives. It'd be an easy vest rig, maybe strap on a few extra pipe bombs and gasoline-filled balloons for maximum burn. Charge in head first, yell, "Vaya con dios!" and then send the whole nasty hive back to hell on a ball of fire. Cops would figure it for a meth lab explosion. A great plan. Maybe it was time to push for it.

But for now, Clem stayed in pursuit. Roger—or whatever it was that now lived inside him—was clearly still learning how to walk, given the change in his vision. Clem never could figure how those bastards could see through all that blackness. Definitely made 'em slow moving at first.

When they were a few houses out, Clem spotted the wife's car in the driveway.

Shit.

Execution would have been easy if he could've dropped Rog inside that house. Now he'd have to drag the poor bastard back to his own place and take him out in the sound-proof basement. That or risk losing the whole family. If Roger even got his arms around them . . .

Clem pulled a syringe full of sedative and got in tight, but Roger sensed him somehow, was already more perceptive than the others had been this early on.

Curse these slow old bones.

Roger had a reach on him, on top of his speed, and he managed to wrest Clem's gun from his holster.

Holy lord, is this how it ends? Gunned down in the street by a brand new convert. And he'll head in and switch the wife. And the kid. The kid. And the darkness will keep on spreading.

But Roger didn't point the pistol at Clem. Instead he looked down at the gun, then back up at the old man. His face contorted as something awful broke inside whatever remained of his mind.

"Tell them . . . I'm sorry."

And then Roger swung the gun into his mouth and pulled the trigger and blasted the back of his sorry skull clean off.

Hell.

Clem had never seen a convert manage such a task. But that's how these bastards were, always changing the way things worked.

There was no solid ground anymore, not so far as Clem could see.

He set to dragging the body home for disposal. The black blood on the asphalt behind him was already melting into the road.

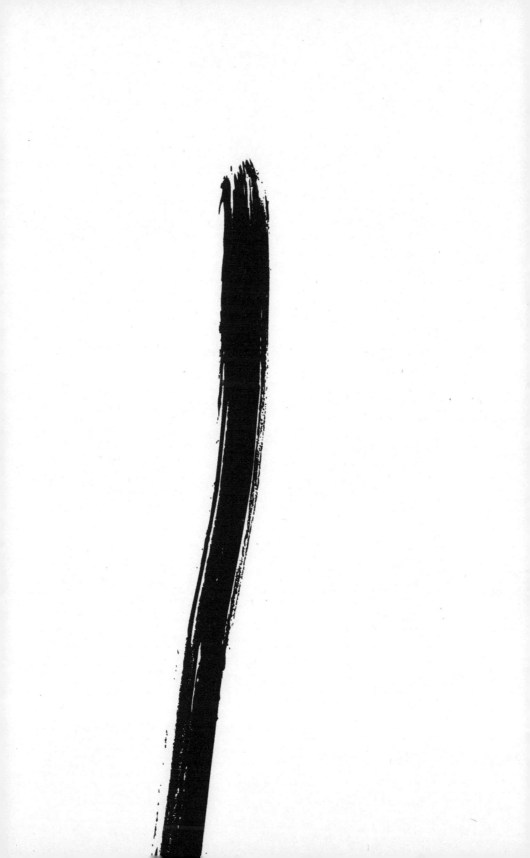

Author's Notes

The League of Zeroes

This is the direction I thought reality TV was headed, and briefly, with the debut of "The Swan"—in which beauty contest competitors first underwent radical plastic surgery—I thought I might have been prescient. However, viewers found the concept repellent and eventually decided they were much happier watching rich people make whining noises at each other. Still, very happy that this story reached so many folks, finding publication in Colombia, Spain, Italy, and France (where someone plagiarized the thing and got it included in an anthology at the Sorbonne [although they changed SaladMan to CheeseMan, which is as French an edit as possible]). Rumor has it that someone adapted the story as a one-act play in Australia, too, though I've never seen evidence. Most of the characters in the story re-appear, some much worse for wear and some with far more malicious goals, in the novel *Skullcrack City*.

Persistence Hunting

It's strange now, living in the same hills our narrator burglarizes in the story, especially since someone broke into my place a year back. If I found out our burglar used the old running-and-prowling gambit, I almost wouldn't be mad anymore. Almost.

The Oarsman

There was a stretch of time where my wife would read books about Buddhism aloud, just before we'd pass out for the night. Some nights I'd find the ideas compelling and comforting. Other nights, when the focus would be ego death and universal oneness, I found myself sweating, tossing and turning, filled with existential dread. It led to me thinking about the idea of weaponized empathy, and what kind of people might be left once that weapon had worked.

The Gravity of Benham Falls

Stephen Gammell's illustration of an eyeless, emaciated specter in the story "The Haunted House" (included in the original run of Alvin Schwartz' *Scary Stories to Tell In The Dark* anthology) has a long echo. When I first received the book as a kid, I was so shocked by that illustration that I asked my mother to tape a thick piece of paper over the grim visage so I could continue enjoying the book. I have no doubt the image was somewhere in my mind when I decided I was going to try my hand at a traditional ghost story.

Dissociative Skills

There's that hoary old joke: Alcoholism doesn't just run in my family, it gallops! It's the kind of thing you can laugh at because there aren't a lot of other options that keep you sane. For a very long time I was that person in an addiction-prone family who managed to beat back his own troubles and then became angry and self-righteous about everyone else's chronic fuck-ups. And so I've written about a decade's-worth of stories like this, and that kept me from completely losing my mind. I think. I hope.

Snowfall

This story has been optioned for film three times now, and once made it quite a distance into pre-production, including a solid script, storyboards, and a classical cellist committed to the score. In that case the director broke up with his girlfriend, who also happened to be the producer/financier, and that was that. On a totally unrelated note, when this story appeared in Spanish the translator had to include an addendum explaining that Tootsie Rolls are a North American candy. Which is to say that next time you're headed to South America, you'd be well-advised to bring your own Tootsie Rolls, if that's your thing.

When Susurrus Stirs

If you would have told me a few years ago that *this*, out of everything I've written, would be the first story adapted for film, I'd have laughed. Nobody is crazy enough to try to put such a thing on film.

That being said, an utterly faithful and disturbing film adaptation from Pandemic Pictures and Outpost 31 Productions premiers at FilmQuest next month. And yes, they retained the "meat sprout" sequence, because director Anthony Cousins and FX wizard Ryan Schaddelee are very troubled men.

Luminary

My mother told me that as a child she used to catch fireflies, twist them in half, and then use their leaking fluids to adhere the glowing remainder to her fingers. She'd wave her hands back and forth in the night air and pretend she was wearing beautiful diamond rings. Years later she gave birth to me in the high desert of central Oregon and there were no fireflies so I just ended up turning over rocks and dodging scorpions. Maybe whacking junebugs out of the air with a stick. It wasn't as beautifully gruesome as my mother's memory.

Trigger Variation

For a brief while, based on my personal interest in not driving myself into an early drug-addled grave, I got really into straight edge. I needed a very stern ideology and some compatriots around who'd help hold me to it. Plus I really liked Gorilla Biscuits. But after a while I noticed that some of these guys, sober though they may have been, were absolutely getting high on violence, whether that meant randomly rumbling at shows or actively hunting the streets of Olympia looking for Neo-Nazis to jump. It was an eye-opener. After that I understood: everybody's looking for a way out of their day-to-day reality.

Cathedral Mother

Once, during a road trip to southern California, my mother decided we'd take the scenic route down and roll through the redwood forest. See some of the largest living things on earth, drive through a tree, all that. However, the majesty of the redwoods had some stern competition in the form of Skipp and Spector's gonzo horror novel *The Scream*. I was so enraptured by the heavy metal insanity of it all, I barely glanced at the forest. Since then I've read Richard Preston's wonderful non-fiction book about the region, *The Wild Trees*, and now I long to return. Maybe I'll take my kid, give him a chance to ignore the miracle.

Swimming in the House of the Sea

A few years back there was a (now-famous) film director who wanted to expand this story into a feature film. He had an excellent young actor attached, a producer excited about the project, and some outstanding ideas about how to turn the tale into an indie take on *Rain Man* with some *Midnight Cowboy* grit in the mix. There was a possibility that one of my top three favorite cinematographers would shoot. Naturally, I was over the fucking moon about the whole venture. Then, two weeks out from the first production meeting, the director was given a shot at directing an adaptation of a *New York Times* bestseller. He took the gig, nailed it, and the film earned more than the GDP of several small countries. Now he's attached to three different tentpole movies and has his own production company. I do not believe I own a computer powerful enough to calculate how small the odds of him ever returning to "Swimming" might be, but it's fun to hold fast to hope.

Saturn's Game

If you come from a family where addiction runs strong in both bloodlines (and so many of you do), then you understand that sense of hopelessness, when it feels as if no one has any control of anything. There's something fascinating/terrifying about self-destructive behavior, and the way the mind can detach into that duality where it can both condemn whatever truly awful thing is about to happen and still send the signals to force its execution. I can barely imagine how much worse it is for people whose frontal cortex damage (or lack of proper development) prevents any sort of inhibition.

The Sharp-Dressed Man at the End of the Line

Or, When a Punchline Becomes a Story. When I was twelve I wrote a short story about a tribe of post-apocalyptic survivors crossing a wasteland to find sustenance, and in the end it turned out our protagonists were cockroaches travelling through a pantry to find the last Twinkie. I thought it was very *Twilight Zone* at the time. Fast forward a decade and GWB's the president and my nuclear war paranoia is at its height and I feel a need to revisit the cockroach/Twinkie dynamic. Later, I found myself wondering what would happen to Dean and his fancy suit if they went on a post-nuclear road trip, and the novella *Extinction Journals* was born.

A Flood of Harriers

I didn't hear of the CIA-coined term "blowback" until 2001, at which time it had gained a certain heavy significance. Since then—given our deeply troubled and oppressive history—I've been fascinated trying to quantify just how much blowback might be owed to the citizens of our country, and how I feel about the truth of that.

States of Glass

There's a semi-curious phenomenon that occurs where, each time I stay at a hotel for work travel, I decide to allow myself the luxury of a long, hot shower, only to inevitably rush out mid-shower to jot down a new story idea on hotel stationery. "States of Glass" definitely found its genesis that way, as have many other stories. Someone postulated that it's the travel aspect; that the new experiences and environments light up your brain's alpha waves. Or maybe there's something in that weird continental breakfast waffle batter. Could be both.

The Sleep of Judges

If you've ever been burglarized (or, say, robbed at gunpoint in a pizza restaurant parking lot) then you know the theft is just the very beginning of a long and unsettling road. I'm officially past my life quota for being stolen from, although I can still laugh about the guy who busted my car window to steal my backpack, since the only thing inside was a multi-year collection of Zoetrope literary magazines. Unless that guy figured out how to trade Mary Gaitskill stories for drugs, he must have been pretty disappointed. Also, a quick note for observant long-time readers: The activities of the residents of 17th (and Clem's mission to stop them) might feel strangely familiar to you. And you might be right to feel that way . . .

Acknowledgments

Huge thanks go out to Cory Allyn at Night Shade whose editorial insights challenged me and pushed the book to a stronger and more visceral realm. J. David Osborne's initial editorial work on "The Sleep of Judges" was also invaluable and helped me convert much of the strangeness from alien to human.

Brian Evenson's Introduction, which manages to be entertaining and humorous and thoughtful (and still end on a hyper-Evensonian crisis of identity and reality) is perfect. I am forever grateful that it opens the door to this crooked house.

I often feel that Stephen Graham Jones and Craig "Nick Cutter" Davidson are the cool brothers I never had (but was lucky enough to find), and their inspiration is central to the existence of this collection. That they also took time out to vet the thing reminds me how lucky I am to know them.

Somehow the only musical artist I listened to while working on this book was Spark Master Tape. *Silhouette of a Sunkken City* has probably infected the work in slow/paranoid/violent ways I can't ascertain. So thanks to Spark for the sonic backdrop.

A big shout out to Night Shade Books for believing in this crazy work enough to create such a lovely edition and to distribute it, for the first time, to unsuspecting readers around the world.

Eternal gratitude, always, to my family, for believing in my writing and encouraging me to do it despite everything else. I love you dearly.

To the magazine editors who took a risk and published these stories on their first go 'round, thanks for digging me out of the slush pile and encouraging me to keep going.

And finally, to the readers who originally discovered these short stories in their primordial form, thank you for believing in and supporting my weird work for over a decade. That this collection exists at all is a tribute to your good will, positive energy, and discerning readership. Here's to the next ten years and whatever madness lies ahead.

Publication Credits

"The League of Zeroes," originally published in *Verbicide #11* (2004).

"Persistence Hunting," originally published in *We Live Inside You* (Swallowdown Press, 2011).

"The Oarsman," originally published in *Dark Discoveries #17* (2010).

"The Gravity of Benham Falls," originally published in *Ghosts at the Coast: The Best of Ghost Story Weekend Vol. II*, edited by Dianna Rodgers (TripleTree Publishing, 2005).

"Dissociative Skills," originally published in *City Slab #6* (2005).

"Snowfall," originally published in *Verbicide #13* (2005).

"When Susurrus Stirs," originally published in *Bare Bone #10* (2007).

"Luminary," originially published in *Darker Than Tin, Brighter Than Sin*, edited by Rabe Phillips (Cafepress Publishing, 2004).

"Trigger Variation," originally published in *The Vault of Punk Horror*, edited by David Agranoff and Gabriel LLanas (Punk Horror Press, 2007)

"Cathedral Mother," originally published in *The Magazine of Bizarro Fiction #4* (2010).

"Swimming in the House of the Sea," originally published in *Angel Dust Apocalypse* (Eraserhead Press, 2005).

"Saturn's Game," originally published in *Angel Dust Apocalypse* (Eraserhead Press, 2005).

"The Sharp Dressed Man at the End of the Line," originally published in *Angel Dust Apocalypse* (Eraserhead Press, 2005).

"A Flood of Harriers," originally published in *Cemetery Dance #56* (2006)

"States of Glass," originally published in *We Live Inside You* (Swallowdown Press, 2011).

"The Sleep of Judges" is original to this collection.

Jeremy Robert Johnson is the Wonderland Award-winning author of cult hits *Skullcrack City*, *We Live Inside You*, *Angel Dust Apocalypse*, and *Extinction Journals*, as well as the Stoker Award-nominated novel *Siren Promised* (with Alan M. Clark). His fiction has been acclaimed by *The Washington Post* and authors like Chuck Palahniuk, David Wong, and Jack Ketchum, and has appeared internationally in numerous anthologies and magazines. In 2008 he worked with The Mars Volta to tell the story behind their Grammy-winning album *The Bedlam in Goliath*. In 2010 he spoke about weirdness and metaphor as a survival tool at the Fractal 10 conference in Medellin, Colombia. Jeremy currently lives in Portland, Oregon, but one day he'll have a cabin in the woods and a silent but respectful relationship with the owl who has long-ruled those territories. For more: www.jeremyrobertjohnson.com.